Natalie,
Keep it up,
believe in
Hannah Williams

Raulin's Oath

The Palidonaya Chronicles Book One

Hannah & Robert

Williamson

Natalie,
Choose to be the hero!
Robert William

1

This is a work of fiction. Names, characters, places, and incidents either are the product of the author's imagination or are used fictitiously. Any resemblance to actual persons, living or dead, events, or locales is entirely coincidental.

Copyright © 2020 by Hannah and Robert Williamson

All rights reserved. No part of this book may be reproduced or used in any manner without written permission of the copyright owner except for the use of quotations in a book review.

For more information visit our website:
https://robertwilliamson41.wixsite.com/website

Shorvista Publishing LLC April 2020

Cover design by Derek Ruble
Edited by Alexandra Ott

ISBN (paperback) 978-1-7348164-0-2
ISBN (ebook) 978-1-7348164-1-9

Thank you for purchasing our book. We hope that you enjoy reading it as much as we enjoyed writing it! Please help spread the word by leaving a review on Amazon.com after reading.

We welcome you to join us in the land that is only accessible through the child's dreamscape. A land that we have traveled to many times. Welcome to Palidonaya.

Prologue

Our venture occurs in a land far from all others, in a place unknown to most. It is past Mercury, Venus, Earth and Mars. Past Jupiter, Saturn, Uranus, Neptune, and many stars. It is so far, the only way of accessing this bright green planet is through a child's dreamscape. Palidonaya was once a place readily accessible to us, once a place that was only a dream away. However, dream walking no longer seems so easy. I long to touch the lush green grass of the Land of Equus once more, to breathe the salty air of the Realm of Belamoris, and to feel the Faendell snowflakes on my eyelashes. I never would've thought it would be closed to me, so now all I have is the bittersweet, fading memory of a paradise I can no longer reach. All I can see are the stars in the sky, taunting me. All I feel is Palidonaya's pull, yet She does not let me come home.

Chapter One

The dream had been the same for the past several days. Arietta stood in a lush green field, the smell of fresh grass mixed with the pleasant scent of clover tickling her nostrils. A warm breeze lifted the hair off of her shoulders, while the sun warmed the skin on her face. In the distance, she could see a mountain range, its tips painted white with snow. The grasses rolled like waves in a vast ocean with the wind giving the scene a hypnotic feel. Arietta took a step, feeling the dampness of the morning dew on her feet and the squish of soil that had recently received rain. She could not remember ever having been here before, yet this place felt like home. She continued walking towards the mountain range, watching dark clouds form, hiding the peaks and promising a storm. Her heart picked up its pace, adrenaline coursing through her veins. A single lightning bolt flashed over the mountains, blinding her for a moment.

***

A large furry head lifted her shoulder, pulling her from her dream and back into her bedroom. A quiet "woof" communicated the sense of urgency as Cooper continued to nudge Arietta from her slumber.

Arietta sighed. "Alright, I'm awake. I'll let you out." She smiled and rubbed his head, sitting up and stretching her arms slowly over her head, hearing the pops as her back straightened.

She stood and shuffled across the bedroom, through the kitchen and to the back door. Cooper had been sitting and waiting, not so patiently, having torn through the house as soon as the words "I'll let you out" had been uttered. He bounced on his front paws, readying himself to sprint to the yard once the door was opened.

"Alright, I'm going as fast as I can," Arietta exclaimed as she opened the door. Cooper didn't stick around to hear another comment as he flung himself out the door.

Arietta went to the refrigerator and got out the can of Folgers, opened the lid, and breathed in the pleasant smell of her morning addiction. She placed three scoops into the filter and started the first pot of coffee of the day. She made a piece of toast to enjoy with her coffee. She glanced down at the floor, and the sight stopped her in her tracks. The tile had smudges of dirt in the shape of footprints. Her first thought was that someone had been in her house the night before. This was quickly dismissed, because Cooper would have woken up the neighborhood had a stranger entered her house. Looking down, she noticed that her feet were dirty. Maybe she had been outside last night and didn't realize that they were dirty before going to bed. How odd.

She sat down and began eating her breakfast, wondering why a sixty-year-old woman would start having weird dreams, when a memory flashed into her mind. This memory was from a time that had been forgotten, dismissed from her mind like a ship disappearing into the mist. She could picture a sterile room, the acrid smell of alcohol attacking her delicate nostrils. The pain radiated through her body coinciding with even the slightest movement. Maybe that was why she had such a hard time remembering those days. Sometimes the mind tried to protect itself from painful memories by making one forget.

Arietta finished her breakfast, then went to the back door to let Cooper in so that he could eat his breakfast. She poured herself a fresh cup of coffee, then made her way into her office and sat down at her desk. She quickly opened her laptop, wanting to record this memory before it faded, and for the first time in three years, she began to write.

***

1972

At this time of day, Arietta's pain was at its worst. She had just finished her physical therapy and was lying in bed after the nurse that she'd nicknamed "Nurse Ratchet" had come in to give her the meds that lulled her into a restless sleep. This was also the time of day that her grandfather checked in on her.

Grandpa Gus' appearance was, in a word, comfortable. He wore a red cardigan that covered a white dress shirt with a black tie, and his black fedora. Every day he wore a variation of this outfit, and every day he looked like the perfect gentleman. His hair had long since faded from a dark charcoal to a speckled light gray. He knew at this time, she was probably either asleep or close to it, so he didn't knock on her door. After entering the room, he took the fedora from his head, setting it with great care on the bedside table, and ran his timeworn hands through his hair. Feeling the obvious dent the hat had left, he chuckled. Arietta stirred at the noise, eyelids struggling to lift. Her vision was blurred, but upon seeing the new frown that her grandfather wore, she wished she could've just stayed asleep. Seeing her eyes flickering open, a great sorrow swelled in Gustoff's heart. How many times had he sat in this seat, watching Arietta suffer through tormented sleep, knowing that he could help her? Though he desperately wanted to help, he feared that Arietta would question his sanity. The prognosis was grim, as this form of juvenile arthritis was extremely aggressive. Over the hushed voices of the doctors and the growing risk of fatality, the situation had become urgent. The fear of Arietta's death was real, and it became a paralyzing thought that was always on Gustoff's mind. He was out of options, out of time, and he felt that the doctors were merely going through the motions. The physical therapy wasn't helping, and chemotherapy was the logical next step, but if her body was too far gone, it would be futile. Time was slipping through his hands, and he would not be able to live with himself if he didn't at least try. He had to convince her to listen, even if that meant she would think he'd gone crazy.

Arietta was still groggy from the medicine and struggled to keep her eyelids open. She was very careful to lie perfectly still as consciousness slowly lifted the fog left from her drug-induced rest. She heard humming, no, it was Grandpa singing softly. She could barely make out the words, as it was as soft as the wind on a warm summer day.

"Good morning, my sweetheart, good morning, my darling, how I love to spend my days with you, though in the night, when I'm cold and lonely."

She loved his voice, and singing was one thing that made their bond stronger. His sweet baritone notes paired with her chirping soprano was a sound always welcome to her ears.

Arietta joined, adding her quiet raspy voice. "All I have to do is dream of you. Hi, Grandpa Gus, I've really missed you."

"Hi, sweet pea. I've missed you too." The days felt long when constant pain was the girl's only companion. Gus smiled and asked, "Are you hungry? I can get you something to eat."

Arietta tried to swallow to ease the burning in her throat, then answered him. "No, but I would love some water."

"I'll be right back, kiddo." She seemed weaker every time he saw her. His idea was crazy, but he knew he would do whatever he must to help her. He only had to think of a way to start such a conversation. She was a smart girl, so he needed to be honest, but she would not believe him. Gustoff had to find a way to show her. He would try before bedtime. First, he must convince her to hold off on taking her medication. He filled a glass with ice, added cold water and a straw to help her drink, then returned to her bedside.

He handed her the water, and she drew it in slowly, a small smile in her eyes. Arietta slowly shifted her position so that she could look at him while they talked. Even this little movement sent jolts of pain shooting through her body. The sickness had progressed, as she became weaker from each passing day. She fought a wince, hating to show the weakness to her worried grandpa. She saw the pained look on his face and despised the fact that he had to look to the window every time she moved so that he didn't have to bear witness to her suffering. The icy water felt wonderful sliding down her dry throat. The medicine sucked every drop of moisture from her and left her feeling like a dry husk.

"So, what do you want to talk about?" Arietta smiled and waited for her grandpa to answer.

Grandpa Gus took a deep breath, looked up to the ceiling to compose his thoughts, and then decided that the best way to start this conversation was to utter the first word and see where it took him.

"You know, when I was young, I used to get terrible headaches. I always knew when they were coming, but nothing that I took helped with the pain. I couldn't stand any light or noise when my headaches hit. I usually ended up in a dark cool room in our basement for two days."

"How did you know that they were coming?" Arietta asked.

"It's kind of hard to say. It usually started with a small spot in my vision, or voices would sound muffled. As soon as I sensed one coming, I would go to my mother and let her know, then it was down to the basement. Mother would bring a drink and food, but I never ate or drank anything. I used to take medicine for them, but I stopped because it didn't do anything but upset my stomach. I found something else that would work to ease the pain."

"You wouldn't take any medicine? Did you go to a doctor or anything?" Ari probed.

"Sure, we went to doctors, and they gave me medicine that was supposed to help, but it never really did. I would just put one of my pillows over my head so that no one heard me crying. That continued for almost two years. Then we tried a doctor that told me not to take medicine. He gave me a coin and told me to squeeze it as hard as I could, envision my hand getting warm, and think of a place that I could go where my head didn't hurt anymore. He had a name for this place: Palidonaya. He told Mother that it was a new treatment that they called biofeedback. I thought it was a bunch of nonsense, but I was willing to try anything." He paused a moment, looking to Arietta to gauge her reaction. "It wasn't long after that appointment that I felt one coming on. I could tell by the signs that it was gonna be a doozie. I ran to my mother and let her know what was happening and stopped in the kitchen to get a cold towel. I then hurried to my room and grabbed my coin and headed to the basement. My mother brought down a glass and my migraine medicine, but as the doctor instructed, I didn't take my pill. As the headache began to form, I took hold of that coin and squeezed with everything I had. I started repeating the name Palidonaya over and over again in my head. I imagined my hand catching fire. My head was really pounding, so I started wishing that I was in Palidonaya."

Ari's eyebrows furrowed. "Did it work? What happened next?"

"I don't know if I can explain it without sounding crazy. I was in a completely dark room, yet I saw a spot of white light appear in my vision. The spot grew until it surrounded me, then I wasn't in my cellar anymore. I couldn't smell the dank basement air, but clean air with a hint of grass. The sun warmed my face, and my head no longer hurt. The best I can tell you is that I went to Palidonaya."

"Come on, Grandpa, I'm young, not stupid." The hope that was written across her features deflated, leaving her expression flat and disappointed.

"I'm telling you, sure as I'm sitting here, I was not in my basement anymore, and my head stopped hurting. I had finally found the one thing that would take away my headaches. I have been thinking about this for a while now, and I want to give you my coin. I want you to try this to help you through the night."

"Why not now?" Against all sense, she wanted to try it.

"The medicine is still pretty heavy in your system. I can see it in your eyes. If we wait until bedtime, there is a better chance that it will work. I want to try it with you to see if I can help you at least get some sleep tonight. What do you think?"

Arietta considered the question. "What if it doesn't work?"

"Then you take your medicine and sleep like you do every night."

"Well, what do we have to lose then, Grandpa? Will you stay with me tonight even if it doesn't work?"

"You bet, sweet pea," Gustoff replied.

The time passed slowly, as usual, for how could time pass quickly when a child was in so much pain? He hated how carefully she did even idle tasks such as breathing. Her face was screwed up with agony. She wasn't the kid she used to be. That had been stripped from her. Gustoff read Arietta her favorite book, speaking in a soft voice yet still using inflection.

For the first time in weeks, a sweet smile spread across Arietta's face, the smile that hinted that hope was still in reach.

"Grandpa?"

"Yes, Ari?" After he turned to her, she sighed. A yawn built in her throat.

"I'm tired. We should try the coin. Either that or I'd like my medicine, I'm ready to go to sleep." Finally she released the yawn, and Gustoff used his pointer finger to guide his glasses a little farther up the bridge of his nose.

"Alright, dear, you give your grandpa a second, and I'll bring the coin over," he exclaimed, rummaging through his pockets. His fingers searched over the shiny gold coin, feeling their way along the ridges, tracing the foreign symbols. He brought the coin into the light, kissing it once before placing it in her hand. He didn't want to go back, not after everything that had happened. It brought back too much for a man his age to deal with, but for Arietta, he would go with her to the ends of the earth. "Do you remember how to get there?" Her eyes closed, she responded only with a solemn nod.

She gripped the warm coin, thought of a place she did not know but already loved. A place away from all her problems, a place that would make the agony of being simply disappear. The world was a chant in her mind, a plea. *Palidonaya, please, please take me. Help me.*

A light brighter than the sun shone in her eyes, yet it did not blind her. She could stare at it all day long if she wished to. It was warm; it was comforting. She left her body, felt her soul drift away, yet it did not frighten her. The smell of alcohol and the Old Spice cologne that would always be the welcoming scent of her grandfather faded into nothingness, and her body felt so pleasantly numb. Gustoff watched in removed fascination, as he had never considered what the absent body would look like as she traveled. Her eyes rolled back, whites showing, and her head tilted upwards. Although he could not see her irises, her eyes darted about frantically.

Chapter Two

Her feet floated gently through the grass blades, softly touching the ground before she sank to her knees. She winced at the pain that shot its tendrils through her, gripping her tightly. A shadow cast over her body as the largest horse that she had ever seen nudged her. The enormous stallion lowered his head so that a horn protruding from the middle of his forehead touched her leg. He closed his eyes, and a soft glow emanated from his horn. A warmth surrounded her, penetrating her flesh and heating her bones. Her heart pounded, threatening to leap out of her chest, and her body lifted from the ground, levitating above the grassy plain. Again, she floated down through the grassy blades. She was now standing without crutches in a grassy meadow. A gentle breeze lifted the hair from her face. She opened her eyes to take in the world around her. The grasses were a deep green, the sky a clear blue with little wisps of clouds adding texture. Arietta stood, breathing in the cleanest air that she had ever inhaled. She took a tentative step forward and discovered that she felt no pain. She let out a delighted squeal, startling the field's other inhabitants.

The animals in the pasture were so beautiful. Though they looked like horses, these were no ordinary herd, for centered on each and every head was a long and delicately pointed horn, twisting towards the sky and gleaming in the sun.

The horse-like being that had placed its horn on Arietta's leg asked, "Are you lost?"

Arietta's eyes widened comically, jaw dropping in awe. "You... you can talk!" she proclaimed in a loud, amazed voice.

He snorted, blinking a few times before speaking once more. "As can you. I welcome you to the Land of Equus. Girl, where are you from?"

"I'm Arietta; who are you?" The girl was dazed and distracted, ignoring his previous question.

"I'm Raulin, Lead Stallion of the Zeus Herd. Where did you come from?"

Her eyes flicked back to him, as she had been scanning the vast expanse of the fields of grass. "Right... I don't know, I was in the hospital. My Grandpa Gus should be here soon."

The stallion did his best not to express his frustration at this. Her fingers traced the tall grass, making quiet swishing noises as the grass seed passed over her knuckles. Arietta pulled in a deep breath and was amazed by the feeling of walking once more. "This place"--she took a breath--"is paradise."

Her appearance had drawn a lot of attention, as a small crowd had gathered around her. Whispers flooded the teen's ears, and she drew together her brows in confusion. She didn't understand the series of events that had led to this moment. From her perspective, the pasture and herd had appeared around her.

What she didn't know was that it had been decades since one had appeared in the land of Zeus. The whispers that she couldn't make out spoke of a prophecy fulfilled. The prophecy spoke of three saviors traveling from a distant land to free them from a tyrant. Nervous whinnies echoed across the herd as they wondered if there were dark times ahead of them.

A small colt hid behind his mother, trying to get a better look at the stranger. Arietta approached slowly and crouched down. His coat was light brown with large patches of white and a spot of pink in the middle of his tiny nose. She could just make out the beginnings of a single horn forming in the center of his forehead.

"It's okay, little one. I won't hurt you." She held out her hand and waited patiently as the colt slowly approached her. Arietta loved the silky feel of the colt's fur as she ran her hand along his short mane.

The colt looked up at Arietta and said, "Hi, my name is Corin."

Arietta smiled at the colt. "Hi Corin, my name is Arietta. I'm pleased to meet you."

Corin nodded. "It is nice to make your acquaintance. Is it true that you are one of the Chosen Ones of the prophecy?"

Arietta giggled before answering, "I don't know anything about any prophecy. This is my first time here."

Corin touched Arietta's arm with the small horn that had just begun to form in the center of his forehead. Arietta could not believe how velvety the horn felt on her skin as he lifted his head to look into her blue eyes.

"You are definitely one of the Chosen." Corin looked at her with big brown eyes, the awe coming through in his shaky voice.

Arietta began to fade, starting with the toes and then up to her fingers, then head, and finally she was back. She was back on Earth, back in the sterile hospital room that had made her forget the smell of an open field and the brilliance of the sky. Back to the bed she couldn't leave.

Ari opened her eyes slowly to find Grandpa Gus enjoying a cup of coffee and reading a newspaper. She tentatively shifted her position judging how her body would react. The pain was instantaneous and intense. She let out a groan, which attracted Gus's attention.

"Good morning, kid. Go slow; once you get your medicine, you will start to feel better."

The morning nurse entered and said, "You will have to wait a few minutes before you get your meds. I am supposed to get you to your treatment as soon as you have had something to eat. I brought you some cereal so you don't get an upset stomach."

Once Arietta choked down her small breakfast, she was placed into a wheelchair and rolled down the hall to receive her first treatment. They had inserted a port close to her collarbone so that they could easily administer the chemotherapy. The doctor had explained the process to her after the surgery to install the port. She was not excited about losing her hair, but if it helped get her out of bed, she was willing to take that risk.

The nurse that Arietta had lovingly dubbed Nurse Ratchet rolled her to the room that was reserved for administering chemotherapy treatments. After the line was hooked up to her port, she settled down for her first three-hour treatment. Arietta sat perfectly still so that she could avoid as much pain as possible and closed her eyes in an attempt to take her mind off of the poison dripping into her veins.

"Hey, my name is Gerald, but you can call me Jerry. Do you have cancer too?"

"Hi, Gerald. If you don't mind, I would like to sit here quietly. I've never had this before, and I am really not in the mood to talk." Arietta's stomach fluttered nervously, as she had heard far too many horror stories about chemotherapy. The boy didn't seem to be unfriendly, but he was obnoxious, and she just wanted some quiet time.

"Suit yourself, but it will make for a looong, boring treatment. You won't even feel sick until later tonight. So, my cancer is in my bones. Makes them break really easily. After my chemo treatments are finished, I get to look forward to them sucking all the marrow out of my bones and replacing it. It's supposed to hurt really bad. I can't wait!"

Ari closed her eyes. She figured that if she ignored him, he would quit talking. She was sadly mistaken.

"So, my favorite color is orange. Kind of a weird color to like so much, but it's just a good color. I'm an only child, and I have a dog back home that I haven't seen in months. His name's Bucky, and if you know anything about Bucky, it's that he's the best dog in the world. Let's see... I like to read."

She huffed, looking over to the boy whose eyes were fixed on her as he blabbered away.

"You really like to hear yourself talk, don't you?" She let out a huff of laughter, and he grinned.

"That I do, cancer girl, that I do."

She crossed her arms tightly against her chest, looking down at the floor. "I'm not a 'cancer girl.' Not only do I not have cancer, but I have a name," she insisted. He quirked an eyebrow at her, leaning forward in his seat. His hair was thinning, which she noticed at that moment. She fixated on the sallow skin and the bags under his eyes. He winced when he moved. She felt a little self-conscious. Could he see all the things she saw in him?

"Interesting. So, if not cancer, then what?" He wasn't interested in her name yet, and Arietta found this to be very rude.

"My *name* is Arietta. Thank you for asking."

The gentle amusement he felt was apparent in the subtle lift of his eyebrows. "Feisty, got it. Very nice to meet you, *Arietta*." The smirk on his face nearly made her want to strangle him, but… she had to admit, it was nice. It was nice having someone to bicker with who didn't treat her as though she was a child. Nice to have someone look at her with a face absent of pity. It was nice talking to someone her age-ish. *Maybe,* she thought, *maybe we could be friends.*

"I have juvenile arthritis. It is a very serious disease."

He cocked his head, listening intently. Folding his hands in his lap, he took a moment to process her words.

"Very interesting. You know, it's kind of nice having someone to talk to during this treatment." He made quote signs with his fingers when he said the word 'treatment.' "It gets really boring, sitting here for hours. There is enough discomfort that I have never been able to sleep like they said I would." While his tone was lighthearted, there was something in his eyes that told her his mood had shifted. The gleam in his eyes had gone. He looked tired. "Let's be friends, okay?"

She paused, considering it for a breath, and he rushed on. "We don't--we don't have to be if you don't want to. If not, it's fine. I just thought, I'm not around a lot of kids my age anymore."

"No, I think it'd be nice. But you need to know that my friends call me Ari. Shake on it?" She extended an arm, painstakingly, toward him, and he grinned. They shook on it, and that was that. That was the beginning of a friendship between two sick kids, between two adventurers.

Chapter Three

Present Day

It was really amazing the way a simple exercise like writing could open up the mind. Memories were coming in waves as Arietta sat at her computer, typing. It was hard to believe that she couldn't remember Jerry's name this morning when she began recording her memories. It was still fairly foggy, but that fog was beginning to lift. They had been through a lot during the time she spent in the hospital.

She stood, hearing the protesting creaks made by her body as she stretched her back. Although she wasn't ready to quit just yet, today was grocery day. She would make her trip to the store, grab a quick bite to eat, and then sit back down this afternoon. She quickly dressed and let Cooper out again before heading to do her shopping.

The grocery store was not overly busy, so the shopping went very quickly, and she had only one item left. Arietta was in the process of picking the perfect loaf of bread when she felt someone watching her. She turned from the shelf full of bread and a tall, slender man dressed in black quickly darted his eyes to the shelf. He had been looking at her, so she approached him.

"Do I know you?" Arietta questioned the stranger.

When the man turned to look at her, Arietta stopped her approach. He had no hair on his face at all, including over his eyes. He wore a black hat that covered the top of his head and was pulled over his ears, which was odd, because it was a very warm day. His nose was thin with a sharp triangular shape, but the feature that most bothered Arietta was the emerald green eyes.

The man smiled, though there was nothing indicating genuine happiness in it, and said, "No, you don't know me."

Arietta's chest tightened, and she said, "Sorry, my mistake." She then turned, grabbed a loaf of bread, and hurried down the aisle toward the register. It was time to leave.

The man laughed and called after her, "I'll see you around, Arietta."

She turned when she heard her name but the aisle was empty. Arietta quickly looked around the store; there was no way that someone could have moved that quickly. He was in the middle of the aisle. She decided that it was time to go back home. She would lie down for a bit after putting away the groceries.

***

Arietta was lying in her bed, staring at the ceiling, mind racing. This had turned into one strange day. The experience in the grocery store caused her to doubt her safety again. Cooper was snuggled up against her, and she knew that the rottweiler would protect her, but there was something about that man that made her feel uneasy. She had tried to take a nap, but sleep wouldn't come to her, so after an hour of lying down, she decided to get up.

She stood up slowly so that she wouldn't get a head rush. For the first time in over forty years, there was a dull throb in her left hip. She then walked gingerly into the kitchen to get herself a glass of iced tea. Arietta needed to stop thinking about the encounter at the grocery store, and decided that writing would help to clear her mind. She hadn't written professionally in over three years, and though this didn't feel like a manuscript that she would be sending to her publisher, old habits died hard. The familiar fever began to build that always consumes her when working on a project. It started with a need to sit down and write. From there it grew to a burning desire to immerse herself in the world that her imagination created. She would spend days without any human interaction. This had really bothered Joey, the love of her life. He would bring her food when he felt that she should eat. She would drink a glass of wine when she got to a point where she felt she could spend a few precious minutes away from the computer. She had lost a lot of sleep writing in her younger years.

Joey had passed three years ago, though she still expected to see him sitting in his recliner watching the news before bed. Not a night went by that he wasn't on her mind as she drifted off to sleep, only to dream of him until she woke the next morning. Yes, his passing created a void in her heart that would not be filled until she saw him again.

It was well past dinnertime, but she was definitely not ready to stop. She poured herself a glass of wine, took a couple of ibuprofens for her hip, and sat back down at her computer. Arietta enjoyed the sweet burn of the wine that made its way into her stomach to create the warmth that she clung to in times of loneliness. The way Grandpa Gus had never seemed willing to leave her side for more than a few hours at a time truly amazed her. If he only knew how much he had meant to her.

1972

Arietta had spent the past day retching. She had never felt so miserable as she did following her first chemo treatment. Grandpa Gus stayed by her side, holding her hair back so that she didn't get any vomit in it. Though this was a horrible day, her pain was not as excruciating as before. The real question was whether it was the chemotherapy or the visit from Raulin that had reduced her pain. She decided that once she finished vomiting, she would ask Grandpa Gus for another trip to Equus. She really didn't want to take any chances with her pain.

That night, the nausea finally passed. She asked her grandfather to get the golden coin so that she could try to venture to Palidonaya for a second time. She wanted to see if Raulin would help her again.

The process went much more smoothly this time, as she knew what to expect. She squeezed the coin tight in her hand and said the words over and over again, "Please take me to Palidonaya. Let me smell the fresh grass and see the open plains of Equus." She then focused on her hand heating up. The weightlessness associated with dreamwalking was unimaginable, and the ascension to the higher plain surrounded her being. The smell of sweet grass danced in her nose, and a gentle breeze ruffled her hair. The light of the surrounding area produced a glow visible through her eyelids. Arietta smiled at the herd that now surrounded her.

Raulin stepped forward, "Welcome. You seem to be stronger this time."

Ari winced as the pain shot from her feet through to her shoulders. She gingerly stepped forward, flexing her toes atop the lush grass.

"No reason to pretend that the pain is gone." Raulin leaned his head down, resting the point of his horn on Ari's shoulder. Heat radiated from his horn, spreading through her body. The pain seemed to dissipate with the heat from his horn. Raulin closed his eyes and slumped in his stance.

"If this is hurting you, please don't do it anymore. The new treatments have really helped my condition. I can take the pain that is left."

Raulin regained his balance and stood proudly. "Nonsense. There is only a momentary lapse of balance. The gift of the Zeus herd is a gift that I give freely. I am glad that you seem stronger today."

Arietta pressed her forehead against Raulin's, closing her eyes, trying her best to convey her gratitude, yet knowing she would never be able to express such feelings to their full extent.

"You have no idea how much this does for me." She stepped back, looking at the stallion with a frown.

"You will repay me a thousandfold."

The words confused her, but she didn't have time to consider them.

"Arietta, Arietta!" Corin cried as he galloped in her direction. Though he was faster than lightning, the colt looked clumsy, struggling with stick legs that were much too long. She couldn't help but grin.

Arietta hurried forward and took the colt into her arms for a hug. "Corin, I've missed you! You look like you have already grown since the last time that I saw you."

Corin whinnied, "I have grown. Check out my horn!" He turned his head so that she could see all of its glory.

Arietta stepped back, placing her hands on her hips. "Wow, it is magnificent!" She reached forward and ruffled his mane.

Corin stood tall and proud, prancing to show off for the visitor. Raulin smiled at the show that Corin was putting on. He enjoyed watching the way that Arietta showed extra attention to the foals of the herd. The two ran through the grass, laughing as Arietta tried to tag Corin. He bucked and whinnied as he dodged before finally allowing her to tag him so that he could be It.

Dimitri, Raulin's son, approached him and spoke so only the Lead Stallion could hear. "Father, do you think that she is a Chosen One from the prophecy?" His muscles tensed as he waited for a response. His eyes darted frantically across the field, praying that no one else could sense his strained energy.

Raulin shook his head in thought. "The prophecy spoke of a dark time in our history. There have been whispers from the mountains, but nothing that leads me to believe that dark days await. I guess that time will tell." He glanced at his son, a wave of pride overcoming him. He knew that Dimitri had no concern for himself, but rather had his herd in mind. One day, he would make a great Lead Stallion.

Arietta jogged over to Raulin, her game complete. "Thank you for helping me, Raulin. It is time for me to go back home."

Raulin bowed his head. "Farewell, Arietta."

***

Jerry was already sitting in his chair, hooked up and receiving his treatment when Arietta was wheeled into the room to get set up. He sat still, his head resting in his hands, without the slightest acknowledgement of Arietta or the nurse's existence. His hair had become so thin that it appeared as if little gnats were orbiting his head. His skin was sallow, with an unhealthy sheen, and there was a sorrow that escaped from him. Arietta gulped a breath of air at the pitiful sight, and she chewed uneasily on her lower lip. As the nurse plugged the chemotherapy line into her port, Arietta risked a quick glance in Jerry's direction, tears and sweat gleamed on his cheeks. She waited patiently until the nurse left the room and then asked a simple question.

"Hi, Jerry, are you okay?"

"Yeah, I'm great, can't you tell?" With that, he shook his head and looked away from her. "Ari, do you ever think about dying?"

She knew that she had to choose her words carefully, as Jerry appeared to be in a very fragile state both physically and mentally. "Yeah, it's hard not to think about it when you're stuck here."

"I think about it all the time. I just wish I wasn't here anymore."

"Jerry, you can't talk like that! You have people here who really care about you." She was honestly at a loss for words, scrambling to give him hope, while frightened to say the wrong thing.

"Ari, have you seen how many people have visited me? One! My mother and no one else. I just can't take this for much longer. I am tired and I hurt all over. Oh, then I get to look forward to vomiting my guts up all night. You know what, that really dulls the pain when your whole body is retching. I am just done." With that, Jerry closed his eyes tightly, tears streaming down his face. Though she wasn't sure what to say, she grabbed his hand without thought. It was clammy, but intertwining fingers with him felt right.

"Jerry." She fidgeted, collecting her thoughts for a moment. "Maybe your other friends aren't visiting you, but I need you. I can't go through this without you." The room smelled of despair, and they shared a long look. He studied her as if it were the last time he would see her, and a feeling of gratitude enveloped him.

Ari decided then and there what she would do. Grandpa Gus had told her to keep it a secret, but if he knew how bad Jerry was, he would make an exception to the rule as well. She would ask again tonight for the coin. She had to see where he kept the talisman.

***

She recently had noticed a marked improvement in her pain, though she knew it wasn't due to the chemotherapy. Arietta's hair had begun to thin out, as she was losing it in chunks whenever she ran a brush through it. The pain that she had felt throughout her body was not as intense, although her hip still ached. She was able to walk down to what she and Jerry called "the chemo room" for her treatment this morning. As the nurse set her up, she let her mind wander, as it was her turn to tell a story. She wanted to make this one great, as Jerry hasn't looked too good the past couple of times and she knew that he was in a lot of pain.

Jerry's nurse wheeled him in and set him up beside Ari, as was the custom once they had become friends. "Hey kid, how ya doin'?" Jerry's voice was barely above a whisper. He smiled weakly at her as the nurse finished plugging the tube into his port to begin treatment. "I believe that it is your turn to entertain me. Will it be another tale of Palidonaya? What type of adventure will the herds of Zeus have today?" He ended the sentence with a dry cough.

Once they were set up, the nurse left the room. She once again reminded them that if they needed anything, they could push the call button. Ari waited until they were alone and then slipped the coin out of her pocket.

"Jerry, I want to try something. I don't know if it will work, but you have to try your best whether you think it is stupid or not. Okay?"

"Sure, sounds like fun," he said in a dry, sarcastic tone. Arietta frowned, but didn't comment. She knew he was tired.

"Okay, I want you to hold onto my hand." Ari put the coin in her hand and reached over to take Jerry's hand, and Jerry lifted his brows. "Now close your eyes and concentrate. Focus on Palidonaya and the pastures that I have told you about in Equus."

Jerry wasn't sure what to make of this, but he was interested to see where this was going. He closed his eyes and imagined the lush green plains that Ari had described in detail to him. He began whispering to himself the words that he could hear Ari whispering. Jerry tried to stay serious, but he felt really silly, and before he knew it, he was full-on giggling.

"Jerry, could you please try to take one thing seriously?" Arietta rolled her eyes.

"I'm sorry, I just feel so silly, like we're having a seance or something. Hang on, give me a second." Jerry covered his face with both hands before breaking into another giggling fit. Arietta couldn't help but giggle a little herself.

"Jerry, please try this, for me." Arietta looked into Jerry's eyes.

That was all that it took to shut Jerry up. He stared back, knowing that no matter what she asked him to do, he would do it.

The two held hands once again, and this time, Jerry took it seriously. When she looked at him like that, he really had no choice.

"Please, take me to Palidonaya." they whispered in unison.

An unnatural heat radiated from their connected hands. The coin was heating up. A bright light overwhelmed his vision, and as he felt an intense pull of acceleration, he thought to himself, "What did they put in my chemo today?"

The first thing he detected with his senses was a fresh smell reminding him of the waning summer days outside; next was the awareness of grass against his feet. Following those lovely sensations was the pain that he carried with him. Peeling his eyes open, he followed Ari, watching her dash off across the open fields toward a group of large horses--scratch that, unicorns?

"Jerry." Arietta summoned him forward to a fiery red stallion. "This is Raulin. This land is what I wanted to show you, and I think it will be able to help you."

"Really?" Jerry was dazed, a foggy gloss over his mind. This was the land from Arietta's stories. The unicorn tipped its proud head, resting about a two-foot horn atop his head. Jerry closed his eyes, unsure of what else to do. After about a minute of waiting, a sniffle from the horse interrupted the gentle quiet of the surrounding fields, and the stallion spoke once more.

"I'm sorry. Arietta, something is interfering with the healing. I cannot help your friend."

"Why isn't it working? Is there another way?" Arietta's voice was passionate and held a mix of emotion, and upon hearing this, a wave of confusion washed over Jerry.

Why did she care? The sunlight danced over her golden hair creating the image of an angel. Fierce passion held her gaze, and her irises swirled seafoam green and baby blue. The ever-present warm breeze swept back her hair, and the sun shone onto her, turning her hair into fiery golden embers. *Wow*, he thought, and while he searched through his memories, he couldn't find another with equal beauty, let alone equal spirit as her.

"I... I'm confused, and to be frank, a little scared, but it's okay. Being here is enough," Jerry croaked, his voice a touch gravelly.

"No," Arietta insisted. "No, it isn't. We're going to figure this out." She focused her gaze on him, that intense fire searing into him, and he found it difficult to breathe.

The sun was high in a bright blue sky, and there was green grass as far as the eye could see. On the horizon, there was a mountain range dotted with white peaks. The air was the cleanest that he had ever breathed. How was this, in itself, not enough? Did she realize that she had given him everything he could aspire for? Had she realized how desperately he longed to smell something other than his own vomit and the stinging alcohol that the hospital reeked of? Could she ever understand what this meant to him?

"Am I dreaming?" he asked breathlessly, as it was the only thing he could say.

A small foal galloped towards them and circled Arietta. "Hi, Ari, I missed you! Who is your friend?"

Dazed, Jerry's eyes turned to the lively foal, which also could talk.

Arietta smiled and turned to him. "Jerry, I would like for you to meet a very special friend of mine. This is Corin."

Jerry stepped forward and bowed. "I'm pleased to meet you, Corin." He quickly realized that bowing was not a great idea, as pain shot up his spine. Jerry winced and eased himself into a sitting position in the grass before lying back and gazing into the bright blue sky. The talking animals had really thrown him for a loop.

Arietta smiled at him, then walked over to Raulin and motioned for him to walk with her. When they were far enough away from Jerry, she asked, "Why were you not able to help Jerry?"

Raulin shook his head. "I am not certain, but there are other sources of healing within these lands."

Arietta looked hopeful. "What do we need to do?"

Raulin sighed. "I have heard of others with healing powers, though they are not of Equus."

Arietta frowned in frustration and headed back to Jerry, who was smiling at Corin. The colt was prancing and obviously showing off for Jerry. Arietta smiled and said, "Well, Jerry, are you ready to go back to the hospital?"

When the two awoke back in the hospital, they took no notice of a third person sitting in the corner of the chemo room. Novalee was a shy girl, and social interaction made her nervous. She watched them in silence, wondering what she had just witnessed. When she came in for her treatment, the nurse tried to set her up beside the two that had fallen asleep, but she insisted that she take a spot in the corner away from them. She held her breath as they woke up and began talking. They chattered in hushed tones, though she could hear every word. Yes, it was an odd thing to do, but she was entertained by them. She tucked her black curls behind an ear, revealing a dazzling blue eye, which many took in with awe, as it contrasted the deep brown of her other eye. Maybe one day she'd summon the courage to talk to them, but a dreamer could only dream.

***

Arietta returned the coin to Grandpa Gus' bag when he made a trip to the restroom. It had been four days since Grandpa Gus had shown her the way to Palidonaya. He had stayed with her every day so that her parents didn't have to miss too much work. They came each evening, ate dinner with her, and stayed until visiting hours were over. That night, when they left, Grandpa Gus made his way into the room and gingerly sat in the chair between her bed and the one he had moved into the room for himself.

She turned to him and said, "I'm getting worse again. I really thought that I would be getting better each day." She showed what she felt was the right amount of anger at the regression. She needed to find out why Raulin couldn't help Jerry. Arietta tightened her hands into fists, then let out a sigh as if the pain wracked her body.

"I think that you need another trip to Palidonaya. I didn't think that you would have to keep going. I really want you to be careful, as it may be beautiful, but it is also a very dangerous place." He was tired too, though he would never admit it to Arietta. He was disappointed, he was angry, but those feelings were irrelevant. He needed to be there for his Ari, and to submit to such negative emotions was like playing with fire.

"I have been many times, but I don't remember anything that seemed dangerous."

"I fell in love with Palidonaya the first time that I went there. I didn't sense the danger either; however, there are some rules that I need for you to follow to keep you safe. Rule 1: Only go when you absolutely have to. Rule 2: When you do, don't leave Equus. Rule 3: Don't tell anyone about Palidonaya. As long as you follow those three rules, you shouldn't run into any trouble. Now, remember to focus on the coin first, then focus on Palidonaya." Arietta cringed internally at the last rule, doing her best to maintain her poker face.

"What is so dangerous about Palidonaya?" Having a set of rules to restrict her path to healing didn't make sense. The lands of Palidonaya were a haven, and she couldn't conjure a picture where they were anything but blissful.

"It doesn't matter, what matters is that you stay safe. Now, please repeat the three rules."

"Rule one was don't go unless I have to. Rule two, don't leave Equus. Rule three, it's a big secret. There, does that make you happy?"

Gustoff's brows furrowed at her tone, but he let go of his frustrations. "You have to swear that you will follow those rules no matter what."

Arietta hesitated, hating to swear to a set of rules that she'd already broken, yet also not wanting to get in trouble. "Okay... I swear!" Guilt roiled in her stomach, but she'd already said the words; it was too late.

Gus took the coin out of his bag and placed it in her palm as she closed her fingers around it. He had already placed her medication under his chair in case she couldn't make the trip. He didn't understand why his stomach was turning over as she closed her eyes and began the process that she had been through every night over the past four days.

Ari focused on the coin and began the simple chant in her mind: *Palidonaya, please, take me there. Please help me.* The heat slowly built up in her hand. She pinched her eyes closed until it felt like her eyelids were overlapping. A single tear ran down her temple towards her ear. She doubled her focus. *Palidonaya, Palidonaya, green pastures, clean air, blue skies. Palidonaya.*

Finally a pinpoint of light appeared in front of her closed eyes. The light grew until it enveloped her. She felt weightless, like she was floating in the air. She risked a quick peek to see the top of Grandpa Gus' head before a pull of acceleration tugged at her core.

"Oh no, I should have kept my eyes closed!" Ari exclaimed as she was whisked away. She closed her eyes as the light shined brighter. She would not make the mistake of opening them again. The light reached its apex and then faded. She smelled fresh grass lingering on a warm breeze.

Chapter Four

She blinked her eyes open and found herself lying in that same green pasture, but to her confusion, she was alone. She stretched, the pain that usually plagued her fading, then hoisted herself up. As she stood, she slipped the coin into the pocket of the white robe she wore. Off in the distance in one direction, there were mountains that reached the heavens. They looked as if they were drawn onto a canvas, as she couldn't see the point that they met the pasture, their cool grays floating against the tranquil sky.

She looked in the opposite direction, which was filled with rolling hills and grass that swayed with the wind. The farthest point her vision could pick up was what looked like the tops of trees. The skies were a royal blue, and she could just make out wisps of clouds over the mountains in the distance. The first sound that reached her ears was a very faint rumbling, like thunder. The only difference was that instead of a rumble followed by silence or rain, it grew steadily louder. In the direction of the thunder, something was moving in the air off towards the mountain range. Her eyebrows knitted together in confusion, lightning licking down towards the ground, and in its trail came a dark fog. From above the lightning, a figure swooped down, resembling a bird, but as it grew in her vision, it became evident that it was too big to be a bird, and it moved through the sky in a serpentine pattern. The rumbling was getting louder, and that was when she saw them. They ripped across the meadow over the rolling hills towards her, all those who had been absent in her surroundings. A wave of panic hit her as she connected the dots. The herd was stampeding. They were still pretty far away, but the line of horses stretched far enough to either side that she knew she couldn't get around them.

"I'm about to become Mufasa," she said to herself quietly, a panicked laugh escaping from her.

A roar pierced through the skies, a violent scorch of flame reached towards the stampeding herd. She was definitely mistaken when she thought it was lightning. The fire was coming from the bird-like creature, though at this point, she was fairly certain that these were no birds. Upon closer inspection, it looked reptilian. *Is it... is it a dragon?* She dismissed the idea, thinking it to be ridiculous, yet in a land of impossibilities, she would soon learn that the realm of fantasy blended with reality. She turned and began running as fast as she could away from the flying creature that had caused the stampede. She risked a look over her shoulder as the ground began to shake with the pounding of hooves. She glimpsed the red stallion, Raulin, leading the pack. As she made eye contact, he veered slightly to align with the direction that she was sprinting.

"You must flee!" he yelled as he approached. *Duh!* Arietta thought fervently. At the last second, he dipped his head and yelled, "Grab onto my mane!"

Ari grabbed the thick red mane and was lifted onto Raulin's back. She held on with a vice-like grip, and terror pumped adrenaline through her veins. As Raulin swept across the meadow at a full gallop, an ear splitting roar made Arietta's ears ache, which was followed by an acrid-smelling dry heat that now blanketed the land, erasing that sweet grass scent she'd grown to love.

After what seemed like hours of galloping across Equus, the herd finally reached cover in the form of a forest that stretched as far as the eye could see in both directions. The trees were colossal, with the canopy reaching several hundred feet in the air. As the herd entered the forest, day became twilight as the canopy allowed very little light to filter down to the ground. With the herd safe from aerial attack, Raulin slowed to a trot, and then a slow walk. Every member of the herd that she could see had a thick white foam oozing out of the side of their mouths. Most had a wide-eyed terrified look that she soon realized had very little to do with the attack. The forest that they had entered was eerily quiet. The noises that the many hooves made were muffled, as was the breathing of the herd. Ari leaned forward and whispered into Raulin's ear, "Are we safe from the creatures? "

Raulin answered in a tired, raspy voice, "Those were no ordinary creatures. They were members of the Draconis, the Dragon race. They come from a land on the other side of the mountain range that has kept them out of Equus for ages. I have heard whispers that the Draconis have been testing their power with small acts of aggression, as they are led by a new, powerful leader. It is a dark day indeed; many brave stallions and mares have fallen to the flame."

Arietta looked at Raulin with wild eyes. "I have to go back to Equus! My grandpa told me that I could never leave it! That is Rule 2. You have to take me back!"

"You cannot go back; it's not safe. We now have to focus on making our way through the Silent Forest. Many have tried to make the trek through, but few have reached the other side, at least with their minds intact. They say that the immortuos roam these woods, feeding on the living. We must keep our wits about us and stay together," answered Raulin.

"I think I'd rather take my chances in Equus, where I know I can get home; this forest certainly doesn't sound very safe." She was getting angry, and honestly was quite scared. "What are the Immortuos anyway?"

"Immortuos are the undead spirits that still walk the lands. The way to Equus is blocked, but there is another path for you to reach home. It lies on the other side of the forest. You need to be brave. While any stallion from the Herd of Zeus lives, no harm will come to you," Raulin answered.

"That sounds horrible. I really, really don't want to be brave," she groaned. Raulin ignored this comment, taking this time to process the events of the day. He'd lost many friends, had seen their bodies engulfed in flames. Yet he knew that this was not the time to grieve, for the entire herd was looking up to him to be their leader, to be brave. Honestly, he didn't feel like being very brave at this moment either.

The herd marched in single file through the dense forest. Raulin led the way, keeping to the same general direction, with the herd following quietly behind. After what seemed like several hours with little to no noise, Raulin announced that it was time to set up camp for the night. A stream burbled nearby, which would supply water for the herd.

The ground crunched under Arietta's feet, and she lowered herself to all fours for a few mouthfuls of water. It numbed her throat as it slid to her stomach in gulps. There was a slight saline taste, but beggars couldn't be choosers. Arietta found a spot near Raulin and snuggled in next to him, trying to keep warm. Sleep would not come easy on this night, and the forest was unnaturally void of sound. The quiet was so complete that Arietta's ears pounded. She sat up and wrapped her arms around her legs, shivering. Through the absolute dark that permeated the forest rolled a thick luminescent fog. When it reached Arietta's feet, the stinging of a thousand miniscule needles that soon began to numb her senses. Her teeth chattered, yet they made no sound. A deeper sense of uneasiness formed deep in the pit of her stomach that quickly spread to every part of her being. She knew that she would never see her family again. She wanted nothing more than to go to sleep, and never wake up. No more softball games, no more victory pizza dinners, just nothingness for the rest of eternity.

She took deep, calming breaths, hands clasping. The cold that had numbed her toes expanded to every part of her body. A soft muffled moan escaped from several in her group. Her breath heaved in and out, wispy gray tendrils exiting her nose as proof she was one of the living. She shivered violently, head jerking towards movement in her peripheral vision. Her lips parted slightly, eyebrows coming together in concern.

"I can hear your heart beating, child. I know why you cry. You are alone, and no one is coming to help you. No one cares but me. You can join us, and we will be together forever," a voice whispered in her ears. *"I can hear the wheezing of your breath. Let us relieve you of the burden of breathing, child. We*

will never let you suffer again." The voices were sickeningly saccharine, and she shuddered further. She couldn't remember a time she had ever felt so alone and afraid.

She took a shaky breath, wishing that Grandpa Gus was with her, and did the only thing she knew how to do: she began to sing. "When I am afraid," she sniffled, "and the fog rolls in, I won't fall to the bitter weight of the sins; just come now and stand by me." There was an awful shrieking noise, but she continued her war song. "Just come now, come and stand by me."

As she sang, her eyes became luminescent, glowing blue in the night. The herd, though far away from the pocket of numbing reality that the Immortuos had pulled her into, took notice, and they understood why Raulin had spent such time with the girl. They knew now that she was the one of which the prophecy spoke.

***

Back in the hospital, Gustoff's eyes opened in a flash, breath hitching.

"Oh come now, stand with me." His haunting notes pierced the air, and the ghost of Arietta's voice sang quietly with him. He closed his eyes, and an overwhelming light clouded his vision. He was being summoned to a place that was dark and cold, yet he knew that Arietta needed him. Her form materialized in the air beside him along with a backdrop of trees. Arietta looked over to him, grabbing his hand.

Singing in unison, they continued, "If you stand with me, the gentle rain will wash away the pain." A loud crack was nearly deafening, and the rain cut loose. It was pure gold, tears of the gods. It was cleansing, and the smell of magic attached to it permeated the air. It washed away the evil beings and broke the trance the pair was gripped in, and they were back with the herd. The blue glow from her eyes began to fade.

"She summoned the Great Wizard! She will be our protector," Raulin announced, hoping that this would settle the herd's anxious nature, not realizing that this only put more pressure on Arietta.

"Grandpa?" She was hushed, but she persisted in a quiet tone. "Grandpa Gus?"

"Yes, dear." His eyes bounced from tree to tree, a nervous energy surrounding him.

"When do we get to go home? I'm done with this place." Her haunted eyes broke his heart. He wrapped an arm around Arietta and pulled her into a warm hug.

"Well, we will need to reach a city called Belamoris. There is an old man there who might be able to help us."

She tilted her head. "What's his name? Why can't we leave now?" she inquired. Her ears pricked at the quiet sobs coming from Corin, whose head was shoved into his mother's side.

"His name is Arkas, but don't let that fool you. He is a very powerful and wise wizard." He took a weary breath before continuing. "I met Arkas during one of my longer stays, when I had my headaches. He really helped me out that time. We need to get some sleep; tomorrow will be a long day."

While the night had blanketed the forest in inky blackness, the sun rose to cast the shadow of twilight throughout the forest. The group continued moving in the same direction during the day, stopping for only brief periods. Progress was slowed by the vast number of trees along with the diminished visibility, and without being prepared for the journey, they all relied on the moss that grew at the base of the trees for nourishment. With each passing day, the herd grew steadily weaker.

The fourth day in the Silent Forest brought with it fresh hope, as Gustoff returned to their campsite with two small furry animals that he quickly made into a nice breakfast stew. Arietta rose with a deep, tired yawn to a smell that made her stomach roar.

"Lucky for us, the herd only eats veggies," he said with a smile.

"That smells wonderful, Grandpa. I am so hungry, I could eat a horse!"

Raulin gaped at her, and surrounding horses whinnied nervously, giving the ravenous girl some space. After sensing the tension, Arietta cleared her throat. "Sorry, it's an expression where I come from that means that you're really hungry. We really don't eat horses." With that, the herd relaxed.

Arietta and Gustoff sat down to the first hot meal that they had eaten in four days. Raulin, finished munching on the tree moss, made his way over to them. Ari devoured her soup, not remembering a meal that tasted so good. She pulled her robe tight, trying to keep in the warmth that spread from her stomach that was now full of soup. She let out a small burp and peered at Gustoff. He stared through the trees, appearing to be deep in thought. His white beard seemed thicker and longer than she remembered.

"Grandpa? Your hair…" She trailed off as he met her. He grabbed at his hair self-consciously. "You look like a real wizard now."

"Do I?" The edges of his mouth curved upward. She nodded and smiled at him.

"This place is full of danger; we must keep moving," Raulin interrupted sternly, but not unkindly. The herd moved in relative silence as they plodded through the forest, with Raulin continuing to urge them on, ever-vigilant to the predators that had made the forest their home.

Chapter Five

In the highest peak of Mons Draconis, the mountain kingdoms that the dragons had ruled over for a millenia, stood the royal palace. Lucius spread his mighty wings and circled high above the throne room. Nearing his landing spot, he metamorphosed midair, shifting to his human form, and landed upon his balcony without missing a single step. His day had come at last. His cape flared dramatically as he paced forward through his bedroom. His mind wandered to the failures of the first great war.

The war had raged for a decade before the weapon was forged. The enemy was on the run, and the pride of this small victory emanated from his father. Even at such a young age, Lucius too allowed the adrenaline-inducing bloodlust to eat away at him, much like his father before they had taken his pride.

The Blade of Atonement, made by dwarven magic, shifted the balance of power. The dragons were now vulnerable to the attacks. When the first dragon had fallen, everything changed. His father was afraid. The day his mother was slain by the wizard was the day his father had been broken. That was when Abeloth agreed to the meeting, and Lucius had followed them to the palace in Lenovia and watched in horror as his father surrendered his power.

The treaty that was signed enslaved them and ensured that all dragons stay in Mons Draconis. They had ordered Aboleth to keep their numbers at or under four. Lucius would never forget that dreary day. Dragons were the rulers, not the ruled.

On this day, none dared look upon the great Lucius save with adoration or fear. Those who looked upon him displaying any other feeling would be burnt to a crisp, as the unicorns and other Equus races had today. All of his life, his kind had been spat on. The elves showed no respect, pixies hated them, the folk of Equus, mermaids, every single creature had despised them. Dragons had been ostracized, forced into the mountains. All this for being the most powerful creatures in the lands. As soon as Lucius had killed his father and took his rightful place upon the throne, he knew his mission. He had to take back Palidonaya and force them to their knees. Soon, every creature on the planet would bow to him; soon the race of dragons would reign. The day of reckoning was at hand, and justice would be served.

He sensed one of the Chosen in the land, felt her energy, yet it was of no matter. She was weak and alone, yet he knew that this would not be the case for long. He must locate her and extinguish her flame before she realized her power. The prophecy called for three, so there was still time to ensure that it did not come to pass. As long as he could keep her separated, she would be of little threat to his dream.

***

"Grandpa?" Arietta called from Raulin's back. The stallion twitched, and his tail flicked to the side to snap away a bothersome fly.

"Yes, dear," Gustoff called from the ground. It was obvious that the stallion appreciated Arietta's bravery. Respect was one of the highest compliments from the unicorns, and the fact that he carried her broadcasted his admiration. Though

Corin was both sleepy and grumpy, he followed Arietta and Raulin at a close distance.

"Tell me, Corin, how is your mother?" Corin's mane was wild after the run through the forest, and leaves and sticks hopelessly entangled themselves in it. Corin ducked his head, smiling at the stallion shyly.

"She's okay, I guess." He shook his head, his mane spraying through the air. Raulin snorted, amused by the foal's bashful nature.

"Are we close yet?" The question from Arietta drew Gustoff's attention from the foal and stallion, and he sighed. He was quite tired of this question. It seemed every four minutes the impatient teen asked it. She was a broken record, a one-track mind.

"Try to think of something else. Think about the candy you'll get back home… I don't know, talk to Raulin. It is, at least, a three-day hike from our current spot to the edge of Belamoris." Even grandfathers who had infinite love for their grandchildren did not always have infinite patience. The stallion, in reaction to this, sniffed pointedly.

"Sweets that sparkle," she hummed, running her fingers through Raulin's hair. "Frosted hills." Her eyes glowed a soft blue, yet she paid no notice, fingers busy weaving the hair of the lead stallion. "Drizzled in chocolate, honey and dew." The ground sputtered, and up sprouted small, shimmering plants, and she continued her song. "All the candy in the world, only a dream away." Finally the plants caught her full attention. "Grandpa!" Both Raulin and Grandpa Gus startled at her shout, and she hopped off the stallion. "Look at the candy!"

The plants glowed like stars, and each was weighed down by the peculiar bounty. Instead of berries or some delicious foreign fruit, from each plant's limbs hung colorful chocolate. Instead of green stems, they were rainbow candy canes. She broke several of the stems off of each of the plants, stuffing them in her robes.

"How... how did you do that?" Gustoff breathed, confusion muddying his thoughts.

"She is a child of prophecy. She is the song spinner." Raulin's reverence was felt by the entire herd as a soft whinny echoed along their lines.

"I'm... what did you just say?" Arietta gaped.

"The prophecy spoke of three that would come during a dark time to bring light. I suspected that you were one of the Chosen when you first arrived in Equus. I have seen the pureness of your heart during your visits. The proof came when you were able to vanquish the Immortuos. It is a rare gift that you have been given."

Butterflies born from excitement fluttered in her chest. She giggled, a grin spreading across her face.

"This is amazing!" She pulled one of the candy cane branches from her robe, taking a bite. "What else can I do?"

"That is for you alone to discover," Raulin said pleasantly, and she hopped onto his back. The hours ahead were peaceful, but the peace was not lasting, and a deadly predator had sensed their approach and was planning their demise.

The foal stared at her with eyes larger than the moons. A million questions raced through his mind. "Arietta." He looked nervously from Raulin to his magical friend.

"What's up, Corin?" He cocked his head at her, careful not to trip over his own legs.

"Where do you come from? I have never seen a creature that only used two of their legs to walk." He froze in his tracks, wondering if his question was rude. At Arietta's light laughter, he could tell that he hadn't offended her.

"These," she gestured to her arms, "are my arms. The ones on my lower half are my legs. You've really never seen someone walk on two legs?" Corin shook his head earnestly.

"No, I have not. I've only seen birds and unicorns. My mother does not let me go out of the meadows; she says it is dangerous." Arietta's brows lifted, then fell in surprise at the statement. Rather than pushing the foal for more information, she simply let it go and decided to answer the second portion of his question.

"I come from Earth. It is a place with creatures like me, and we also have other animals. The animals from Earth can't speak, though; they usually just make different noises," she offered.

"Can they not speak, or do you not listen?" Corin stared at her for an odd amount of time, and she cleared her throat. "Will you do more magic?" The strange, mature seriousness had evaporated, and she was left with the playful and rambunctious colt she was used to.

"I promise I will later, but that bit of singing I did wore me out. Would you like to try a sweet?" She offered him a sugar vine, and he accepted graciously.

"Very generous, thanks!" Corin said around a mouthful of vines. Though the mood of the travelers was light, despite their recent tragedy, Arietta had a deep pit of dread that twisted her stomach. The hair on her arms stood on end, and the energy around her pulled taut with dark intention. Something was watching them. Listening to them. Waiting.

Chapter Six

Spirits began to lift after Arietta conjured the candy plants. Small animals rustled by them and the forest hummed, which put everyone at ease. The herd walked with raised heads as Ari hummed to herself, thinking about songs that she knew. Grandpa Gus had insisted that she wait until they made camp to try singing another song, but she could think of little else. This was definitely the most pleasant day of their trek through the forest. Soon the light faded, and Gustoff made his way to Raulin. "We need to start looking for a good spot to make camp."

"I hear the burbles of a stream ahead. The herd will need to drink. We can camp near the source." Raulin made his way to the lead, raised his head and pulled in a giant breath, drawing the air through his flaring nostrils. "There is water on the other side of this ravine. We can camp there for the night."

As they began the trek down the ravine, the gentle crunch of the herd's hooves meeting the ground was the only noise left. Before they started their descent, crickets, owls, and some other noises accompanied them. She gently tugged on Grandpa Gus's arm and whispered, "Why is it so quiet?"

When there was no response, Arietta looked up at him, eyebrows raising with concern. His eyes had turned a pearly white, and his mouth hung open as he moved forward. To her right, Raulin's eyes had also turned to that same, horrible milky white. Arietta could just make out a soft melody that seemed to come from everywhere. The music reminded her of a harp playing quietly in the distance. Her body swayed with the rhythm. She slipped away, struggling against the seductive siren song. Her soul was at rest, her entire being tranquil as she moved down the embankment. Arietta wanted nothing more than to embrace this peaceful feeling. This tranquility, however, was met with a fear that began to creep into her subconscious mind. With the last bit of resistance, she did the only thing that she could think of. She dropped to the ground and grabbed two handfuls of dirt, filling her ears with the damp soil. This new quiet cleared her mind, and terror replaced peace as her eyes followed the slack-jawed faces of the herd as they meandered down the slope. Her eyes paused on Dimitri, Raulin, and Corin, who was pressed against his mother's side. They were zombies, trudging along quietly.

Her breath turned ragged, impending doom casting a heavy blanket around her. Her instincts told her that she needed to get off this path. She couldn't hear the soft melody, and while the dirt that clogged her ears made her feel as though she had a layer of grime all over her, and the urge rushed forward to cram more dirt into her ears to further distance herself from the alluring notes. She followed the herd from a distance, finding difficulty in keeping to the sides of the path, as water long ago cut the walls of the ravine to be steep. It was crafted to trap the wanderers who made the grave mistake of following the enchanting noise. What further disturbed her was the feeling of being watched, of eyes burning into the back of her head.

As the path led to somewhat of a clearing, her skin throbbed, a shiver forcing its way down her back. Of all the creatures of the Earth, there was one that turned her blood to ice, that instilled a panic so extreme that rational thought was not possible. Arietta flattened her back to the wall of the ravine, taking in the horrific sight. The arachnid could not be described merely as a spider. She was as big as a car; a ruby red spot painted her abdomen, and the rest of her was night-sky black. Even from there, Arietta could see her needle-like fangs, prepared to suck all of the essence out of Arietta should she give her the opportunity. She was the mother of all spiders.

Arietta's stomach twisted, understanding what that alluring noise had been. The goliath's web stretched from treetop to treetop, its intricate design morbidly pleasing to the eye, and she was the centerpiece of her macabre work of art. The weight of the goliath curved branches as she moved closer. Eight button-like eyes flashed with an intense ferocity, a pure hunger as she inspected the herd. She used all eight legs to weave her siren song and they danced over the web with a grace that could not be matched as saliva pooled on her fangs, dripping from her vast, shadowy maw.

Arietta watched in horror as the massive spider, with a shudder, opened up the great red droplet on her abdomen, and millions of spiders, varying in size, poured out of her and onto the web. They moved as a black mass, a calculating unit. She released her cluster, and they spiraled down the trunks of the redwood trees. Numbly, with their milky white eyes, the herd stood still; Arietta wanted to scream when she saw what happened as the spiders descended on the first horse, a beautiful palomino mare. The one thing that pierced her shield of soil were the screams of the mare as she was engulfed by the black mass. The spiders pierced her flesh, injecting her with venom. All Arietta could do was watch in blank terror as the horse was reduced to a twitching mass of flesh. Busybody tarantulas worked steadily, weaving threads and using their combined strength to take the horse, the prized meal, up to their master. The spiders and Arietta alike knew that this horse would not be enough; they knew that she was insatiable.

Arietta cursed herself for being frozen. She was pathetic, afraid, and useless. Her fear swelled for a moment as a hand clasped onto her shoulder, and she nearly jumped out of her skin, taking in the boy that gripped her.

"Jerry… is that you?" Her eyes were round as saucers, grateful to be temporarily distracted from what horrors lay ahead of her. He wore large earmuffs to block out the noise and was donning a cloak made out of fine navy-blue fabric. He had been prepared, which meant either that he had some incredible luck, or that he frequently visited. Her eyes flicked over to several horses who had already been strung up in the trees, like gruesome ornaments.

"Fancy seeing you here, Ari; you've gotten yourself into quite the mess, haven't you?" His voice purred, and regardless of the dirt, she was able to hear him.

"How can I hear y--"

He put a finger to his lips, urging her to be quiet.

"Arietta, I have the ability to slip in and out of minds. Now, you must listen to me. Adeline may have eight eyes, but she doesn't see very well. She relies on touch, the vibrations through the web, hearing, and smell."

"Okay." Her voice felt bigger inside her mind.

"I must admit, you were very clever shoving the dirt in your ears. I'm impressed that you were able to hear the music without fogging immediately."

Her ears detected a chime, and the boy brandished two beautiful daggers. They were carved from night-black obsidian, and a large ruby stone featured as the centerpiece. *"Do you have any weapons?"* he questioned, tilting his head.

"No... well, I have my singing. When I sing, magic happens. Why can't you just break the spider's mind? I'm... I'm terrified of spiders." It hit her how childish she sounded, but dismissed the embarrassment, because she was entitled to sounding childish. She was only thirteen, after all.

"I have already tried to enter her mind. It is blurry. It's like she has divided it into each and every one of those millions of spiders you see skittering up the trees. It would be impossible to break them all. Look, Ari, I know you're scared, but if we are going to save your grandpa and the rest of these horses, we are going to need a plan." His usual impish smirk returned to his face. *"All good plans have a distraction..."* Arietta wasn't sure she liked the sound of that, especially after he explained his plan. She didn't understand how he was here with her, but she was relieved to know that she didn't have to face this alone.

She glanced over her right shoulder, where he had been standing seconds ago, yet he was gone. Her heart was a bass drum keeping an erratic beat, and the spiders were working busily on incapacitating yet another horned horse. Out of the corner of her eye, he reappeared, shadows oddly pooling at his feet. He tossed one of the obsidian daggers, catching it swiftly, showing off with a newfound confidence that she had never seen in him. He drew back his elbow, slamming it through the air, flicking his wrist, and following through. The dagger whistled through the air, slicing through several thick strands of the web.

While this world defied many laws of nature, gravity, unfortunately for the lady spider, was not one of them. Her weight became unequally distributed, causing her to lose balance. She toppled with a hiss, pulling the majority of her intricate web down with her. The impact of her hitting the ground shook the earth, leaves coughing into the air. A shriek tore through the atmosphere, and her back left leg snapped and began to ooze a blue shiny liquid.

"Who *dares* attack me in my home?!" she roared, confusion and anger seeping into her words. The sound was like broken glass, clear and cutting, making Ari shutter violently. Several horses shivered, and her grandfather's head twitched. She released a sigh of relief as the ghastly white eyes leaked color, returning to their normal forms when the music stopped. At this moment, Jerry froze with his eyes enlarged as if the grim image of the arachnid had finally confronted him. "I am *the Great Adeline,* and you threaten me in my court?!" Her voice had midnight silk woven through it, and she enunciated her words greatly, doom painting itself in the minds of all who could hear her. Everyone, including Arietta's grandfather, backed away from that roar, all except for Jerry. He remained frozen. His breath had been snatched from him, a deer in headlights, and as she took a clumsy step forward, he gasped, a small whimper forcing its way out of him. Her looming head snapped in his direction, each of her eternal eyes focusing on him. Her mouth formed into a snarl. "*You will pay for this!*" Finally, his brain caught up with him, and he re-extracted the twin dagger from the warmth of his cloak. Her acknowledgement momentarily snapped him out of his daze.

Speaking with forced bravado, he exclaimed, "A gentleman always pays when entertaining a lady?" Due to her impaired vision, she couldn't see how unbridled his shaking had become. Arietta, in this moment, realized that alone, Jerry was fighting an impossible battle. Her mouth formed a small 'O' as the goliath stalked forward, Jerry lunging out of the way. She was distracting him, long legs stabbing at the ground around him. He hadn't seen the ocean of spiders gathering behind him, their writhing bodies stacking, forming a wave to crash down upon him. Words couldn't form, so Arietta did the only thing she could seem to force herself to do: run.

Her legs pumped, pushing from the ground, moving as quickly as she could. His yelps cut through the thick air, the terror strangling his throat as the wave of spiders crashed upon him. She didn't want to think about the spiders that had sacrificed themselves, pouring into his mouth and forcing their way down his throat, biting and pumping their venom into him. Arietta leapt, tackling him to the ground, batting at him, taking handfuls of the spiderlings and flinging them through the air. Jerry convulsed, and Arietta shrieked as the spiders started their way up her legs. The small stings of bites overwhelmed her senses, a cry building in her throat. No longer was she focused on ridding Jerry of Adeline's minions; she was now tearing at her own legs. She was close to hyperventilating, and she looked out of the corner of her eye to Jerry, whose full focus was directed at her. There was a drowsiness in his eyes from being subdued by the venom.

His words were choked from the spiders squirming over his tongue, "Fight it--you can." His eyes resisted the urge to roll back, and the mass forced him to the floor. The spiders used their combined effort to wrap him as a mummy in their silks, and his words echoed through her mind. *Fight it.* She felt so small, so weak; the hot tears on her cheeks reminded her she was just a child. A child that had everything stripped from her: her summer, her softball, her ability to move freely. How was she supposed to be the one to save the day? Her chest heaved, the feather-light feet of the small army tickling her skin. She closed her eyes, not wanting to acknowledge that her skin was barely visible under the heap of black bodies clinging to her.

Arietta began to sing, "When there is danger, he comes." Her lips quivered, and a sob tore through her as the spiders infiltrated her mouth, tasting salty on her tongue. "The wind it stops, the mist rolls in on wings the dragon soars." A heavy fog coughed from the ground, and a hissing sound filled the air. She skipped lyrics, as she was having trouble focusing her thoughts. "The ships, they would l-lower their flag when he lets out a mighty roar." Her singing was garbled and weak, but she hoped desperately that it would be enough, that it would save her. The mist rose higher, and golden eyes shone brightly like lanterns, their eerie glow stinging the flesh of the spiders. A mighty roar blasted through the air, and panicked spiders fled, causing Jerry and Arietta to drop to their knees, clutching their ears.

The spiderlings raced to their mother, evacuating into the pulsing, open abdomen of Adeline as her howl of pain filled the air. She scaled a nearby tree, her body swaying back and forth as she compensated for her missing appendage, small and large spiders alike fighting for refuge within her, following her up the tree. Regardless of their absence, Arietta, eyes still filled with terror, furiously swatted at her body, still moaning in panic. One of the horses rushed towards one of the far trees, retrieving Jerry's dagger between her teeth, and Grandpa Gus grabbed Arietta's wrists.

"Arietta you need to stop! We need to leave this wretched place!" He had finally seemed to force his mind away from the venom. Her eyes were haunting, and she struggled against his hands. Seconds passed until her eyes seemed to clear.

"Jerry." A rushed whisper sighed from her, and she flicked her wrists, demanding to be let go. She dropped to the forest floor on her hands and knees, forcing herself to his side. "Jerry!" With her bare hands, she ripped through the webbing. She screamed his name once more.

"We must flee! We haven't the time for these games," Raulin chastised, yet Grandpa Gus immediately came to her aid. He lifted the frail-looking boy, slinging him over the back of Raulin's heir, Dimitri, who was the closest, fixing the horse with a stern look.

"Please take care of this child; he saved us all today," he growled, blazing white cloak flaring. Gus then turned and placed Arietta onto Raulin's muscular back, and she clung to his neck, trying to soothe the overwhelming fear coursing through her. The mist had dissipated, and a frenzied look came over Raulin. Arietta then lost her battle with consciousness, her eyes slipping closed.

"Onward!" He galloped with a purpose and led the herd away from the carnage. As they reached the hill leading out of the ravine, signs of life flooded their senses once more. The chirping of crickets and the gentle soothing song of birds reassured her that they had escaped the Reaper once more. About a mile out from the nightmarish trap, the horses slowed to a brisk walk, and Arietta woke from her trance and slid from Raulin's back. She stumbled, fighting the lingering effects of the venom still coursing through her system next to the horse that carried Jerry. She shivered, a phantom itch raking over her body. She asked Dimitri if she had permission to mount, to which he nodded, and she climbed upon his rump. She then worked, slumping Jerry upright. His body tilted dangerously to one side before she caught him. Facing him, she brought a harsh hand to his cheek, and he released a soft whimper.

"Jerry, wake up." She shook his shoulders, and his eyes opened, still out of focus. He wiped foam from the corner of his mouth, nose wrinkling, and he wiped it on his pants.

"Hey, Ari," he slurred, struggling to keep his eyes open. She wrapped him in a tight hug, avoiding cringing at the cobwebs still tangled in his hair. "O-oh," he exclaimed in shock, settling into the hug. His heart broke for the girl as her shoulders shook with sobs. He propped his chin on her head and whispered, "Hey, now, you're okay. You're safe now," over and over. They had only been friends for a few days, but they had just been to hell and back together, and that had to count for something. Arietta slid off the stallion, thanking him, and made sure the venom-filled Jerry could safely get off the horse.

After collapsing to the ground, she managed to sputter, "I'm really glad you're okay, Jerry. When I heard your screams… saw all the bites…" She inspected his swollen face. "I was really worried."

"Thanks for saving me," he replied with sincerity. She shook her head briefly, then turned to her grandpa, whose eyes hadn't left her since the event. He was sick with guilt over not being able to do anything, sick that his mind had wandered far enough away that his ability to protect his granddaughter, the most precious being in the world, had been compromised when she needed it the most. How could he ever apologize for leaving her to fend for herself? How could he ever cope knowing that she'd likely have nightmares for the rest of her life over the events that had passed?

Little did he know, Arietta needed no explanation, for she knew it was not his fault. She knew that if he had the opportunity, he would've killed each and every spider before they laid a single spindly limb on her, and would've sacrificed himself if it had been necessary. She held no resentment, nor did she place any blame upon his shoulders.

"Grandpa Gus?" Her small voice reached out to him, and his eyes sparked nervously. "I love you." His bushy eyebrows shot up in surprise at the words, and he immediately understood what she meant to convey with them. A small portion of the burden lifted from his shoulders. He was able to breathe once more.

"I love you too, dear. You were very brave, I'm so proud of you, sweetheart," he said, a relieved smile ghosting his face. Although they had seemed to escape the hurricane of danger, they were merely in the eye of the storm.

The massive spider used the last of her strength to climb to her nest high in the tree canopy. The rest of her finally made its way into her great red spot as she snuggled down into her nest. Her leg screamed with a white-hot intensity as she began the process of healing. Her anger burned brighter than all of the stars in the sky. She had made that ravine her home and had fed for a thousand years. None left her home alive until today. She had envisioned a great feast as that group had been wandering through the forest. It had been so easy to guide them to her. Once awakened, the hunger was always great, but as she quivered in her nest, the hunger racked her body. She fractured herself to claim the beasts that she had taken. She opened her mind, sending slivers of her down to the valley floor. She needed to feed before she could heal. As her main body awaited the much-needed meal, an emotion that she had never felt in her long life ripped through her. She had never been bested before, and for the first time ever, Adeline was afraid.

A sharp pang of hunger ran through Adeline's body as the first unicorn was placed at the opening of her nest. She quickly approached the panicked foal, and her fangs pierced the outer cocoon. The brain was tender and dripped down her throat, delicious and satisfying.

Corin's mind filled with a dense fog as he was lifted up to the nest where Adeline waited. The sting of pain was brief, and there was a pull of acceleration when she began feeding on his essence. He repeated the traditional saying of the herd of Zeus: *May my legs run strong, and may I be one with the wind.* Brilliant white light flooded his vision as Corin of the Herd Zeus galloped into the great meadow.

The euphoria of feeding did little to ease her mind. She would begin the preparation for her vengeance once her body was whole again. She would venture out of her home for the first time, then she would feed as she had never fed before.

When she found them, they would suffer a slow, agonizing death.

Chapter Seven

Lucius sat upright in his bed, drenched with sweat. Two of the Chosen had traveled to Palidonaya. They must be found before they realized their potential. He quickly made his way to the lower levels of the palace, where the high priest of the order loyal to the throne slept. As he approached the room, he found that the door was locked. Overtaken by rage, he engulfed the door in flame rather than knocking. The door disintegrated in a flash of orange light, and the flames kissed his scaly skin. The priest flew from his bed and bent at the knee as Lucius entered.

"Please forgive me, Your Majesty. I did not realize that you had summoned me."

"Another of the Chosen has entered Palidonaya and has joined the girl! We need to close the gateway now."

"This is not an easy task, My King. Closing the gateways takes old magic; I need more time."

With that comment, Lucius clenched the priest's robes in his right hand, lifting him into the air. Smoke curled from his nostrils as his gaze burned into the priest's eyes. The high priest screamed in agony, a searing sensation overwhelming him. His eyes lost their color, from pearly white to charcoal, and the smell hung nauseatingly in the air. Lucius tossed him across the room, the priest crashing into the stone wall and sliding down. Black smoke rose from the empty ebony sockets that once contained his eyes.

"Close the gateway, priest, before my mood darkens. I will not be as forgiving if another joins them." As he turned and strode out of the room, he summoned the healer to bandage the priest's eyeless sockets.

Sleep would not come to Lucius again that night. As he sat in the throne room, his mind wandered. He could almost hear the voices of the leaders who met on that dark day a hundred years earlier. He was just a prince then, not allowed to attend the great meeting. His father, Abeloth agreed to meet with them near the capital city of Lenovia. The leaders from the regions of Palidonaya sat in seats spaced evenly around a large round table. He had signed the treaty that enslaved his own people. He felt himself slipping, the world losing its meaning as he was swept by the ebbing pull of the past.

Lucius had begged his father to avenge his mother's murder, yet Abeloth followed the orders of the council and chose which dragons would remain. The rest were slaughtered like cattle. How could his father allow this? Abeloth was a coward! Little Lucius burned with hatred, watching his friends and family be slaughtered by that caitiff king that he would never claim. There the boy sat, a prince in ruin, covered in the blood of those he held dearest to him. Even at such a young age, he knew that he would be the one to claim Abeloth's life.

That scent of burnt flesh interrupted his thoughts, and Lucius stirred. He wondered what would become of the priest, and if it was even necessary to have sent him to the healer.

The order of the priests had been around for millenia. Their sole purpose was to serve the dragons. They had tirelessly slaved to build the fortress that now stood atop the tallest peak of Mons Draconis and had served Lucius well since his father's death. He had slowly built up the dragon population as the priests had rebuilt the city. Lucius kept their numbers a secret, ensuring that no more than two dragons hunted at the same time. With the help of the priests, Lucius had again brought pride to the once mighty race of dragons. They helped him develop hunters that were smaller and more agile than the dragons and had an uncanny ability to track prey, also helping develop the weapon that would spell doom for the lands of Palidonaya. The Shadow Walkers would be unleashed upon the land like a plague.

In a room distant from the mighty Lucius's chambers, the healer slumped in frustration. She could do little to save the priest's eyes; while she bandaged the seared sockets, no amount of magic could save the delicate material that had been melted. His injuries had proven too severe, and the healer ended the priest's suffering. She hoped desperately that this wouldn't spell her doom, but even if it had, she knew it mattered not. All that mattered was King Lucius, and should it bring him joy to slay her where she stood, she would gladly lay down her life.

A new priestess was transferred into his old room, the door left off. The priests were an odd order, completely and fully devoted to the dragon kind. The priestess, Clarette, gathered her robes of green, assorted them to pool perfectly around her feet and pulled her hood to cover her hair. She awaited the king anxiously, straightened her back, and willed her body into perfect posture. The normal sounds of destruction at Lucius' feet pressured her to create the image of an obedient servant.

"Priestess!" he barked, aggressively entering her room. A feline smile came over her mouth, eyes sparkling.

"Yes, My King?" Her voice was velvet, and he glared at her with distaste.

He took a moment to himself, eyes blazing quizzically. He knew that she understood that her success or failure at the task that was assigned would determine her longevity as both high priestess and as a living, breathing creature. "Is the gateway closed yet?"

That same feline smile returned to her face. "It closes at sunset, though it requires a small sacrifice, if you will."

His eyes narrowed. "What kind of a sacrifice?" He pinched the bridge of his nose, ignoring the pulsating sensation in his head that made him want to roar, pacing back and forth in her cramped room.

"Oh, it's nothing, really. Some of your blood and the ritual is as good as complete." Her voice lilted, and he immediately stopped his pacing. He turned on his heels to fully face her.

"Why *my* blood?"

"It requires the most powerful blood in the land, My King, your blood," she insisted. For a moment, his headache receded, and a lazy smirk came over his face.

"Naturally." He drew the bejeweled dagger he kept on him at all times, looking up to her. From inside her cloak, she produced a small vial, handing it over to him. Without hesitation, he grabbed the blade, sliding it down the length of his palm. He did not wince as he watched the glistening black blood flow into the vial, and he filled it to the top. He inserted the cork, sealing the blood, and handed it back to her.

Clarette took the vial of his blood, securing it to a chain around her neck. "I've sent the hunters into the Silent Forest, and should all go well, the closing of the portal may be unnecessary."

He nodded approvingly at her words.

"I hope their slaughter is brutal," he said, exiting the room without another word or glance.

Chapter Eight

Arietta struggled to breathe, a weight pressing down on her lungs. Every little sound, from the rustling of bushes to the wind in the trees, was off. When she closed her eyes, the spiders traced her skin, threatening to pierce her with their fangs. Arietta shuddered, forcefully pushing out a breath. Jerry took notice, eyes turning to her. He placed a hand on her shoulder firmly to separate it from the light needles of spider legs.

"You okay?" he asked softly, so that only she had heard him. It was different than the sarcastic banter that she was used to. She winced.

"My skin is still crawling; something feels... *wrong*," she said, and that sense of being watched still bit into the back of her mind.

"We are safe now. You don't have to worry about it; I'll protect you," he offered, that bravado coming back full force. She wasn't sure why, but that... that bothered her. She knew they both had nightmares, she knew they both were vulnerable right now, so why was he all of a sudden acting like he had everything together?

She rolled her eyes. "Yeah, like you did that so well last time." More venom seeped into her voice than she had expected, and his eyes darkened for a moment.

"Hey," he said forcefully, and her eyebrows lifted at his tone, "I made the best out of a bad situation. It's not like *you* had any better ideas."

"It wasn't like you had any ideas either; you went out there, threw your dagger and froze," she retorted. Neither acknowledged the nervous whinnies, their argument's volume rising until…

"Arietta!" Grandpa Gus shouted, gaining her attention. To her horror, when her eyes flicked towards where his voice came from, there was nothing. Her eyebrows furrowed, like daggers preparing to crash. Suddenly their argument ceased completely, was forgotten, and she grabbed at his cloak to steady herself. There were no trees, no herd to be seen…

"Where… where did it all go?" Jerry's voice had lost all of its fire. Before she could reply, a voice sounded from all around them.

"*You have entered the One's domain and have bested two of my guardians. Safe passage through my domain comes with a substantial cost. The One has chosen you to represent your group. You may choose safe passage for yourselves only, or you can save your traveling partners if you complete a challenge. None have passed this challenge, as I can trust none to tread my forest with peace in their hearts, but I assure you that the trials are fair. Should you succeed in the challenge, One will grant you and your traveling party safe passage and you will gain a powerful ally. However, should you fail, One will consume you and all who travel with you. Do you accept the challenge, or will you choose safe passage for yourselves only?*" Its voice was the night sky, never-ending and dark. It was the depths of the ocean, drowning them in fear. It held the beginning and the end and long-lost secrets that had the power to abandon the listener to insanity. The children eyed each other nervously, knowing what they must do.

Simultaneously, they stated, "We accept," and while they could not see the thing that was all around them, yet nowhere, its toothy grin spread wide.

In a blink, Arietta and Jerry were in a room with no windows or doors. In the center of the room stood a table with two large jars of liquid and two containers of different sizes with strange markings on them. Directly across from them, there was a fireplace with a fire heating a cauldron. The One began speaking as a tablet appeared on the table with a quill and the markings on the jars swirled until the larger of the empty jars had five dots and the smaller had three.

"The first test is a test of the mind. A potion you will mix and brew, with four cubits red and seven blue. Mix it true you're on your way, but mix it false and you're here to stay."

With the message delivered, the room filled with a silence so complete that Ari's ears almost ached for sound. She turned to Jerry and he appeared to be talking to her, yet the silence remained complete. She pointed to her ears and shook her head. Jerry looked at her quizzically, so Ari clapped her hands as hard as she could. No sound transferred through the room, so Arietta pointed to the quill and paper on the table, picked up the writing utensil, and wrote down the message delivered from the One.

The two largest containers had changed, with one now red and the other blue. Ari pointed to the caldron and motioned for Jerry to bring it to the table. Jerry lugged the caldron over and set it down. He motioned for the quill and began writing.

"I have two questions. Do the dots on the jars stand for the number of cubits that each one holds? How do we measure seven cubits and two cubits using those jars?"

Ari shrugged and began examining each of the containers, trying to see if there were any clues that they had missed. As she was doing this, an hourglass appeared on the table and turned so that the white sand began to sift through the small opening, piling up in the lower half. A pit opened in Ari's stomach, as she knew that all of their lives depended upon their ability to mix this potion.

Ari motioned for the paper. She began by recording a three and a five. She then added them together, as it would be easy to fill each jar, then dump them into the caldron. Jerry motioned for the quill and wrote, "Then pour half of it out!" Ari shook her head and pointed to the phrase *mix it true*. Then took the quill and wrote "It has to be exact!" Then she subtracted three from five. That didn't work either. She tossed the quill back on the table and strode away from the table in frustration. They were running out of time! How could she measure exactly seven cubits and exactly four cubits?

She looked at Jerry, who looked totally defeated. His head was in his hands and she saw that he had been writing on the paper. It simply said, "I hate math." As she read those words, the answer rushed into her mind. She looked at the hourglass and frantically grabbed the five-cubit jar and filled it from the red pitcher. Next, she poured from that jar into the three-cubit jar. Once it was full, she then dumped the leftover liquid from the five cubit jar into the caldron and then wrote *two cubits red*. She quickly repeated the process. She smacked Jerry on the arm and motioned for him to put the caldron over the flames as she began the same process with the blue liquid. She emptied the three-cubit jar on the floor so that she could use it to store the two cubits left in the five-cubit jar, then she quickly filled the five-cubit jar from the blue pitcher and emptied both into the caldron. Jerry stirred the concoction as it began to simmer. As the potions boiled, she watched in horror as Jerry collapsed to the floor. She bent down, shaking Jerry to wake him. As she did, everything went black.

Arietta sat up sometime later with her head spinning circles atop her neck. Jerry moved nearby and she sighed in relief as he said, "Sleeping beauty is finally waking up!"

"Jerry, I can't see anything!"

"It is pitch dark in here. Do you think we passed the first test?"

"Either that or we are both dead and have to spend an eternity together… I really hope we passed the test!" Ari stood and stretched, being careful not to step on Jerry as she did so. It wasn't hot or cold, and there was no breeze. She yelled, "Hello!" and listened for an echo.

"I already tried that while you were out. It's like there is nothing but ground, and there's no wind. I have no idea what we are supposed to be doing here."

The One's voice boomed in the inky darkness. *"The second test in the Challenge is a test of the heart. Terror waits at every turn; stray from the path and you will burn."*

Ari looked to where she thought Jerry stood. "What do you think that means?"

Jerry mumbled that he had no clue. As she strained to make sense of her surroundings, the one thing that stood out from the darkness was an iridescent trail. She gazed down where her feet met that path and she couldn't even see her feet, but she saw the path beneath them. "I think that we are supposed to walk this way." Groping through the black, she grabbed Jerry's shoulder, causing him to yelp. She walked her hand down his arm to his palm, explaining that it was her and that she figured it'd be best to stick together.

They held hands and walked down the mysterious golden path. "What do you think it means by 'terror waits at every turn?'" Jerry said.

"I think that is pretty self-explanatory." Ari did not like the look or the feel of this test. There was a dreamlike nature that she noticed in both of them. The only thing she knew to do was to keep putting one foot in front of the other and see where it led her. Whatever awaited them, they would face it together, and that gave her the strength to continue.

***

Gustoff examined Arietta and Jerry as they lay motionless in the fallen leaves. They had left Adeline's territory yesterday and had been keeping a slow and steady pace. They set up camp on the second day when a coldness had surrounded them.

The two children were in some kind of deep trance. He had tried everything that he knew of to wake them up. He found that his magic did not work in this area, so he had asked Raulin if he could carry the children so that they could continue their journey. If they could get out of this mist, then the children would come out of the trance. That had been two days ago. It seemed that even when walking due west, they ended up circling back to the camp. Gustoff furrowed his brow and looked to Raulin with concern etched deeply into his face.

"Raulin, what do you make of this?"

Raulin shook his head. "There is old magic in the air. It appears that these children are the key. Our fate seems to be tied to theirs. We will have to wait until the entity that has a hold of us shows its intentions."

Raulin then instructed the herd to make camp, knowing now that it would do no good to keep walking in circles. The two children were made as comfortable as possible while Gustoff and Raulin stood watch and waited for the entity to show itself.

***

"Jerry, where are you?" Arietta asked quietly. He'd let go of her hand, not paying attention.

"Right here," he said, and her head swiveled towards the sound. She reached out, and he jumped with a yelp as her hand connected softly with his face. "Ari!" he exclaimed, laughing a bit. She worked her hand down his arm so as to not lose him and linked arms with him.

"Okay, let's see if your heart is strong enough to pass the test," she said sarcastically, and he sighed heavily.

"One foot after the next, that's all we have to do. Don't step off the path or I'll ring your neck before the scary monster gets to you," he retorted. To this she simply smiled, a change in her features that was impossible for him to notice at the moment. "Hey," he said softly, and her attention turned to him. "Whatever happens… Whatever we see, know it's going to be okay. We'll stick it out, so far we have, right?" She mumbled a small yes, and they continued their walk. The path glowed a soft gold, and suddenly, the straight line they had been walking forked. The gentle comfort they'd found in that moment twisted into something more horrific.

"Terror waits at every turn," she murmured softly, and she closed her eyes. Next to her, Jerry whimpered. "Let's go…" She thought it over, then decided, "Let's go right." He mumbled his agreement, and they headed right. Suddenly, light flooded the path, and they could see everything, and it took all of the restraint Arietta could muster not to shriek, for a mutilated Nurse Ratchet stared into her soul. Jerry's face held the same expression of terror, but something told her deep within that he likely saw a different individual staring back at him. The Nurse's legs were far too long, face suddenly oblong, and a gruesome smile dripped off of his face, pooling on the path.

The voice of a demon assaulted her ears as that maniacal smile widened. "You seem to have arrived early for our next session." His head swayed to the side, and he fell to the floor, skittering towards her. "First the legs," he purred, pushing her over. He took the leg into his mighty paws and snapped it with ease. She screeched, the sound echoing, and writhed in agony.

"Don't you hurt her!" Jerry roared, furious, launching himself at the demon. She bawled, rolling on the floor, and watched the nurse produce a belt out of nowhere. Jerry's breath seemed to be snatched from him, but he forced steady inhales and exhales, shaking his head. "You're *not* real." His whisper cut through the air, and the demon thing laughed.

It sniffed the air deeply, and suddenly it was no longer a malformed Nurse Ratchet, but a great spider. "You do not fool me, child; I smell your fear, and I must say it is quite *delicious*." Jerry's face didn't seem to change at the beast's shift, and she wondered if the two shared the same vision. The thing wielded the belt as a whip, and it struck the boy across the cheek. A hot, angry welt rose as he fought back tears. He knelt next to her and lifted her up. She made a small noise at the shift in position for her leg, but he hauled one of her arms over his shoulder, providing support. He forced her to a sprint, running as fast as the pair could manage, and finally, everything faded back to that blissful dark and golden glow.

"What--what did you see?" She tripped over her words, pain overcoming everything.

"I saw my father." His voice was grim, and she decided not to say any more, to let him continue if he wished. "I was the one that found him after he hung himself with his belt." He took a breath. "I was six." She squeezed his arm.

"I'm so sorry." It was the only thing she could force out.

"You know, that's what everyone says."

"Well, I mean it. You shouldn't have had to go through that, especially so young." He tensed.

"I did, though. I did go through it." His voice was stone, no longer seeming quite so afraid, just cold.

She shifted uncomfortably. A light rustling in the darkness echoed, but still they soldiered on. Arietta's leg throbbed in tune with her racing heart. She squeezed her eyes closed and gritted her teeth as they continued down the path.

"The first trial was difficult, but you will surely find, as the challenge progresses, you may lose your mind." The One's voice had a rich vibrato hiss that haunted its words. A chuckle filled the chamber, and its presence dissipated into the darkness.

As those words had the time to replay in her head, and the support of Jerry's shoulder vanished, and she yelped as her full weight was distributed to both legs. She nearly dropped but quickly shifted her weight to her good leg. The path curved ahead of her, and rather than taking a moment to collect herself before moving forward, she made the turn without hesitation.

"Jerry?" There was no answer, only dead silence. Hands dragged down her face, tickling her throat, and then the path disappeared. Hands of shadow, cold and unforgiving, ran over her. There was a deep pit in her stomach, and she groaned. A sense of hopelessness coursed through her, and that unbearable ache that she faced day to day on Earth hit her full force, sweeping her off of her feet.

You never told them what you were willing to risk to feel nothing, did you? Something had intruded into the darkest depths of her mind, using her memories to taunt her. *They never realized how far that little girl would go to stop the pain.* She squeezed her eyes shut, the darkness so consuming that she felt as though it wouldn't be too bad surrendering to it and fading into the void. *Why was such a meek child sent to a world full of wonder and horror? Only the bravest of warriors cross into these lands, and yet they pulled a whimpering, insolent child through the gates. Are you capable of anything other than crying and moaning, child?* the cruel voices asked her, and suddenly she couldn't remember. She couldn't remember any of her abilities, any of the things she took pride in. The only pictures in her mind were those cold hands and her whimpering, pathetic self. Through the fog of despair, a voice roared, and it had the element of warmth. It combatted those cold hands, and it cut through the never-ending night.

"Fight it, Arietta! They tell lies!" *Jerry,* she thought, shaking her head. The pain lessened, as his voice seemed to extinguish the majority of it. *He will hate you; he is only using you. He doesn't want you to succeed. He will betray you. He will take away everything that you love.* The voices shivered in the void.

"Shut up. Every word out of your vile mouth is a lie," she snarled, and the voices laughed. *You wish they were lies, yet every word we have spoken is the truth.* She told herself she wouldn't listen anymore, and so she did not. Crawling through the darkness, hoping desperately she would move past these hateful entities, she shielded her eyes as once more the room glowed. She must have made another turn without realizing it. "Jerry?" But Jerry was still nowhere to be seen. With a shudder, she pondered the possibility of him failing the previous turn and hoped desperately that he hadn't wandered from the path.

"Your second tribulation is nearly through; face the truth, the challenge lies within you." Arietta's face dropped, and she was suddenly not so sure she was ready to face what lay ahead of her, certain she didn't want to face it alone. Still, on her hands and knees she crawled. On the path in front of her lay a puddle, the golden glow of the room reflecting from it and casting diamonds and stars against the walls. The puddle didn't seem inherently evil, and yet it did not seem purely good either. As most things in the world were, it was a mix of the two, sitting firmly in shades of gray. Her instincts told her to circle far around it, to not look into its gleaming reflection, and yet somewhere deeper within her she knew she needed to seek the truth.

She dragged herself closer, inch by inch, her body and mind battling for dominance, but when she reached the looking glass, it was far too late. Shards of memories were the pools, confirming everything she hated about herself, confirming the possibilities of failure, of a life in which the only ground she moved was the ground they dug to dispose of her corpse. Images of a future family who would leave her, and a miserable life spent alone shone back at her. The memories contained her greatest sins, her worst faults, and the monster she knew she would always be, and yet… There was more. There was so much more than the pitiful excuse that many of the memories painted her to be. There was light within the darkness, beauty in the repulsive, and as she stared into that painful puddle, she learned something new. She learned to love. She saw herself in its most sickening form, saw everything she hated about herself confirmed, and yet still she came to peace with it. She learned while staring into the looking glass to love herself as she truly was. While she first hated it and felt like screaming into the puddle that it wasn't true, the longer she stared, the more acceptance bred in her soul.

The mood of the room changed, disdain and frustration lighting a fire in her soul, and its grim frown spreading on the back of her neck. *"A deal is a deal; this challenge is complete. Reunite with your companion and face your final feat,"* the One growled into her ear, and she sighed in relief as Jerry's wonderfully familiar face appeared next to her.

"Are you okay?" she asked as he helped her up. Her knees and hands were scraped and bloody, something she hadn't noticed until that moment.

"For now, yes. You?" A stranger could've told him he wasn't looking well. The warmth seeped from his face, and he looked positively dead.

"For now, yes," she parroted, and the ghost of a smile graced his face, the most she would be able to get out of him in this tortured world. It was a relief not having to face this last challenge alone, and while she wasn't sure she would be able to continue the torture, she braved on, for the herd and for her Grandpa Gus. It was their only option.

The two marched onward, hand in hand, with gaunt faces and dried blood covering their legs and arms from various scrapes. They limped towards the final challenge that would prove to be the most difficult. The path forked ahead, giving them one last direction to choose for their final destination.

The voice boomed overhead as they approached this fork in the road.

The final test is a test of honor. No passage comes free of cost; one of your group must be lost.

Arietta screamed into the void, "We've done everything that you have asked! The deal was that if we chose to complete the challenge, we would be able to save everyone in our group. This is not what we agreed to!"

No passage comes free of cost; one of your group must be lost. YOU MUST CHOOSE.

Arietta and Jerry collapsed to the ground, exhausted both physically and mentally from the Challenge. Ari looked to Jerry. "How can we just choose someone from our group? I thought that we could save them all. I don't think I can do this."

Jerry sat for a moment with a pensive look on his face. "Easy, we choose the oldest of the group. The one who proves to be the weakest. We are almost through the forest, but there will surely be other trials along the way. Plus, from what I hear, the dragons have declared open war on everyone. The older, weaker of the group will not be able to give much help in the war. Who is the oldest?"

A grim, yet determined expression spread across her face. She knew of only one way that she could choose and live with her choice. This was one of the hardest things that she has ever had to do, but this decision felt right to her. With her mind made up, Arietta leaned into Jerry and kissed him on the cheek. "Could you please tell Grandpa Gus that I love him?" With that she limped forward and said, "I have made my choice, Demon. Do your worst!"

What started as a low roar built steadily to an ear-piercing scream. Arietta put her hands over her ears as tears slid down her face. The scream built in intensity until it was all that remained. Arietta's vision faded to inky blackness, and following that came total silence. Everything hurt as someone turned her over onto her back. Her eyes opened to a dazzling white light, which was blotted out by a huge face. There was a muffled sound followed by a cool damp cloth stripping dirt off of her face. Grandpa Gus looked down at her from above. Her guardian angel had arrived.

Gustoff looked down at his precious granddaughter. There were trails of dried blood from her ears that dripped into her hair. He gently cleaned her face and then picked her up to place her on Raulin's back, while the boy, Jerry, was on Dimitri's rusty red back. Gus looked to Raulin to lead the herd. "We must leave this evil place. I believe that the spell has been broken, but we must go now."

With that being said, the herd continued the long trek through the forest, wondering what horror they would face at the next turn. Arietta looked down at her leg, which had been ruined by the reincarnation of Nurse Rachet. She pulled it up to get a better look at her injuries.

"Wow, I really thought that my leg was broken!" Arietta was amazed to find that her leg, though aching, was fully functional and that the injuries that she had sustained were injuries of the mind, not the body.

Chapter Nine

They marched through the day without stopping, wanting to put as much distance between the One and themselves. As the sun melted into the ground, its golden rays dripping like warm butter, Raulin told the herd to prepare camp. The horses looked haggard, but the humans looked like the walking dead. Arietta knew that it had to be hard being so scared but having the expectation of always acting brave. Sometime after midday, Arietta and Jerry decided that they needed to walk. Arietta's hearing was still muffled and a constant ringing interrupted her thoughts; her leg was sore regardless of the fact she'd only been injured in the plane they'd been pulled to. Gustoff left the camp to look for a special plant that would ease the pain while her ears healed.

Arietta and Jerry sat in silence as they warmed themselves by the fire. Arietta could not get past the fact that Jerry was ready to pick someone from their group to sacrifice, and she was pretty certain who he had in mind. She knew at some point, she would need to talk with him about this, but she didn't know how to even begin that conversation. She turned towards Jerry and conflict danced in his eyes as he gazed through the fire. The voices had told her that he would betray her, and though she couldn't imagine him doing so, there was a shadow of doubt lurking in the back of her mind. He had shown up at a time when she needed help, and had risked his life to aid her. Yet there was no explanation from Jerry as to how he was able to travel to Palidonaya without her, or how he had healed himself. One question loomed that was dominating her thoughts and could provide the insight that she desired. How well did she really know Jerry?

She decided that she needed to go for a walk and speak with her grandpa. Maybe he could help her with this problem. Arietta gingerly rose from her sitting position and stretched her back, trying to ease the soreness from her overworked muscles. She slowly made her way in the direction that Grandpa Gus had gone. She couldn't help but notice that Jerry's gaze didn't falter.

As she meandered through the forest, two thoughts entered her mind. First, she realized that her leg no longer hurt, though she was positive that it had been broken by the One. The second was that she could once again hear the sounds of the forest. This was very soothing, and she was soon lost in her thoughts. Before she had even noticed that she was no longer alone, an arm reached out from behind a tree and grabbed her, covering her mouth as it pulled her in.

"Shhh, don't make a sound," a familiar voice whispered. She stifled a scream. Ahead of her a creature perched on the bank, looking intently into the middle of a creek that cut through the forest. It was not any bigger than a large cat, but walked on two legs. There was no hair that she could see, and it had a bluish, slightly iridescent hue to its skin and large saucers for eyes. It seemed to be talking to itself while focusing on the water and wandering through the trees. Suddenly, it lashed out with its right arm, which stretched to a length that was at least twice what it should have been. It jumped in joy as it pulled its hand to its mouth, devouring an animal that resembled a mix between a lizard and a frog. This creature then happily skipped away, never straying too far from the creek bed.

After the creature was out of earshot, Arietta was released, and she immediately turned to see who had grabbed her. A long white beard blazed a path to twinkling blue eyes that belonged to her grandpa. He held his finger to his lips, then motioned for Ari to follow him to the creek bed, where he bent down and scooped a cup full of water.

He then crumbled a plant into the cup and whispered, "ignis." A blue flame danced from his index finger, which he pointed into the cup. Soon, a minty smell drifted up to Ari's nose. Gus raised his hand to his mouth, making a gun with his thumb and index finger, and blew the flame out. He then handed Ari the warm cup and whispered for her to drink the mixture. "It will help with the ringing and pain in your ears."

Ari took a tentative sip, then decided that it didn't taste like the medicine that she had to take back home and continued sipping as they made their way back to camp. She asked the first of many questions that she had as they walked. "Do you know what that thing was that captured Jerry and me?"

"I really don't know the answer to that. It felt like a spirit, similar to the Immortuos we first encountered in Palidonaya. Though I don't remember seeing any spirits that powerful. What happened to you? You were walking along with Jerry, and suddenly you were out. I had two of the herd carry you and Jerry when we noticed that the temperature had dropped several degrees. I really thought that the Immortuos had returned. We were stuck in some kind of a loop. No matter how far we walked, we ended up in the same spot."

Arietta began recounting the tale of the challenge. Gustoff walked quietly by her side, taking in every word. She finished by talking about the final challenge and how she had decided that she couldn't sacrifice one of the herd or him and live with the choice. After she had made up her mind, the spirit screamed as if it was on fire. She had rehearsed how she'd tell her story, trying her best to remove all emotion… to just lay out what happened. Gustoff didn't need to know how terrifying it was, didn't need to know the pain she'd been through. His sad eyes and concerned nods made it more difficult to verbalize.

"That was the test of the soul, Ari. Your sacrifice proved that your soul is pure. Your choice was the only option that would save everyone."

Ari took a deep breath and spoke of Jerry, and how he was so quick to sacrifice another, which verified the voices' warnings.

"Remember that Jerry has not had the same experiences in life that you have. Don't be so quick to judge him just yet. The spirits feed on fear. They sow the seeds of doubt and mistrust, which, if left to their own accord, lead to fear."

"Grandpa, how do you know so much about this forest?"

"I am one of the few living beings to cross the Silent Forest, survive, and not go mad," Gustoff said with a smile and a wink. Arietta considered this, thinking back to the stories he used to tell her, many set in a "deep, dark, and spooky" forest, that he used to describe to the much younger Ari. "My best advice for you, Arietta dear, is to talk to him. Just don't be confrontational. Ask him what happened on his half of the journey the two of you experienced, and remember that those spirits' goal is to drive the two of you apart, and to keep their forest safe. They sensed your combined power, and a pair that strong is dangerous. No one really knows the extent of your abilities, dear, but as soon as you came here… that raw energy connecting with its home rang throughout this world. As for Jerry, he is extremely powerful as well. It's a beast under his skin, scratching to be let out. I am certain that those who practice the darker side of magic don't want the two of you so close," Gustoff explained, his weathered hand clamping on her shoulder.

So with that, Arietta set off to have a conversation with Jerry. When she arrived at the camp they had set up, she was surprised to see what she had returned to. Next to the small fire they'd made sat Jerry, legs crossed, levitating two feet off the ground. He had sweat on his brow, and his palms faced the sun. Shadowy wisps gathered at his fingertips, weaving along his body. The pull of his magic felt familiar. The shadowy wisps had begun to take form when Arietta interrupted his concentration.

"Jerry?"

His eyes snapped open, and he dropped to the ground with a small cry.

She laughed. "I'm so sorry!"

He rolled onto his side, dazed, sending her a glare.

"I can see how sorry you are!"

He couldn't hold his serious face for long before he burst into a laughing fit himself. "Okay, what do you want?" His face returned to a neutral smile, yet his eyes didn't quite match his easy-going spirit. He held her gaze, assessing her intentions. She knew that he was a mind reader of sorts, that he likely suspected her suspicion.

"I wanted to talk to you about what happened when we were separated." She helped him to his feet, and the corners of his mouth drooped.

Chapter Ten

Lucius paced the palace grounds coolly, the rage inside him no longer boiling, just simmering. Clarette, the newest High Priestess, met him in the courtyard, her green robes billowing behind her.

"My King." She bowed deeply, but those impish eyes never left him. He glared at her, but she held her icy gaze to his contrasting fiery stare.

"Priestess," he bit out. "Do you have any updates on the Chosen?"

"The hunters were released as you asked and were tracking them through the Silent Forest when there were...complications." Clarette cringed before Lucius posed his next question, knowing what his reaction would likely be.

"Complications? Have the Chosen been found?" He would keep his composure this time, for a king was not prone to tantrums as a child would be. A king was regal, poised, and elegant. Though angry, he held a cool anger; he was a lake frozen over. Clarette was, however, on its thin ice. She shifted, yet kept her neutral expression, smoothing her cloak and gathered her wits before speaking. She knew that again she must choose her words carefully.

"The Silent Forest is full of dangers. Our small party came upon an ancient being; something older and darker than anything that we have encountered. The hunters have been lost; nothing but dry husks remain." She winced, her eyes dropping to the ground. His pacing was continuous, and each step burned into the earth, leaving evidence of his rage in the blackened ground where he stepped. He forced himself to a deadly calm, but the smoke curling from his nostrils betrayed his inner feelings.

"Clarette." She hummed softly at her name, not daring to meet his eyes. "You know that I do not take kindly to failure." Though he spoke in a calm, reserved voice, Lucius' face flushed with anger. "I will give you one last chance, but only because you have served me well so far. I will not remind you of what happens to those who do not meet my expectations." His voice was not raised, it was quiet, for he knew he had her full attention, and the beast inside of Clarette grinned, but her face betrayed no such chaotic glee.

"Understood, My King," she said, turning on her heel to leave the courtyard and head to her room.

"Has the gate been closed?"

She turned back to him. "Yes, My King, the portal was closed last night as promised." She needed to tread lightly if she wanted to keep her head intact.

"One more thing, Priestess," he called after her, and she turned on her heels to face him. She waited expectantly. "Gather the Generals, but do so discreetly."

That same Cheshire cat grin came over her face. "Is there a reason for your wish for discretion?" His eyes flickered at this as he whirled around to face her.

"You dare question me?"

She held her hands up, eyebrows raised. "Never," she breathed, and his shoulders dropped. He sighed, pinching the bridge of his nose. He chuckled, the unfamiliar sound rumbling from deep in his chest.

"Of course you wouldn't." He shook his head, and this was the first time he caught Clarette off guard. "I've been acting like such a brute. Apologies, my lady. My little birds have detected some schemers within my court. I don't..." He sighed once more. "I don't need spies to make this war more difficult than it already is." Clarette ate up this information voraciously. She twisted the elaborate ring on her middle finger, deep in thought.

***

"So..." Arietta said, observing as he poked a stick into the campfire.

"I would like to talk about the challenges that we faced yesterday. I saw a lot of stuff. I know we saw the same thing for the first challenge. The second challenge..." Jerry closed his eyes and rubbed them, dropping his head as Arietta continued.

"I'm sorry, I shouldn't be pushing you like this. It isn't fair; you haven't been pressing me to share what I saw." She backpedaled with her words, a ball of guilt in her stomach.

Jerry sighed. "No, stop. It's fine. You will tell me if I tell you, though, right?" She nodded grimly. He took a breath, preparing to share the horrors he'd encountered when they separated. "The thing that broke your leg... what I saw was my father. When I was six, he hung himself with a belt on his closet door. There was no note, only a blue face and drool dribbling out of his mouth." He took an unsteady breath, shaking his head, then forced himself to go on. "At the next turn we made, I was blind. I couldn't see, only could feel these cold hands. They confirmed my greatest fears, told me that you would betray me. They said many things, proclaimed it as truths, but when they said that you would betray me... I knew they were lies. I heard you crying, it was louder than all of the whispers, it seemed to drown out everything else, so I yelled to you and dragged myself further through the path. Anyway... the next thing I saw was the worst of all of it. I'm not sure what you saw at the next turn, but I saw this... this mirror, I suppose is what I'd call it. It had this beautifully elaborate golden framework. It didn't show me my reflection, though, it showed me bits of my past and future. I saw every single one of my fears confirmed, saw all the horrible things I thought about myself to be true. It told me to let go. It taught that there was nothing in me to love, and when I accepted that, and only when I accepted that, would I be released from it." Arietta's eyebrows furrowed, and she contemplated their difference. Both of their keys to freedom required acceptance, but it broke her heart that his acceptance led to self-loathing.

"And the final challenge?" He turned to her, searching her eyes in confusion.

"What do you mean? You were there." She fixed him with a look, as if to ask him to explain. Jerry continued, "Alright. When we were told to choose, I tried to find someone who had a long life, someone who would understand that it was a sacrifice we needed to make. We are kids, we haven't gotten the chance to taste life yet, we have that right, you know. When I said the oldest, I wasn't referring to your grandpa, I promise.

95

I was thinking about one of the horses; there are so many of them, it didn't seem *that* bad." Jerry had grown defensive, and they both knew it.

"It's okay. I was just… curious." Her voice was strained, and he tipped his head.

"When you offered yourself to the thing… I was terrified. The challenges were nothing compared to that moment. Please, promise me you'll never do anything like that again, not without telling me first." His broken heart showed in his eyes. She gave him a promise she knew that she could not keep.

"Of course, I promise." A grim smile of appreciation spread across his face, and she averted her eyes. Things grew quiet between them, and tension hung heavily in the air.

The sound of silence was something foreign to Arietta's ears. It was too quiet, and her eyes wandered over to Jerry. The boy was staring at one of the charred trees, deep in thought after their conversation, and she was curious as to what he was thinking. Leaves blanketed the ground, and tree nuts decorated the forest floor. An idea popped in her mind, and she grabbed at the ground. The leaves were wet, which was gross, but she had her little fingers secured around the bumpy, roughly ball-shaped object. Jerry's light humming filled her ears, and a grin spread across her face.

She had to go easy, as she had a strong arm and often underestimated how hard she could throw. Winding back, she sent the nut in an arc towards the unsuspecting boy, and *plunk*. "Hey!" he yelled, his hand immediately traveling to the back of his head. He whipped around to face her. "That hurt?"

She let out a low whistle, averting her eyes from him. "Haven't you heard? It's raining tree nuts. Really figured the horses would've let you know." A sly smirk quirked her face, and he let out a low groan of frustration. A few paces away, Raulin snorted, insisting that he wasn't a lowly horse.

"You're gonna pay for that, Beaufort." His pointer finger flicked upwards, and three of the tree nuts shot into the air, levitating at his sides.

"Impressive. Want to teach me how to do that?" Her eyes were glowing a bright blue, but the nuts nearest to her stayed firmly grounded. She knelt quickly, picking up a thick stick, adjusting the weight in her hands. The three nuts soared at her, and she wound up, cracking one of them through the air. Arietta had timed it perfectly. The nut flew straight back to him, and he had to dive out of the way to avoid being struck again.

"Game on, Beaufort." Arietta grinned, lowering her butt and assuming batting position. Though they were in an alien world, she quickly found that her softball skills were better than ever, and a stick was not all that different from a bat if held in the right hands.

"Stay classy, pitch," she sneered, and he waved an arm in a pitching motion. Like a puppet, the tree nut was obedient to the boy and shot towards her. She stepped aside, allowing the nut to hit a tree behind her.

"Strike!" He drew out the words, making it sound more like *stee-rike*.

"That wasn't a strike! You have to swing and miss for it to be a strike."

He twisted his face, mocking her. He lobbed another nut, and this time she swung, hitting it with a boom of thunder.

Jerry smiled and said, "So she *can* hit the ball after all. Interesting."

"I'll aim for your forehead next time. I'm sorry I missed," Arietta snorted, and for a moment they had forgotten they weren't home. The silence of the forest wasn't as deafening.

***

The next morning, Arietta awoke, finally feeling rested for the first time since she had arrived in Palidonaya. The mood of the camp changed from grim to hopeful. Grandpa Gus and Raulin were deep in conversation as she approached. Gustoff turned to Arietta with a large smile and gave her a hug, asking how she was feeling this morning. Ari replied that this was the best she had felt in days. Grandpa Gus announced, "We have two more days at most in the forest if we make good time. Let's get moving!"

With that, the herd began a slow walk to the west. Grandpa Gus hummed as he walked. This further brightened Ari's mood as she caught up with Jerry. "Hey, Jerry, how are you feeling today?"

"I am pretty sore. I think that thing really hurt my ears. They have been ringing and aching since we returned. Don't your ears hurt?"

"No, Grandpa Gus made me some weird mint tea last night. It seemed to dull the pain immediately. I woke up with no pain or ringing at all. Let me ask him if he can make you a cup."

Arietta then picked up the pace, falling between Raulin and Gustoff. "Grandpa, Jerry's ears are really hurting today. Do you have any more of that tea that you gave me last night?"

"No, I don't. I will keep my eyes peeled as we continue walking. Could you run down to the creek and fill this cup with water? That way, when I do find the dreadnought, I can have the tea ready."

Arietta skipped away, heading for the creek. She had to use some of the smaller trees to brace herself as she made her way down the incline to the water below. As she bent to scoop up some water, a noise caught her attention. That same little blue creature that she had seen with Grandpa Gus the other day, was trudging along close to the water, engaged in an intense conversation with itself.

"Yes, I hear the unicorns up there. They won't hurt us, I promise. Unicorns are nice to us; they always be nice to us. Oh, I bet they would even give us a ride!" The small blue creature had a smile on his face, hands clasped hopefully in front of him.

The smile quickly turned to a sneer. "No, they won't! They hate us! They fear us because they don't know us. We must hide!"

"Hello, little guy, my name is Ari."

The creature looked up in horror as it finally noticed the terrible creature reaching for him. He closed his eyes and puffed out his cheeks, then began stretching. The creature grew to twice his size. Arietta pulled back the hand that she had offered the creature, when the sheer terror shone in his eyes. When the creature realized that she was not a danger to him, he blew out the air in his cheeks and immediately shrank back to his regular size and scampered up to meet her.

"My name is Rogar the Strong! I am very glad to meet you." He placed one arm across his waist and held the other high and performed a deep bow. "I am at your service, my young lady. Do you like shizbiz? I can catch you one."

"No, thank you, I just ate and am very full. I am looking for something called dreadnought. Have you seen any?" Ari decided then and there that with some help she could get all of the ingredients for Grandpa Gus' magic tea so that Jerry wouldn't have to suffer longer than necessary. Arietta was careful to keep her voice down and to look non-threatening. She didn't want the little guy to get all puffed up again. Rogar seemed very happy when she mentioned dreadnought. He jumped into the air and out into the water, swimming to the other side in seconds, where he sprang out of the water and ran parallel with the creek to a large moss-covered tree. There was a plant that looked like some kind of vine with purple flowers growing up the side of that tree. Rogar quickly plucked a few leaves and one purple flower, then repeated the process of springing into the water. In seconds, he was in front of her, shaking the water off of his hairless blue body. His smile stretched completely across his face as he handed Ari the dreadnought. "There you are, pretty princess. What do you have to trade?"

Arietta pensively took note of all of her possessions. She then reached into her robe and grabbed a penny. She looked at it to make sure that it wasn't the golden coin that allowed her to travel here from home. She then handed Rogar the penny. He was delighted. "It is so beautiful! We are so lucky to have met the princess with the precious coin."

Arietta thanked Rogar for the dreadnought and hurried back up the hill. She had to hold her hand over the cup so that she didn't spill any of the water as she jogged to catch up with Gustoff. "Grandpa, I got the water, and a little guy named Rogar the Strong helped me find some dreadnought! You can make the tea for Jerry."

As she approached Gustoff, she reached into her pocket and produced the dreadnought. When she neared her grandpa with the plant, he quickly hit her in the hand with his staff, knocking the plant to the ground. "Did you put any of that in your mouth?"

"No, just in my pocket," Arietta said as she shook her hand. Her hand was purple and quickly swelling. "Grandpa, look at what you did to my hand!" The swelling was moving unnaturally fast. Gustoff grabbed Ari, tugging her down the slope towards the water.

"I never should have sent you alone!" Gustoff raced to the edge of the creek. The swelling had made its way to her shoulder, and Ari could not flex her fingers, nor could she bend her arm. The swelling had halted at her shoulder, but her arm felt as if it had been stung by a thousand bees.

Gustoff worked quickly, picking up a handful of moss, a few leaves from a nearby tree and a few red berries. He tossed those into his cup and used a stick to work the mixture into a paste. Next, he added water from the creek and mixed again.

Once he was satisfied with the consistency, he carefully applied the paste to her arm. The pain immediately began to subside. "What else did the nightingale touch?"

"I think just this hand, but I did put it in my pocket."

"Did the creature reach into your pocket?"

"No, but I gave him a penny for helping me find the plant."

Gustoff shook his head. "This is not good. What did the creature look like?"

Arietta sighed heavily. "He was blue, like a small, frail man. He was the creature that we saw by the creek last night. He was scared of me at first, then was very nice."

Jerry was sliding down the embankment as Gus positioned Arietta's swollen arm into the water. "That creature is called a Shebaat. Their sole purpose in life is mischief. He gave you a poisonous plant and got you to offer something in return. That exchange bonds the two of you together. We definitely have not seen the last of Rogar." Gus turned towards the herd and yelled, "Raulin, can we rest for a few minutes so that I can make more paste for Arietta's arm? I can also make Jerry some dreadnought tea to ease some of his pain." With that said, the herd rested by the creek while Gustoff worked his magic for Arietta and Jerry.

Chapter Eleven

Present Day

Arietta walked into the kitchen, needing a break from sitting at her desk writing. She slowly reached for the top left drawer and gently pulled it open. Cooper saw this and let out a low-pitched howl as he hurried to her side and sat, cocking his head to the right and patiently waiting. Arietta then snapped the leash onto his collar, and the two made their way to the front door. Cooper loved going on walks, but he knew that he had to travel at Mother's pace, or he would be left at home. Arietta gently opened the front door, followed by the screen door, and locked up before heading down the sidewalk with Cooper.

Memories kept sailing in, and Arietta kept recording them. She needed to know why she was suddenly able to remember a time from her childhood that had always been shrouded in mystery. She had known that she spent time in the hospital, but really remembered little else. She was struggling to make sense of the strange tale that was unfolding as these memories resurfaced.

Arietta had to slow Cooper down so that she wouldn't fall. The dull throb in her hip had been steadily worsening, and if she fell, she didn't think that she could make it back home. Ibuprofen had been her savior, though she was careful of how many she took each day. Her hope had been that her hip would quit hurting after a couple of days of rest. She knew that she should be taking it easy, but one could only stay cooped up in a house for so long. She stopped at the first intersection from her house and decided that she would turn around and head home. If she went the full distance around the block, she would definitely pay for it in the morning.

Cooper let out a low growl as they approached her house. There was a car parked along the road in front, and a man stood at her door, looking through the window. Arietta gave a tug to Cooper's leash to quiet him. If this was a visitor, there was no sense in scaring him.

Arietta yelled to the man, "Can I help you?"

The man flinched, as if he were startled. "Hello, Arietta, is that you?"

He seemed friendly enough, but the hair standing up on Cooper's back caused her to approach with caution.

She answered, "I am Arietta. Can I help you?"

This man looked similar to the one that she had seen at the grocery store, except he had a pencil-thin mustache, though he had no eyebrows. The eyes were that same emerald green that she remembered. Cooper let out a low growl, stepping between this stranger and his mother.

The man smiled, though the look was more wicked than friendly, "I hope so. My name is Tim, and I collect antique weapons. I have heard that you may be in possession of something that I could purchase."

A confused look came over Arietta's face. "No, I don't have anything like that. You must be mistaken."

The man shook his head. "We know you have the weapon. We can make you a very wealthy woman if you would just let us have it." He took a step toward Arietta.

Arietta looked at the man and frowned. "Tim, I don't know what you are talking about. If you don't leave now, two things are going to happen. First, I will let go of this leash and you will have a chance to meet the business end of Cooper, my Rottweiler. Once he finishes introducing himself to you, I am going to call the police."

Tim smiled again. "No need to be hostile, Arietta. I was just leaving. It would be much easier if you would give us what we want, but we are patient. We will be in touch." He then made a wide berth around Arietta so that Cooper didn't have a chance to make his acquaintance. He got in his car and left.

Arietta limped up the stairs, unlocked her house, and wondered what would have happened if she had forgotten to lock up before she left. She let Cooper off of his leash and settled in her recliner, turning the heating pad to high and wrapping it around her hip.

The heating pad began to ease the physical pain that her hip was causing her, though it did nothing for the emotional pain that she was feeling. Tonight would not be a night of writing, but of grieving. Arietta and Joey met on this night, thirty-one years ago. She remembered it as though it were yesterday: the excitement of fireworks climbing their way into the night sky, bursting into glorious plumes of color. The vibrancy stung her eyes, the sound booming across the lake that the boat sat on. It was a dangerous night to go out on the water, so many boats crammed into the bay like sardines to watch the fireworks, but it had been worth it.

Joey had been a friend of a friend, and he had been invited to join them to watch the fireworks. It had been a magical night, and she agreed to go out with him a week from that day. Together they had twenty-seven beautiful years of marriage, the last filled with hardship and heartbreak.

She wept when they learned of the terminal cancer that was slowly but surely taking over his body, but they had come to terms with it. They vowed to make their last stretch of time together as good as it possibly could be, but they had forgotten the effect of disease could have on a person. Their first few months were lovely, filled with traveling and bittersweet moments. As time progressed, however, she watched the love of her life wither away.

A groan escaped Cooper, and she looked down to see him looking into her eyes, the top of his mouth curled under, showing his teeth in a doggy smile. She sighed wearily. "You always know how to make me feel better, Cooper." As the loving companion Cooper had always been, he could tell when Ari was upset. He eased himself onto the chair alongside her and rested his head in her lap.

Arietta extended the legs of the recliner and floated into a restless sleep. Visions came to her mind, flooding her senses. Her family room was replaced by a vast pasture filled with lush greens. The seeds from the tall grass tickled her legs as the wind swept over and around her The same mountain range with the peaks disappearing in the dark storm clouds towered over the land. Lightning clashed as flames fell like rain, igniting the farthest reaches of the meadow. Arietta turned and began moving away from the firestorm. The first hint of smoke permeated her nostrils as the flames approached. She knew that she would not be able to outrun the storm, but she would not lie down and accept her fate. Arietta grabbed a handful of the still-green grass and held it to her nose, hoping to lessen the effect of the smoke.

Flame blocked Arietta's path, so she turned, looking for a way out. The flames stung her skin, and smoke filled her vision.

***

1972

Gustoff wasted no time as he gathered extra ingredients for paste and tea. He quickly made Jerry and Ari both a cup, which they sipped while he made more paste for Ari's arm. "You are a very lucky girl. If you had even touched your mouth with your hand, the swelling would have made it difficult to breathe. Men have died from one of the purple flowers being ground up and added to their food. The tea will help with the stinging, and the paste will continue to pull out the toxins. Dimitri, would you mind letting Arietta ride at least until our next break?"

"Anything for our savior." Dimitri held still, allowing Ari to climb onto his back.

"So, Dimitri, tell me about yourself," Ari started, beginning a conversation between the two, and Gustoff walked ahead, his mind wandering.

He sighed with worry and thought to himself, "Some wizard I am. I can't even keep my granddaughter safe." With that he continued walking with the herd to the west, knowing that soon they would be back at the hospital safe and sound.

The trees were thinning out the longer they walked, and by the time the traveling herd set up camp for the night, oranges of the sunlight bounced off the twilight blanket the forest was constantly wrapped in. Grandpa Gus grabbed at his knees, lowering himself slowly to rest on a nearby log. "We are less than a half day's walk to the edge of the forest. Once we clear the trees, we will make much better time." Raulin nodded approvingly.

"Yes, we will, wizard, but we will also lose our cover. Let us pray the Dragon King is not waiting on the other side of the forest." Raulin then began to graze on the moss growing at the base of a large tree.

Arietta was starting to get some of the flexibility back in her arm, as the swelling was barely noticeable. Jerry already seemed to be feeling better. He had been so quiet all day. Originally, she figured he was mad at her, but after several hours of walking it became evident that he was just hurt worse than she'd realized. "Hey, you okay?"

Jerry looked her way and yawned deeply. "I will be after I get a good night's sleep." Gustoff approached the two and handed each a glass of tea for them to drink before lying down for the night. The minty flavor relaxed their bodies and minds. Soon, they were both sound asleep dreaming peacefully.

When Ari's eyes opened, she stretched and took in a deep breath. There was no pain anywhere in her body. Jerry stirred and asked how he felt.

"I feel great! Nothing on my body hurts. I think that this is the first time in the past year that I woke up with absolutely no pain."

The camp came to life. Arietta and Jerry both helped Gustoff make a breakfast stew. "Just think, kids, tomorrow at this time we will be eating breakfast at the inn after sleeping in a bed!" There was a quiet excitement that stirred in the air, and the pace of the herd reflected this. The children walked together and spent most of the morning deep in conversation. They were excited to finally see civilization after this long and dangerous walk through the forest.

"When we get to the inn, what kind of food do you think they'll be serving?" Arietta pondered excitedly.

"I hope they have chicken... and vegetable soup. You don't think they'd have ice cream, do you?"

Arietta lifted her brows as the boy listed several more food items, most of which she doubted they would have.

Arietta turned towards Jerry. "Someone's hungry. Have you had your ration today?"

His face drooped, desire in his eyes. "I wish, but no. I've been saving them until I get so hungry I can't stand it. It's too bad, though, because while it lasts longer, it's made me into this constantly hungry monster, and while everything I eat seems to give me relief... It's never enough."

Her own stomach turned uncomfortably. "I'd try to summon us food, but the only song I know involving food is the Candy Dance. Last time I sang that, I gorged myself on so much candy I nearly threw up, but junk food doesn't really make you full," she said, but his face lit up at the idea. She rolled her eyes. "I'm assuming that you want me to try the spell again?"

"Please." And so she began singing. The results were unexpected to say the very least. In place of the wonderful candy sprouts, an egg pushed its way out of the ground on the end of a long brown stem. Arietta walked over to investigate, and as she neared the strange plant, the egg started twisting, trying to free itself from the stem. She let out a yelp of shock, and she backpedaled when a hand shot from the creamy white shell. With a moan, a bald man in a pinstriped red and white shirt freed himself from the egg.

"Who are you?!" she demanded, arms crossed.

The man looked her up and down in an assessing manner before he said, "I'm the candy man." A wicked grin spread across his face. Upon further inspection, each of his fingernails were a different color of the rainbow, and his eyes were a startling blue. Before she could say another word, he sprinted deeper into the forest, taking refuge in its darkness.

Arietta was frazzled to say the least, her eyes wide and brows furrowed. "Well, that… that was not what I was looking for?" Her voice turned upward, suggesting the statement to be a question. Regardless of Jerry's empty belly, he burst into laughter.

"I think we should begin training together," he said through his laughter.

Arietta smiled and said, "Hey, I may not be experienced as a spell singer, but I get the general point across!"

Jerry did his best to look serious. "So you wanted a bald man rather than heaps of candy? Look, Ari, it's not an insult. I need practice too. We just need to be able to sharpen our gifts, to keep us safe."

She crossed her arms at this. "I tried getting you candy," she said, suddenly sad.

"Hey, I know you did. It's okay, though, soon I'll be able to eat my ration, and not long after that we'll be feasting on real food, right?" Jerry said hopefully.

"Yeah, I guess," she moped, and he wrapped an arm around her.

"You've got to admit, that was still pretty awesome that you were able to produce a whole being with your gift," he chuckled, and she shrugged.

"The clearing is ahead," Raulin's voice boomed from a few paces away. The kids looked excitedly at one another, hope glimmering in their eyes.

The sun was at its apex as the weary group stumbled out of the silent forest. The herd's numbers were decimated both by the initial attack of the dragons and the long walk through the forest. They gathered at the edge of the tree line to wait for the stragglers, to rest, and to eat a small dinner. They would then bend their path northwest towards Waterhaven, where they would arrange travel to Belamoris.

The strength returned to what was left of the mighty Zeus herd. She counted twenty unicorns in their group. She tried to remember how many were in the herd when she had arrived in Equus. It seemed like there were thousands, but that couldn't be right. "Grandpa Gus, how many horses were in the herd before?"

"I am not sure, honey. I do know that the herd numbered over five hundred when I was a boy. The day of the dragon attacks was the darkest day in the long history of the herd. They lost more than their families and friends; they also lost the home that had served the herd for many generations."

The group had been under constant threat over the past several days as they crossed the Silent Forest. There had been no time to grieve for the lost. Raulin called the herd together at the edge of the forest. The three humans kept to themselves as he addressed what was left of the once mighty Zeus herd. "We are all that remains of the line of Zeus. There will be time for us to remember those who fell, but now we must continue to survive. You will travel with the humans to Belamoris, where you will find refuge. The path I must take leads through the Sword's Edge and into Aridol. I must call a meeting of the Council of Elders. They must know of the treachery of the Dragon King. With the treaty broken, there will be open war. I must convince the great nations to stand together."

"My King, where you go, I go. You cannot make this journey alone," Dimitri exclaimed as he lowered his head. The rest of the herd whinnied and pranced in agreement. "This journey is too dangerous for you to make alone." Dimitri's voice rose to a commanding level as he looked to the others.

Raulin gazed off to the Western skyline. "Dimitri, you are a brave stallion, but you are my heir. Should I fall, you must lead." Dimitri stamped, ready to protest. Raulin added, "It is done! Now we must part ways. I will not return until I have united the seven kingdoms of Palidonaya. Our herd will be avenged!"

With that, Raulin turned to the north, leaving Dimitri to lead the remainder of the herd west to the city of Waterhaven. Dimitri was lost without his lead stallion, but he understood that the fate of the herd of Zeus rested squarely on his back. He gathered the remnants of his kind together, and they took a moment to mourn the lost. After several minutes of silence, the herd chanted in unison. "May their legs run strong, and may they be one with the wind."

Arietta bowed her head, tears streaming down her face as she remembered the colt that she had befriended in her first travels to Palidonaya. "May your legs run strong, and may you be one with the wind, Corrin."

Chapter Twelve

Lucius awoke well rested, knowing that this would be the day that the next phase of his plan would be put into action. He summoned Hestia from her resting place, as she would play an integral role in this mission. As he entered the throne room, he transformed into the magnificent black dragon. Footsteps on the landing outside of the throne room broke through his thoughts and he turned in time to see Hestia enter and lower her head to the king.

"You summoned me, My King."

"Indeed I have, Hestia. You were once known as the Queen of Fire to the races of Palidonaya. That was before my father allowed us to be imprisoned in these mountains. Today, we leave for Belamoris. Our mission is two-fold. First, we cripple the seven kingdoms by burning their center of trade to ashes. Then, we will find the Chosen that have united and end the threat that they pose to our kind."

Lucius spread his magnificent sable wings and took to the sky. Hestia galloped forward, launching her violet form upwards and followed. It had been an eternity since she had ventured out of Mons Draconis. Energy pulsed through her veins as she soared through the clouds. She tasted the anticipation as she followed her king. It was an honor to be chosen to embark on such a monumental quest for dragonkind. She longed to burn the infidels. Yes, she would follow her king wherever he led; whenever he needed her, she would be there without question. Dragons were meant to rule, and they had bent the knee to the Council far too long.

According to Gustoff, the city of Waterhaven was a two-day trek from where they had exited the forest. They finally felt safe, as they no longer worried about the dark spirits that reside in the forest launching attacks against them. They were tired to the bone, but the hope of reaching Waterhaven kept them moving. The sun continued its journey to the west as the group trudged on, and as the sky turned to twilight, they entered a small village that went by the name of Dell Meadow.

Dimitri and the herd made camp on the outskirts of the village in a grassy meadow while Gustoff led the children to the local inn, aptly named The Dancing Pony, to arrange rooms for the night. Gustoff entered an office and asked Arietta and Jerry to stay in the main room. There were no objections as they quickly warmed themselves by the fire. A few minutes later, Gustoff emerged from the office with a smile on his face. He led them to a table, where they were served the most ambrosial, savory stew that they had ever eaten.

"I don't know if this really tastes this good or if I have eaten so many dry rations that anything would taste like this!" Jerry laughed as he scooped the last of the stew into his mouth. He washed it down with a large mug of cider, eyes closed with enjoyment. Ari laughed as she finished her stew. Her eyelids were heavy, threatening to close, and her stomach was so full it was uncomfortable. Gustoff smiled as he finished his stew and sipped on a tall mug of ale.

"Grandpa, would it be rude for us to just go to bed now? I am really tired." Ari yawned as she spoke. Gustoff smiled at her and nodded.

"We hope these rooms will be satisfactory; the discount seemed necessary for the man who had saved this inn all those years ago," the inn owner said pleasantly.

"Thank you, we have not slept in a bed for weeks, and this was the first real meal that we have enjoyed since our journey began. Now, if you don't mind, I would like to retire for the night." Gustoff padded off to his resting spot He stopped by the children's rooms to ensure that they were still asleep and safe. He locked their door, and once he hit his bed, he immediately fell into a deep sleep that would be the last restful night of his journey.

The herd had eaten their fill of the rich grasses that grew in the plains. The innkeeper arranged for the horses to enjoy a good brushing and an almost endless supply of water to replenish them before they slept. Strength returned to Dimitri, and his mind settled on his king's quest to call a meeting with the Council. "Come home safe, Father," he whispered into the night as he drifted into a deep sleep.

Feeling the effect of one good night's sleep in a warm bed with a full belly was simply amazing. Arietta woke as the sun drifted from the right corner of her window to the left. She reached both hands high in the air without a single creak or pop from her back. Grandpa Gus had arranged for a hot bath before breakfast, so she felt clean and energized as they packed extra supplies into backpacks furnished by the innkeeper. They were again on their way before the sun had reached its highest point in the sky. She walked with Jerry while Gustoff strode alongside Dimitri at the front of the herd.

"Hey Jerry, want to see what we can do?" Arietta was thinking about a song that she could try out that could help her control her power without causing any major issues. Jerry nodded curiously as Arietta gazed pensively in the distance. The herd chatted amongst themselves as Ari began singing. "Hello darkness, it's nice to see you again..." As she began singing, the heavens swirled, and massive clouds formed. Day turned to twilight as sound ceased to flow, the only audible noise coming from Arietta as she continued to sing.

Jerry stared at her with wonder as an energy seemed to build around her. Her eyes shone bright in the sudden darkness. The herd had come to a halt. Ari continued singing.

"Then the lightning splits the darkened skies. The wind and rain came down to claim their prize." Lightning zagged its way across the sky with a loud crash. Arietta blinked, realizing what she had done, and quickly switched songs. The temperature had fallen several degrees with the absence of sunlight. "I like to see the sun shine, down on me. The warm brightness makes me so happy." The sun suddenly appeared, bringing with it an increase in temperature.

This got Gustoff's attention, and he quickly joined the pair. "Ari, as you sing, try to focus on the result that you are wanting. Otherwise, the magic will make its own sense of the words. You could do something like making day into night and turning your entire party mute. Try something a little less drastic."

"Something like this?" Arietta began singing, "I see the trees reaching to the sky. The flowers bloom and it makes me sigh. The beauty of nature takes my breath. It makes me feel that we've defeated death." Suddenly roses sprouted and bloomed around them. A tree sprang from the ground, reaching skyward. Ari stopped singing.

Gustoff shook his head. "Think about a specific result." He swung his staff about his head, and the trees and roses disappeared. Ari looked down at her feet, then smiled at the worn shoes on her feet. She closed her eyes, concentrating on the desired effect, and began, "I've been-a walkin'. Down the beaten path, but my feet just hurt me oh so bad. My new boots they feel so rad." She stopped the song there and looked down at her feet to see a brand-new pair of Palidonayan walking boots on her feet. Gustoff smiled and gave her a wink.

She then turned to Jerry and said, "Let's see what you can do." The spirit of competition flared in his eyes. Jerry was there one second and gone the next. The air shimmered like a mirage in the distance. She could almost see his shape, but couldn't make it out. A breeze whispered in her right ear and she jerked around to see him smiling on the opposite side of where he began. "That is so cool!"

"Well, I can't change the weather, but I can enter someone's mind and make them see, or not see, things."

Gustoff had a quizzical look on his face and said, "You didn't just enter her mind. I couldn't see you either!"

Jerry smiled. "I have found that I can have the desired impact on a group as long as they are close together. I have that ability along with some pretty radical skills with my blades." Jerry produced two ebony blades as if from nowhere and began spinning through several lethal moves.

"I pray that you will not need to use your skills with the blades again, though I fear that they will be needed before our journey comes to an end," Gustoff murmured solemnly, causing the conversation to come to a halt. Uncomfortable with the silence, Arietta let out a laugh.

"Way to kill the mood, Gramps."

At this, Gustoff released an uneasy chuckle.

Chapter Thirteen

Lucius and Hestia saw the great city of Belamoris in the distance. Lucius soared towards a small uninhabited island off the Eastern coast of the main island. Hestia followed. "My Lord, we're not to raze the city and set it ablaze?"

"You will remain here while I infiltrate the city. I need to prepare an army that can hold Belamoris once it has been conquered. There is plenty of wildlife here for you to rest and keep your strength. When the sun sets for the seventh time, you will come to me. The city will be destroyed and rebuilt for our use." Lucius transformed and waited until nightfall. He would swim to the island city tonight and begin the preparations. He found a quiet place to rest through the day, as he would not rest again until the next sunrise.

Lucius awoke as the last rays of sunlight glimmered off the waves. He silently slipped into the water and began the hour-long swim to the coast of Belamoris. His heart beat heavily, a drum of war in his core. He would don a cloak to blend in, hiding the scales that glimmered in the sunlight, though he wouldn't be out much in the daytime. This work needed to be concealed by the cover of night.

The inn's bell rang, alerting the shop owner of the new customer's entry. Lucius pulled up the hood of his cloak and wrapped its fleece-lined body tighter around him.

"Hello, good sir, is this your first visit to Belmoris?" The man behind the desk said these lines tiredly, as though he'd delivered them a million times before and knew he would say them a million times more.

"Your finest room. I want everything you can offer me," Lucius demanded, and the man felt uneasy at that tone, at the thunder in his voice. Not realizing the consequences, he showed the hidden king to his finest room.

Once there, Lucius inspected a delicately pointed claw, then in a swift motion slashed out, slitting the man's throat. Blood sprayed Lucius's fair skin, and his tongue emerged between his rogue lips, tasting the essence. The man's eyes went wide with surprise and pain, and he wrapped both hands around his throat. He made a pathetic gurgling noise, his breathing wet and difficult. His gaze never left the emerald eyes of Lucius, and when he dropped to his knees, Lucius gripped his shoulders.

Lucius ran his fingers through the man's hair, the blood on Lucius's fingers making the hair a sticky red, and the king made a soft shushing sound. "Now, now, it'll be alright. Let go, it'll make things faster." The man closed his eyes at these words. "That's it." The man's heart slowed, and Lucius heard when it stopped completely. While holding the man upright, Lucius slit his wrist and held it to the keep's mouth. As the warm liquid slid easily down his throat, his eyes fluttered. They flashed open, and emerald green shone out in a burst. The gaping throat wound sealed shut, and the luster in his eyes seemed to return, but no longer did his heart beat, and no longer did he need to trouble with breathing. He scanned Lucius', taking him in.

Lucius extended a hand to him, helping him back on his feet. "I have given you the gift of eternal life. I am your master now."

"Who are you? What are your intentions?" His voice was gravelly, yet his eyes held steady to the king's.

"My name is King Lucius. I have a very important mission for you." For those he summoned from the grave, there was a deep inner compulsion to do his bidding, and this was no different for the keep.

"Yes?" he asked, and the thing couldn't help but feel a pure joy out of having a purpose in the king's eyes.

"You have a very important task. We will descend upon Belamoris like a plague. You will help me to build an army that will take this city." The keep nodded his head eagerly. "You simply need to share my blood to resurrect the slain. You must hurry, as you will need to take shelter when the sun rises. Now go and build my army!" The man who rose from the dead bit and clawed his way through the peaceful town; he tore through marketplaces and through the plaza. He was one with the night, a whirling nightmare. By the time the sun rose out of the eastern sea, the two had turned fifty able-bodied men, women and children to the cause.

The next time the sun set, the ghoul invaded a familiar house. It was his home, where his family slept. Had his eyes not been blinded by the strong coveting mask Lucius had thrown over him, he would've stayed as far away from this place as possible. He crept into his youngest daughter's room, standing by her side. She stirred at the sound of him, sleepy eyes peeling open.

"Daddy?" Her eyes squinted, and her little fists rubbed at her face. She knew something was wrong, and she cowered, scooting away from him. "Daddy? Are you okay?" His hands were around her throat, the vice-like strength unknown until that gloomy night. She let out a choked cry, and tears streamed from her forest green eyes, and she watched him as he stole her life. Her face turned an ugly blue, and finally, when she breathed no more, he forced his wrist to her plump lips. The toddler swallowed the black blood, and then he left her to turn the rest of the house.

Her mother screamed when the little gremlin-like girl climbed from the bottom of the bed, tiny baby teeth ripping through her throat. The child relished the taste of fresh blood, and offered her own in exchange for it. The cycle of death and blood continued as Lucius slept peacefully through the daylight hours and wreaked havoc after sunset each evening.

***

Arietta loved her new boots, as they were shiny and incredibly comfortable. She had forgotten how wonderful a bed felt under her compared to the back of a horse or the ground, and while the room was cramped, since she shared it with her grandfather and Jerry, the bed was all her own. It was warm, cozy, and in her mind, there was no place closer to heaven than between those ratty sheets.

"Ari?" Jerry whispered into the velvet dark. He heard a stirring in the bed to his right and knew he had her attention. "Where do you think we go after we reach Belamoris?" His voice was soft, as to not wake Gustoff, who was snoring loudly.

"We go home. While this place is full of wonder, it's just not the same as being home," she declared. Jerry's face dropped, but his movement was obscured in the pitch black of the room. He released a pent-up breath and turned on his side. "What's wrong? Don't you want to go home?"

"No, everything back home was hard. Life was painful, and I was always exhausted. This place is beautiful. I can *walk* here, I can even run. Earth took that away from me," he confessed, and she thought upon that for a few seconds.

"Won't you miss it, though? Your mom, your friends… school?" A silence filled the room, and Jerry drew in a shaky breath.

"That was taken from me when I got cancer. My friends stopped visiting me, I couldn't keep up with my assignments when I missed all the lessons… My mom became a ghost. I miss the past, but I can't win that back." He was just a shell, that hollowness he felt on earth traveling to Palidonaya. Arietta wasn't sure what to say to this or how to help, so she remained quiet. "It was so lonely, you know. The only anchor I had was my mom, but even she changed. I don't blame her; it's hard seeing someone you love suffer."

At this, Arietta sighed. "Look, Jerry, I know you are angry. This place is no different than home. Everyone dies, and people get sick; the place you go doesn't matter. You can't blame it on the stars, not on the planet… that's just life. It's just stuff we need to deal with." She tried to be reasonable, but what he was saying was beyond reason. She knew he was angry, but she needed to guide him towards the truth. He was dying, but he knew it was just life, so why couldn't she understand?

"Maybe you're right, but it doesn't change what will happen to me once I go back. It doesn't change the pain I will have to suffer through." This place was everything, and even in its scariest moments, it was far better than the alternative. He could be who he wanted to be, *do* what he wanted to do. There were no rules, and certainly no limits to his indulgence.

"I know."

They slept through the night, and when they awoke, sunbeams danced through the room. Arietta laughed when faced with Jerry, whose bedhead was untamable. He tried running his fingers through his hair to smooth it out, yet somehow seemed to make it worse.

"Try to use your magic," she suggested through her laughter. Grandpa Gus laughed as well, but unlike the young man before him with the messy hair, he had been up for several hours and had already tamed his white mane.

Jerry's face screwed up, and he cast a glamour over his hair. To Arietta's surprise, it took one try for him to master his intention, and she couldn't help but smile at his success. The kids scrambled downstairs to the inn's living hall, where breakfast was set up. Grandpa Gus trailed behind to fill himself another cup of coffee while the kids gorged themselves on delicious rolls and foreign purple fruit.

When Arietta filled her plate for a second time, she asked another guest what the wonderful fruit was called. The lady paused in the line, turning to the little girl with wide eyes.

"You've never had an Uganlan fruit?!" she asked wildly, but not unkindly.

"No, we aren't from this area. It's very good though!" Jerry chirped, mouth stained purple.

"Well, like I said, it's an Uganlan fruit. They grow off of an Uganlan tree, which is native to Lenovia. I grew up working on a tree farm there," the tall woman said gleefully.

When the pair were out of the woman's earshot, Jerry wisely said, "I didn't realize we asked her for her life story." At this, he received a sharp pinch from Ari.

"Be nice! She was being helpful." He held up his hands, one gripping yet another Uganlan fruit. "How many of those have you had?"

"Arietta, I hadn't eaten anything but rations for the last month! I *deserve* to eat as many of these tasty little things as I want," he harrumphed, and Arietta laughed.

"A whole month in the woods? We met up with you after a week's worth of hiking," she said.

"Yeah... I got lost and had to figure out how to survive. I, well, let's just say that I would just as soon forget the first few weeks of my stay. I am stronger now than I have ever been, and I plan on staying here."

Gustoff finished off his hot cup of coffee and nodded to the children. "Arietta, Jerry, are you ready to head out? We are only a few miles outside of Waterhaven, and if we make good time, then we can arrange for passage tomorrow." With that, the group left the inn and headed out.

The herd moved at a quick pace, as they could sense the end of their long quest. Dimitri was weary from a restless night. It was now his job to lead, and the weight of the herd was upon his broad shoulders. He didn't feel as though he was ready. He didn't think he could fill his father's immense shoes.

The sky was clear and the trail was smooth. Arietta hummed as she walked, feeling both full and safe for the first time since she had arrived. She was really enjoying the day as they made great time on the first road paved with stone that she had seen in Palidonaya. She worried about the herd. How would they stay safe, and where would they live? There were some plains on this side of the Silent Forest, but Equus was their home. Surely Raulin would be able to meet with the Council and they would agree to help the Zeus herd. She would have to worry about that later as she breathed in the fresh air and increased her pace to catch up with Dimitri.

***

Raulin continued north, heading towards the distant peaks of Swords Edge. This was the highest pass in the known world. This pass led to the capital city of Aridol. There in the northwest tower was the meeting place of the Council. The Council had disbanded after the last dragon wars, with its members scattered across Palidonaya. Only the King and his court remained in Dragon's Bane, the castle that lay just beyond Swords Edge, the highest point in the mountains of Lenovia. It has been said that one could see the entire continent from the Northwest Tower. Once called, the representatives from each of the seven lands that made up Palidonaya would gather at Dragon's Bane. The council would offer the Zeus herd protection.

He had been traveling for the better part of three days and was just now entering the foothills of the Iron Mountains. Raulin knew that another day of hard travel would see him beginning the long climb to the Sword's Edge, where he could cross the mountain pass that led to Aridol. He slowly made his way to their last, best hope.

The temperature continued to fall as he approached the pass. The wind was steady and extremely cold, slowing the travel. His hooves were sore and his mane was tangled, but it would be worth it. It would be a harrowing journey, but Raulin, like any other great leader, was willing to do anything for his people.

Chapter Fourteen

The herd had finally reached the outskirts of Waterhaven. The crisp morning air had morphed into a warm, breezy day. The town came to life with merchants selling goods that were brought in from Belamoris. There was a bazaar with every color of the rainbow represented in clothing. Turning the corner, Arietta could see shops of every size and shape all along the street. Citizens moved with a purpose whether they were shopping, selling or heading to work. Gustoff took the lead, as he was the only one from the group who had been there before. He was looking for a certain inn that was along the shores of the great ocean. The inn served as a central hub for traders from both the north in Casparnia and the island traders from Belamoris. Arietta had never seen a city as busy as Waterhaven.

Gustoff entered the establishment known as the Wayward Pelican. He quickly made his way to the barkeep and asked for Gilly. The barkeep lifted a hand and pointed out the door. "He is at the docks securing his boat. He will be in shortly. In the meantime, would you like something to eat or drink before he arrives?"

Gustoff nodded and took a cup of warm ale to drink. He watched as Arietta and Jerry found a place to sit and wondered how close they have grown over the journey. Many a day, the two gravitated towards one another. He downed the remainder of his ale and headed for the door so that he could touch base with Gilly to see if he could arrange for passage to the island for the group. After some haggling, the two reached a price that was acceptable to each. Gilly would be leaving at dawn for Belamoris.

Gustoff then made his way back to the Wayward Pelican to procure a place for the group to sleep. That would give them the better part of the day to explore the city. Arietta would really enjoy the bustling city as traders entered the harbor delivering goods to be sold in the mainland. There were a few places that people would go to for entertainment. He remembered jugglers and dancers as well as the trainers of the Yabis, the deadliest serpent save a dragon in all of Palidonaya.

Gustoff had the rooms paid for and then took the children on a tour of the city. They ate baked Chani along with biscuits for lunch and enjoyed watching the entertainers as they performed exotic dances, juggled knives that were on fire, and acted out intense dramas to the cheers and jeers of the crowd. This had quickly become Ari's favorite place in all of Palidonaya. By suppertime, the children were ready to eat and head off to bed to get a good night's sleep before the ride in Gilly's ship.

Dimitri and the herd again stayed on the outskirts of town and awaited word from Gustoff that he had arranged for transportation to Belamoris. From that point, Dimitri really didn't know where they would go. Why the herd didn't just stay in Waterhaven, he did not know. There was plenty of shelter, and once one left the city limits, there was also plenty to graze on. The longer Dimitri considered his options, the more certain he was that they would remain in Waterhaven. He would touch base with Gustoff later before he retired for the night.

"Hey," Jerry intruded into her mind.

"What are you doing in my head?"

Jerry externally winced at the irritation in her voice.

"Sorry... I was wondering if you'd like to sneak off, see if we can find anything interesting in the town," he offered, and Arietta looked nervously at her grandpa, whose steady eyes bored into the ship they would soon take. *"Oh, don't mind him. He's focused, you know, trying to figure out our plans. He could use a break from the two of us."* At the hesitation he sensed within her, he prompted again, *"Come on, Ari, it'll be fun!"* Begrudgingly she agreed. She was curious as to how the pair would sneak off, yet didn't have time to question Jerry before finding her answer.

"Hey, um, Mr. Gus?" Jerry's voice sounded tired, and when she looked over, his posture hinted at exhaustion.

"Yes, Jerry?"

"Look, Ari and I are pretty tired. We were wondering if you would escort us to the inn?"

She tried masking her confusion, but when Gus turned his back after agreeing, Jerry lifted the intention he had over himself and looked as lively as he was moments before.

"Okay, I'll see you kids to bed. I will retire along with you soon, I just have some loose ends I need to tie up before tomorrow's voyage," Grandpa Gus said. His walking staff clicking down the cobblestone road, he led them to the modest inn in which they'd be sleeping. After the kids were tucked safely into their separate beds, Gus wished them goodnight, murmuring that he'd be back in around two hours. Nearly ten minutes after that, they executed their plan.

"It's clear." Jerry threw off his blankets, jumping to his feet. "Two hours of freedom in the town! Are you ready for some fun?" he said enthusiastically.

"Not to be cheesy, but I was born ready."

Jerry chuckled, and Ari's wry smirk turned to a grin. They walked down the hall, and Jerry cast his intention over the pair. Neither looked to be themselves, and that was exactly what they needed.

"So, I heard that there was this amazing place in this town that no tourist would want to miss…"

"I'm listening." Arietta felt a stir of excitement.

"It's called the Wishing Well," he said in a hushed whisper.

"What's so special about that? We have those on Earth." She knitted her brows in confusion. Jerry's grin softened into a sweet, excited smile.

"It is supposed to actually work, but only for the purest of wishes." His tone was filled with awe, and Ari's eyes lit with stars at the words.

"Really?" she breathed, trying to imagine such a thing. Her heart fluttered, and suddenly, sneaking out was more than worth it.

"Really. What do you say we go try it out for ourselves?"

In order to catch a wagon, Arietta sang a song to the wagon puller, a horse by the name of Eduardo. When singing, she willed a single gold coin into existence, and to her delight, it worked.

"Thankee', ma'am, that'll do, that'll do." The horse nickered. "T'was a lovely little ditty you did there."

"Thank you very much, sir." A rosy blush came over her cheeks at the praise.

"Sir," the horse said thoughtfully, "why, no one has called me that in quite some time. Working horses like myself don't get no respect in these parts. Your words are kind, ma'am, very kind indeed." Arietta lifted her brows at that, shock written across her features.

Arietta said, "Well, sir, where I'm from, everyone's equal, and everyone deserves respect." Eduardo, the respectable working horse, swished his tail.

"Had I a horn they'd treat me like royalty, ya know, but no simple horse from here that does a lowly job has the pleasure of being called sir on the average day. Where are you from, girl?"

Jerry pursed his lips, bouncing as the wagon traveled down the uneven road.

"Earth, it's... not around here," she offered. And Eduardo whipped his tail at a fly that had landed on his rump. The coin pouch attached to his wagon jingled delightedly.

"No, I suppose it wouldn't be, never heard it before."

"Are you sure you should be telling him that?" Jerry questioned her privately, a sense of urgency in his tone.

"Why wouldn't I?"

"Haven't you noticed that people, well, unicorns, are calling us the Chosen Ones? We have these amazing abilities here. Look, I just think remaining as unnoticed as possible, giving out as few details as possible while we're at it, would be the smart thing to do."

Arietta shifted on the wooden bench, considering his words.

"Alright." Jerry released a heavy sigh. *"I suppose it wouldn't hurt to keep to ourselves."*

Eduardo seemed to notice the long silence from the pair and decided not to prompt them with any more questions. They were likely done talking with him, he assumed, and that was mighty alright with him. All he needed to do was earn a good coin and return to his family once their trip was through.

"Was my coin enough for a round trip, or should I find another?"

"No, m'lady, I told ya, the coin was far more than I usually get in a whole week. I just don't have that much change, if I'm being honest," Eduardo replied.

"No, no, keep it, that's fine. I don't need it anyway," Arietta said nonchalantly, and the horse whinnied gleefully. Arietta's breath was stolen from her as she finally saw the Well. The wagon rolled to a stop, and Arietta took in every detail of the Well. The sun had set; Jerry and Arietta figured it'd been about half an hour since they'd left, and the milky moon was high in the sky.

The Well seemed to glow in the moonlight, and Arietta's mouth was still agape when she hopped from the carriage. Jerry, the same awestruck look on his face, followed her footsteps. The pair stood at the mouth of the well, staring into the abyss. It was so deep that even when they strained their eyes, they couldn't see the water at the bottom. Once more, Arietta began to sing, and the sound swelled and echoed back at her from the mouth of the Well. This time, two beautiful gold coins floated in the air. She took one for herself, and handed the other to the impatient Jerry.

"Remember, the wish has to be pure. Nothing produced from greed or spite or selfish intent, not that I'd think that you'd do that," Jerry whispered. He kissed his coin and flipped it off of his finger.

"What did you wish for?"

"I can't tell you that or it won't come true," he said, and he hoped desperately that his wish would work. He had wished for his mom to be happy, despite whatever physical condition he was in on Earth; he had wished for her to not worry as much, and for her to know that he was safe and being taken care of.

Worlds away, Jerry's mother sat up abruptly. She gasped and heard the words from who could be none other than her son. Tell my mom that I'm okay. Tell her that I'm coming back, and to keep hope. Tell her to be happy. *Her hand reached to her plump face, and she wiped the tears that had steadily leaked from her for nearly a month now.*

Arietta followed suit, kissing the coin, and then she tilted her hand, letting it slide off. She had wished for her pain to disappear back on Earth, but as soon as the wish was made and the coin left her hand, it defied gravity, cementing itself to her skin.

"I guess that was selfish," she said with a tone of despair. She kissed the coin once more, and it unglued itself, sliding off her hand and disappeared for good. They got back onto the wagon, both staring longingly at the Well, then disappeared into the night. The stars glittered like the dust of angel wings, and Arietta rested her head on Jerry's shoulder. "I hope our wishes actually come true," Arietta whispered at a volume only he could hear.

"I have this feeling in my gut that they did. Can you feel it too?" His eyes never left the stars.

"Yeah, I do." The road rocked them back and forth, but there was not a moment that their stares left the stars. They had never seen this many in their lifetime. The sky was a landscape of diamonds, and they burned into the children's eyes.

***

Nova had finally found the missing ingredient and made the trip to Palidonaya. There were two treasures she'd uncovered upon arriving. The first was the amazingly impossible fact that she could transform into a wolf when she was in this world. Her first transformation from her human form to her wolf form was terribly painful. The jolt of all her limbs tensing and her entire body turning malleable nearly sent her into shock. The high she rode after completing her transformation made it more than worth it.

The second treasure she'd uncovered came in the form of heightened senses. There was a familiar scent in the air that she had begun to follow. The two that she had seen in the hospital left a scent behind that was familiar. She decided that they would be her family. Destiny whispered into her fluffy ears, and she was off to find them.

The two that she had followed here were close; she could smell their scents mingling in the air. She paused, listening to the flutter of a moth as it flew across her path and landed on a blade of prairie grass. The heat signatures of every living being made the night as visible to her as the day. Her paws met the cool cobblestone that led into the seaside town. She trotted evenly through the streets and was surprised by how many vendors were open so late. Once she hit the square, Nova's mind bounced from booth to booth, anticipation thrumming through her veins.

The wolf form had impacted her much more than she'd realized. In one booth, a squirrel was selling candied nuts, and a surge of predatory delight flooded through her. Her eyes dilated, nostrils flaring obnoxiously. That squirrel was a jerk. She fought the urge to hurtle herself through his stupid candied nut booth and make him pay for his squirrely sins.

"Nova, no." The sound came out as a growl. She'd seen a talking owl, and the squirrels were chatty, so she wasn't sure why she couldn't talk. She prowled the streets, and the others' scent stretched thinner. Where were they? Green eyes met her own, and another growl escaped from her. That man smelled bad. His eyebrows were missing from his face, and the moon reflected from his hairless head. Those horrible green eyes bore into her own, and the sudden urge to protect those that she followed ran through her.

Meeting her eyes, the man smirked at her and turned on his heel, marching down a narrow alleyway. Her hunt had changed; she would need to find her pack later. She flung herself through the night, running faster than she ever had before. There was a building at the end of the alleyway; she had him trapped. She panted heavily after screeching to a stop, and for once the man looked scared. That smug grin had vanished into the shadows. A sly hand slipped up the arm of his robe, and she let out a low snarl.

"Little wolf, I would advise that you leave now. I'm going to kill you and your Chosen friends, and when I'm done, I'm peeling that pretty coat of yours off and wearing it as a new cloak. One Chosen is far less dangerous than three; you will never amount to anything without your friends." Rage filled her vision, and her claws lengthened. The hair along her back bristled, and the human half of her backed down, surrendering to the waves of anger that pushed her forward.

Her vision went out for a moment, but after waking up, her snout and teeth were stained with blood, and she stood over ribbons of the man. He was a bad man who was endangering her pack, and he needed to die. Her grin looked more like a snarl, but she was the victor. She had protected her pack, and she had lived to protect them another day.

Chapter Fifteen

Outside the inn, Gustoff paced. How had no one seen the kids leave? Not a single soul within a three-block radius had seen any teens that fit their description, so where did they go?

Along the cobbled road, eyes torn from the sky, the children shared a look of understanding that they were in deep trouble.

"How are we going to do this? Are we coming clean or sneaking in and greeting him from inside?" Jerry asked, and she masked her surprise at the question.

"We aren't going to *lie* to him," she said harshly, and he raised his hands as a form of surrender.

"Alright, alright." He released his intention over the two, and Gustoff's eyes lit dangerously. They hopped out of the wagon, walking shamefully towards him.

"What were you thinking?!" he roared, more to Arietta than to Gerald. "You don't understand the dangers of this world; you simply haven't been here long enough to understand! Not only did you deceive me, but you went off on your own and put your lives in danger!"

"We were just going to the Wishing Well—"

"I don't care! Don't ever sneak off like that again!"

After receiving a good old-fashioned scolding, Arietta and Jerry went to their rooms, where Gustoff provided a watchful eye until they were sound asleep. Their journey was coming to an end, and he was not about to let any harm come to these two children.

Gustoff tried desperately to rest, but sleep did not come easily that night. As soon as he had given up and begun to get out of bed, a soft clunk sounded at the door.

"Hello?" Gustoff questioned cautiously, looking through the peephole revealed an anxious Dimitri waiting patiently for an answer. "Dimitri, it is always good to see you. What are you doing here so late?" Gustoff questioned the stallion pleasantly.

"I have come to ask for your wisdom," Dimitri offered.

"Let's discuss this elsewhere. Arietta and Jerry are sleeping." Gustoff grabbed his cloak, following the red-coated stallion out of the room, through the halls, and out of the inn. They moved silently to avoid waking any of the inhabitants, but once out of the inn, the town still purred with activity. Buildings were still open, and nocturnal beings were doing their nightly shopping.

An owl on the corner called out from his perch, "All books on shelves one through three are fifty percent off! Come on in and get yourself some good summer reading material, spell books, and genres from mystery to historical fiction!" Gustoff regarded the owl with fascination and excitement at the deal; he would have to stop there later.

"Gustoff, Waterhaven has everything that the herd would ever need. They are exhausted from the journey here and need time to rest. The plains outside the city offer plenty of space and grasses to graze upon. This is a safe haven that will allow us to rebuild our numbers. We owe you our lives, but I do not feel that we could offer much help in the journey across the sea," Dimitri said carefully, and Gustoff stroked his beard.

"I understand. I do agree, as well; it makes sense for you to stay here. Take the time to heal and rebuild your numbers. There will be a time when you can return to your lands in Equus, but until then, Waterhaven will offer you the respite that you need." Dimitri nodded.

"Thank you, Gustoff. We really do appreciate everything you, your granddaughter, and Jerry did for us. We could never repay you, but we will try once we recollect ourselves. Have a safe journey." With that, Dimitri dismissed himself, saying goodbye and trotting off toward those who remained in the herd.

Gustoff, thinking he deserved it for all his struggles, traced back his steps to the bookstore for which the owl had been advertising. Digging deep into his pockets, he counted out the coins that he had remaining from his childhood. It was illegal to make coins from any spells, though several had tried. He hoped that Arietta hadn't attempted conjuring coins in order to make the passage to the Wishing Well. Just thinking about it made him sigh deeply; after all, inflation was *not* a joke.

While Gustoff didn't sleep that night, he did have a pleasant and relaxing time reading the new book he purchased for fifty percent off the original asking price.

**

Jerry yawned, his tongue searching the roof of his mouth. He had the worst taste in his mouth. Morning breath was a killer in a land without toothpaste. "Good morning," he groaned, rolling on his side to face the older gentleman in the bed to the right of his own.

It was evident to Jerry that Gustoff once more had been up, and downstairs to the main room, as he had coffee that was still steaming in his hand and several books at his side. One he had open in his hand. "Good morning, Jerry," the man exclaimed, licking his finger to turn the page.

"You ready for the boat ride?" Jerry asked quietly, glancing over to Arietta's sleeping form.

"Seeing that I have nothing to pack, yes, yes I am," Gustoff said wryly. "Is this going to be your first time on a boat?"

"Yes, it will be. I'm pretty excited," he said, running his fingers through his dark hair.

"Once we arrive in Belamoris, I must warn you that it will be strictly business. We have no time to wander, nor do we have time to shop. It is a beautiful place, and once I get you kids out of here and back on Earth for a bit, I don't mind showing you around there next visit, but we don't have time for that now." Jerry nodded at Gustoff's words. "Hey, kid, you mind waking up Arietta? I'm trying to finish this chapter." Gustoff's eyes connected with Jerry's and flitted down to the finger that was saving his spot.

"Okay." Jerry slid out of his bed, moving towards her bedside. He shook her shoulder, and she shot up with a gasp. Once her eyes seemed not so lost, and she appeared to recognize her surroundings, he began to laugh at the hair sticking up on the back of her head. "Arietta, my good pal, pack your things. We have an adventure to go on," Jerry said with a flourish, and regardless of the sleepiness that weighed down her eyelids and shoulders, she laughed lightly.

Once more, the pair, plus Gustoff, required the services of Eduardo. Gustoff flagged the beige horse down, and Eduardo knickered pleasantly, for he saw Arietta.

"My, my. I didn't think I'd have the pleasure of seeing such a generous spirit twice in a row!" He directed this at the girl. She grinned widely.

"It's nice to see you too, Mr. Eduardo."

"And Jerry, was it? Good to see you as well!" Jerry exchanged pleasantries with the horse and Gustoff frowned slightly. This must have been the transportation service the kids used to sneak away, and that meant Arietta likely used her powers to summon some coin.

"What is the toll?" Gustoff questioned anxiously.

"One bronze coin please." Eduardo eyed the elder man with caution.

Gustoff asked, "How about a silver instead?"

"You're negotiating in the wrong way, mista'," the horse quipped, yet he seemed to lose the caution in his gaze.

"I'm sure I am," Gustoff laughed, and popped a silver coin in the empty pouch that collected the money the horse would earn through the day. "We're off to the docks, if you will."

"For a silver, of course." And they were off. Once reaching the docks, the trio took in their surroundings. Arietta inhaled deeply, and she could smell the salt in the air. Seagulls swooped around the port, and Arietta watched with humor as one swooped down and stole a pastry from the hand of one of the salesmen on the wooden walkway.

"Filthy bird!" the man cried, and the seagull laughed. "Get a job like the rest of us! The other birds earn their pay!" he spat in the air, only for the spittle to crash back onto the creaky wood walkway.

The bird banked hard to port, swooping back over the angry merchant. "How do you like that?" the bird shouted through a mouthful of pastry as he sent droppings that splattered on the man's bald head. He then banked to fly over the ocean to avoid the man flinging a rock he found through the air, which plopped uneventfully back into the sea.

"Ah, the wonders of nature," Jerry chuckled, prompting the other two to burst into nearly uncontrollable laughter. The sea twinkled, and there was a playful energy radiating from the rolling waves. Lined through the docks were boats of many different sizes with beautiful sails of varying colors. Scanning the line, Arietta's eyes connected with a ship with the words "The Pink Lady" scrawled in gold lettering across its starboard. Its sail was a pastel pink.

"Is that the ship we'll be taking?" she questioned, gesturing to The Pink Lady. Her grandfather nodded.

"She's beautiful, isn't she," he said dreamily, eyes filled with appreciation for the ship. "I've always wanted a boat," he admitted quietly. Attached to the ship's side was a ramp that several beings were using to board the boat.

The trio got in line with the swarm, getting lost in the crowd until they were on the boat.

"I've got to admit, I'm really excited to go home," Arietta said quietly, and Gustoff nodded slightly in agreement. Jerry couldn't share their enthusiasm. He would've stayed there forever had Arietta and his mother not been in his life.

Arietta watched the ship's anchor as it was tugged from the depths, slick with water and weighed down with slimy green seaweed. The boat rocked comfortingly, yet when Arietta looked to Jerry, he was as green as a Granny Smith apple.

"Are you--"

Jerry clutched the side of the ship, hurling vomit towards the sparkling blues of the water.

"Okay," she finished, not really seeing the use of asking anymore.

"*Peachy*," he panted, vomiting. "Remind me to never get on one of these things again." His knuckles had turned white gripping the ship's railing. Arietta frowned, not quite sure what to do for him. She didn't think anything would settle his stomach from the rocking, and no words would stop the vomiting, so she just stood quietly.

"The Mer won't be very happy with you vomiting into their living space," Gustoff chuckled, and Jerry just moaned, too sick to question who exactly the Mer were, and definitely too sick to care. A tail flipped out of the water, and a scaled humanoid figure with sharp teeth and seaweed-like hair burst from the water. Though her words above surface sounded like gurgling, she gestured violently to the floating vomit and shook her fist at the departing ship before diving back to the depths.

Eventually, there was nothing left in Jerry's stomach, and he slid weakly to the floor, sweat percolating on his forehead. This was a lot less fun than what he'd expected. On the other side of the ship, a little girl was in the same position as he, and he averted his eyes as she too gripped to the side of the ship. "I'm going to go check out the bunks we've been provided. We'll be here all night, and by early afternoon we should be in Belamoris— sorry, Jerry," Gustoff said jovially.

Arietta gave Jerry a look of sympathy, then turned to Gustoff. "I'll stay here with Jerry; it doesn't seem like a good idea leaving him. Can you check to see if they'll get him a spare bucket for the night?"

"I'm going to see if I can do him one better: I'll find some ginger tea infused with black pearl dust. It should fix his nasty case of sea sickness if we are lucky."

Arietta nodded, and Jerry did his best to show his appreciation, but Gustoff simply turned on his heels and strode off, moving like he was on a mission.

It wasn't long after he left that Gustoff came back with the tea in hand. Jerry grabbed it from his hand greedily, chugging the dark mixture, grimacing. After finishing the tea, he seemed to relax.

"I still don't feel great, but I feel a little better," Jerry offered, and a light came to Gustoff's eyes at this.

"Good, an hour from now you should be perfectly fine." Gustoff smiled, knowing that they would not be needing a bucket for the night.

When Jerry was feeling much better, the trio elected to roam the ship. Sea out to the right side, sea out the left, and unsurprisingly, sea to the front and back of the boat. They had already spent several fairly uneventful hours on the ship, and at this point, neither Waterhaven nor Belamoris was in sight. The sun lit the entire sky on fire: oranges, reds, and yellows like a painting on a canvas. Out at sea it was especially beautiful, as the blue water reflected the passionate colors of the sky, a looking glass of its own right.

Chapter Sixteen

Present Day

Arietta woke from her nap with a fit of coughing. Tears welled in her eyes, which were burning, and her face felt flushed. Smoke filled her nostrils and she reached to wipe the tears streaming down her face. She lunged out of her recliner, and when her feet touched the floor, a sharp pain exploded from her hip, both taking her breath and causing her to collapse. She tried to lie perfectly still, hoping the pain would subside. Arietta brought her hand to her head causing something to brush across the floor. A handful of grain stalks topped with feathery seeds littered her family room floor.

Arietta let out a moan as her body was wracked with another explosion of pain from her hip. Falling had definitely not helped her situation. She needed to focus and decided that she would worry about how she brought grasses back from her dream later.

The kitchen counter. Cooper barked at her, licking her face. He was incredibly concerned. She tried to move her legs, tried to stand, but she could not. She pulled herself across the rug that covered the wood floors and onto the cream tile of her kitchen. She was lucky it hadn't been farther.

She whined, arm pawing at the counter, and knocked off the phone onto the floor. How had she let it get this bad? *When* had it gotten this bad? First it was her hip; nothing impossible to deal with, she just would pop a couple aspirins and go to sleep. When her other extremities began to ache, she blamed it on the transition from the milder summer to a hot and arid, unforgiving heat that the land had been experiencing.

She punched in the buttons, each taking too much effort. She took a deep breath, trying to steady her hands. She mentally criticized herself for the reaction; she'd been through much worse, after all.

"911, what is your emergency?" a polite woman asked on the other end of the line.

"I'm in excruciating pain." Her voice was uneven, but who would blame her?

"Okay, it's going to be alright. Now, where are you?" Arietta told the kind lady her address. "Help is on the way. What's your name, ma'am?"

"Arietta," she replied, trying not to make the fact that she was crying evident.

"Okay, Arietta, everything will be alright. My name is Sarah. Will you tell me what happened?" Arietta pictured the woman with a neat, professional bob, but with kind eyes.

"I've had pain in my hip for a few months now. It progressively got— it got worse. I just ignored it, though, gave myself a couple aspirin and would walk it off. Soon, the pain was everywhere. I thought that it would go away; had I known it would get like this, I would've made an appointment much earlier."

"I'm sure," the lady said comfortingly.

"I woke up and could barely move, barely breathe. It--it feels how it felt as a girl. I had juvenile arthritis. This isn't quite as severe, as for the most part when I was a girl I had been nearly paralyzed with the pain, but this is up there," she groaned.

"They'll be there in twenty minutes tops," the lady said politely, and Arietta wanted to cry at this. Twenty whole minutes until anyone would help her. She wondered if she would pass out from it before they arrived. "So, Arietta, tell me about... tell me about your family." Arietta grimaced, but obliged. Anything to distract herself. Cooper lay next to her, both sprawled out on the tile.

"Well, my husband's name is Joe... was Joe," she corrected herself, something she still wasn't used to. "Joey was a good man. I miss him with all of my heart. He passed away a few years ago; no need for apologies though. I was lucky to have him. He was the love of my life. We had two kids, two little boys. They are all grown up with families of their own. Grayson and Levi. Love them to death, wish they would call more. Of course, my third baby is Cooper, he's my dog." She caught herself rambling and interrupted her thoughts. "What about you, Sarah? You have a family?"

"I have a husband and a little girl. Tom is a wonderful man, and Maggie is my world." Sarah kept it short and simple. "How about hobbies, you have any of those?"

"I write. It's not really a hobby, since it's my way of making a living, but--"

Sarah interrupted her. "You aren't *the* Arietta, are you? You wrote all the fantasy and horror novels?"

Arietta smiled through her pain at this. "Yes, that would be me," she forced out, trying to move as little as possible.

"Wow, I--I can't--"

Arietta heard a hushed whisper across the line, informing a nearby coworker that she was on the line with her favorite author.

"Sorry. Anywho, tell me about your other hobbies and about your writing," she offered.

"I mostly just write. I have a little flower garden outside as well. Writing takes up the majority of the day, but I like movies too, and of course I love to read as well."

Sarah sighed dreamily at this, but Arietta did not hear. The ambulance arrived early, red lights flashing and casting eerie shadows through her house. "Oh, they're here."

Sarah told her goodbye and that she hoped she felt better soon. The slight disappointment shone in the woman's tone at ending the conversation so soon.

She was loaded into the ambulance and whisked away into the night. Cooper was left in a dark house, confused and afraid.

***

1972

Jerry, while feeling better, was still a little shaky. He was grateful for their arrival in the city. The captain was currently docking the ship into one of the ports. The city was far less bustling than what he had expected, and the air was tainted with an oppressive taste. The streets that could be seen by the boat were empty, and in Waterhaven everything had seemed to be in motion. How was this dreary place supposed to be more alluring and energetic than Waterhaven? How was *this* supposed to be the largest trading center in the world? This place was pathetic. A sickness weighed down the streets, a beast unseen but lurking within the city's heart.

Gustoff was disturbed as well, to say the very least. He knew this center like the back of his hand, and there was something deeply wrong here. His wrinkle-creased face twisted into a look of concern, grasping Arietta's hand protectively. He wouldn't let anything bad happen to her this time. The solid ground felt wonderful to stand on, and while something might have seemed off, Gustoff still allowed himself to relax. They were so close to escaping and getting back to Earth. He smiled at the seashells and pearls embedded into the walking paths that sparkled in the sunshine. To his left, a child with emerald green eyes was watching the trio, then snapped the blinds of the cottage windows shut. She would feed tonight.

Gustoff led the trio to the nearest inn to get a bite to eat. Navigating through the winding streets, Arietta's grip on her grandfather's hand tightened. "This place is off; I don't trust it." Gustoff nodded to her and pointed to the next street corner.

"The Fishermen's Port is down Ocean's Passage. We should be able to get some information there." Daylight was fading as the sun gently settled into the horizon. Gustoff was ravenous, so he knew that the children would be very hungry as well. Once they ate, he would be able to get the information that he needed. Finding Arkas was his number one priority, but he would also inquire as to why Belamoris looked like a ghost town. Gustoff pointed out the sign with a picture of a large ship with the words *Fishermen's Port* written in large white letters.

As they entered the inn, a wonderful smell permeated the air and Arietta's stomach roared in anticipation. She didn't realize how hungry she was. The great room was mostly empty, with only a few tables seated with patrons. A hush fell over the room as the three entered. A plump lady with thick brown hair tied in a bun scurried from behind the counter to welcome them. Stray strands escaped her bun and outlined her rosy cheeks as she introduced herself to the travelers. "Hi, welcome to the Fishermen's Port. I'll be taking care of you today." Her voice was pleasant enough but seemed weary.

The three were seated and brought potatoes and eggs. As they devoured their meal, Gustoff signaled the tired woman over to the table. "I couldn't help but notice that the city seems rather empty. The last time that I was here, the streets were full, as was the Fisherman."

Her eyes fell as she spoke in a hushed tone. "Some say that a curse has fallen over Belamoris. I fear that it is some sort of plague. Many have fallen ill and stay in bed through the working hours. The city feels like a ghost town. Some shipments have remained in the docks for two or three days, as we don't have enough able-bodied workers to unload them. Some of the younger families have packed up and left for fear that they will fall ill."

Gustoff sat in a pensive silence, and he swallowed thickly before he spoke. "How long has it been like this?"

The kind waitress answered, "Not long, maybe a week. I have never seen an illness sweep through the city this fast. I fear that there is dark magic at its roots. I would leave myself, but all I have is here."

"Do you know an old man named Arkas? I would visit him in my younger years."

The woman tilted her head to the side in thought for a moment. Her eyes sparkled at the old man's name. "Are you referring to the Wizard of the Wharf?"

"Aye, that is ole' Arkas. Do you know where I can find him?"

"He has a small shop on the north side of town. I can't remember the name, but it is the only shop that sells potions in all of Belamoris. If you take Ocean's Passage to the next street and turn north, it should put you in the vicinity of his shop. I think that the street is called the Northern Way. We are not very imaginative with our street names," she said with a wink.

Gustoff thanked her and paid for their meals. The three left the Fisherman and headed up Northern Way. The sun had completely sunk into the horizon as dusk had fallen over the city. An uneasy feeling sent a shiver down Gustoff's spine. The hairs on the back of his neck stood on end as he stopped the group. Gustoff whispered under his breath, "By the pricking of my thumbs, something wicked this way comes."

"Is that... Is your grandpa quoting Shakespeare?" Jerry asked.

Gustoff completely ignored the boy, ensnared in a trance.

"He's a reader, so probably," Arietta said warily, and though Jerry's voice held amusement, she couldn't muster such courage. Gustoff scanned the street, then began looking at the buildings lining the walkways. Shadows danced in his peripheral vision, yet when he turned, there was nothing.

"We need to get moving." At Gustoff's words, Arietta could've sworn his flowing beard transformed whiter than before.

A coldness embraced Arietta, and an ominous feeling pressed into her core. Movement flitted in the corner of her eyes, but the streets were empty; they were quiet as death. Something was out there, watching them. They picked up their pace from a brisk walk to a jog. A growl rumbled from the south, and Arietta's heart dropped. Frantically, they searched for the potion shop, the "Wizard of the Wharf," moving like shadows in the night. That was when everything went horribly wrong.

As they ran, Jerry's eyes kept searching for the movement that he was missing. He held Arietta's hand as they sprinted north. He closed his eyes and took a deep breath. Time slowed, and when he opened his eyes, he could see into the shadows. From windows in the dark alleys, perversions of the city dwellers crawled toward the ground, spilling and falling as though they had no sense of self preservation. They were everywhere.

Emerald green eyes glowed hauntingly in the night, gathering and waiting for something… something to consume. Hungry eyes that watched the three running, preparing to strike. Their nostrils flared, inhaling the raw power that distinguished the group. A great darkness swelled over the town; suddenly the milky glow of the moon was missing, as if the night had been swallowed into a great void. None of the twinkling stars, no moonlit streets, only darkness. Arietta raised her eyes to the heavens, seeing a great, deep purple dragon swooping, its mouth opening in an eardrum-shattering roar. A great light from the depths within the dragon swelled, fire spurting forth and pouring from beneath its dagger-like fangs.

Buildings on both sides of the street erupted in flames. She could see their eyes glowing emerald green with fury. This had been planned carefully, Gustoff realized; for as the buildings burned, those who were left unturned flocked straight to the danger of the Shadow Walkers, the horrible creatures of darkness. Fire and blood, blood and fire was all to be seen-- that was all Arietta could register, anyway. It made her head dizzy, made her feel as though the world beneath her strayed. She was screaming, choking on the smoke, and her feet and legs were splattered in blood. Was this hell? Was this what bad guys feared for their afterlife? An eternity of blood and fire? Jerry was her tether to reality, though; he held her hand, tugged her from her mind, from the fire and blood, and brought her to the streets. One foot in front of the next, picking them up and putting them down. "You're okay." He said the words like a prayer, and she wasn't sure if they were targeted at her or himself. Either way, she drew strength from them.

The raining fire lit up the ebony sky, and Arietta could just make out two figures flying high in the darkness. The city was a torch in the night; the dragon flames spread quickly and wildly, like an intrusive weed. Arietta feared that if they found Arkas, his shop would be burned to a crisp. She needed to do something to give them more time. As she ran, she focused her thoughts and began to sing. "Rain in my heart, wash away my pain. Rhythm coursing round me, let it drown, let it surround me, let it pour." The sky opened up with a torrential downpour. The once-bright flames began to smolder as the fire subsided. The song was ethereal, weaving magic through the nightmarish cityscape.

Lucius roared in dismay as a violent rain pounded the streets. The skies were clear only moments ago. The rain smelled of magic! The Chosen had arrived in Belamoris. No matter, this town was his anyway. The city had fallen, and his army would slaughter whoever remained, including the Chosen. Lucius was a two-birds-with-one-stone type of guy.

Hestia felt whole again as she continued doing what she did best. She had engulfed the entire south end of the island in flame and was making her way to the north when it had begun to rain. *No matter, the rain will only slow the burning.* She smiled as Lucius's army swept into the streets as her flame destroyed the buildings. There would be no survivors. The rage that had built over her years of captivity finally had an outlet. Satisfaction that could only be attained through vengeance coursed through her veins. The people of Palidonaya would feel her wrath. The debt owed to her for being caged would be paid in full. They would all burn.

The rain meant nothing to her. Her fire quickly turned the water to steam and buildings to dust. She flew with a purpose. The city would be turned to ash, then rebuilt in the image of Draconis. A great rebirth. Her terrible roar filled the night as she laid waste to Belamoris.

Chapter Seventeen

The three ran down the street, searching for Arkas's shop. As they ran, the screams of the fallen sliced through the streets and fire turned the rain into steam. The heat surrounding them swelled, and they were running out of time. In a matter of minutes, Belamoris had changed from an eerily quiet town into a war zone.

Gustoff locked on the sign on a building ahead that read *The Potion Master: All are welcome.* He turned to the children and yelled, "Arkas's shop is just ahead. We must hurry!" A wall of fire blocked the street ahead, and a mighty black dragon dropped from the sky to interrupt their path. His roar spelled a terrible death for all who approached. Through the flames, the emerald green eyes glowed in a cool rage. A plume of flame swelled from the dragon, charring the streets and stretching out to meet the trio. The light was brilliant and all-consuming.

As the flame hurled through the night, Arietta's eyes were on her grandfather. She knew without a doubt he would know what to do, and she trusted that he would protect her. She lifted her gentle song to the air; now, rather than lyrics, she released a high humming. The rain responded to her song, picking up in intensity. Gustoff lifted his staff, slamming it into the cobblestone. A white light burst from the bottom of his staff, weaving an intricate ball of brightness around the trio. Arietta watched in removed fascination as the flames licked up the walls, unable to reach its target.

Again, the dragon drew breath and launched flame. The molten fire engulfed the trio, surrounding them, yet not touching them. Arietta couldn't even feel the temperature rise; Gustoff's shield held. Sweat beaded on his temples and ran down into his long, flowing white beard. When the flame subsided, Arietta looked to the blackened ground. Beyond it, the Shadow Walkers gathered, rushing at them. The dragon considered them tentatively, cocking its head before blowing yet another sea of flames that encircled the field that Gustoff held around them, its heat unable to touch them. It was curious, testing to see what would crack the egg of light. The anger it had displayed was absent now, replaced with a tactical calm.

When the light subsided, the silhouette of a man stood where there was once a mighty dragon. He had a cape that trailed to the ground and stood with a regalness about him. He walked through the wall of fire, emerging unharmed, and continued toward the trio. The Shadow Walkers locked arms, forming layers and layers of boundary between the trio and any possible escape.

A gravelly, humorless laugh boomed, and the caped figure strode toward them. There was something different about his walk: it was a glide with power emphasized in each step. He held his head high, and there was an air of arrogance to him. Though she was terrified, when she looked to her Grandpa Gus and saw only strength and determination in his gaze, she grew more resolved. He slammed his staff down, emitting a blue flash, and the approaching army stopped in their tracks. They hissed and growled, shielding their eyes from the light. Arietta could not see a way out of this, couldn't see an end where her corpse wasn't charred amongst the ruins, where Jerry's blood wasn't splattered across the cobblestone, where her grandfather didn't have to watch his grandchild die before he himself perished. Her voice was shaking now, and the glow was absent from her eyes. Hot tears formed, and her nostrils flared, extending a hand to her grandfather's arm, and her fingers intertwined with Jerry's.

They were completely surrounded and cut off from any help. This dark, menacing figure continued his approach until he was ten paces from them. He smiled dauntingly, a hateful teasing smile that made Arietta feel even smaller. Her grip on Jerry's hand had her knuckles turning white, and rather than looking at the terrifying being, Jerry focused an intense gaze on Arietta. If he would die, his eyes would be set on her, only her.

Gustoff stood his ground determined that they would not meet their end in the streets of Belamoris. What had happened to Arkas? There was little hope of reaching the Earth now. How could he have been so careless to lead Arietta here? She was only thirteen. His grandbaby was never going to drive, never going to college… He should have gone to the capital and met with the Council. They would have helped them find a way home that was safe. No! He had to fix this. He pulled in a deep breath and slowly let it out. He needed to stop all of the background noise and focus on getting them out of this.

"Wizard, we meet at last. I have heard so much about you and your companions. It is a pity that we are meeting as foes instead of allies."

***

Raulin stood before the gates of Dragon's Bane, the castle that had once served as the center of the Council during the first Dragon Wars. The castle spiraled to the skies, and the bricks were scrubbed shiny clean. If they had put as much effort into the trails for the way here as they had put into the appearance of the castle, his hooves wouldn't be aching quite so severely. He did not have to wait long.

The hall in which the nation's leaders congregated produced a soft hum as the Council debated what should be done about the dilemma at hand. All wore their finest clothes, and all looked regal and incredibly elegant.

Timara was the first to speak to the group as a whole. Her voice, which was as smooth as silk, declared, "Do you realize that the attack on Equus was an attack on us all?" Everyone seemed to stop mid-sentence, mid-drink, mid-breath, as she said what no one else was brave enough to say.

Brannan, High Liege of the Casparnia, sneered at her. "No, the attack on Equus was planned as revenge against those that slayed the queen. They would not be foolish enough to make open war with the Seven Kingdoms. We need to assess our losses. The attack could have been just on Equus," Timara released a glare that lesser men would have surrendered to, yet his gaze remained strong.

"Do not be foolish enough to think that they will stop with Equus, Brannon. I said what everyone else was too afraid to say aloud. I'm not sure you all comprehend how dire this situation is. They were condemned to the mountains because they were too powerful." Her voice held her barely contained rage, and she tightened her fists. She smoothed out her golden gown, readjusting the crown with which her head was adorned as a way to tame her aggravation.

"Look, Timara, I mean no disrespect," Brannon countered. "Lenovia, and many more of our homes, border Draconis directly. Your lands are far to the south. The Zeus herd protects your lands from invasion."

"My country borders the majority of the Silent Forest. Creatures of the night frequently invade villages near the border, but our guards keep it in check," she hissed.

Brannon argued, "Yes, but--"

His statement was promptly interrupted by Javaron, the King of Lenovia, who slammed his fists against the bocote wood table. "Enough of your bickering!" he exclaimed, and both snapped their heads to focus on him. "We are discussing a *war of nations*, and you two are bickering like children. The only way that we can win this fight is if we stand together." He glowered, the heavy eyes of all who sat at the table ripping into him. The fiery redhead straightened his back to fix his posture, folding his hands on the table.

Timara shifted, crossing her long mocha legs. "You are right, Javaron. Let's resume the conversation." She tipped her head ever so slightly to the tempered man, and he did the same.

"Okay, let's get to the point. What are we doing about this dragon king?" Timara's eyes stayed on Javaron as he opened his mouth to reply. There was a loud pounding that could be heard through the great halls, and it echoed all the way to the dining room. Brannon stood, brushing off his pants, and went to confront the ones who had interrupted their important meeting.

"Raulin," Brannon gasped, showing the shock that struck his heart. He had been positive that the stallion had been slaughtered. "You're alive," he said flatly, not betraying himself by exposing the feelings.

"I am. I have come to call a meeting of the council." There was a wildness in Raulin's eyes that hadn't been there before, haunting memories engraved into them. The urgency, if not conveyed by his voice, was pushed further through his body language.

"The King has already called the Council together. Right this way." Brannan extended a delicate hand, inviting him inside. He did not judge the knotted mane, nor did he judge his bedraggled state. It was obvious that Raulin had been through much, and had valuable stories to share with the Council. The dining room fell silent, most not resisting the urge to gape at the proud stallion, who still held his head high entering the room.

"Raulin!" Neoma exclaimed happily. "We thought-- we thought... Well, that doesn't matter. We are so glad that you made it out alright. You must tell us what happened."

Chapter Eighteen

Lucius had not noticed the change of energy, the powerful hum that radiated from the city. Belamoris had reeked of terror and suffering, so much so that this change had been buried in it. The wolf had tracked the trio here, her nose working endlessly to scent them out, and finally she had found them.

Her instincts had told her that they were heading into grave danger, and she always trusted her instincts. They were usually right, after all. She held her fear of fire at bay; the city burned bright all around her, but she focused on the three that were now surrounded by the dead. Her white coat was streaked with ash, and her paws stung, rubbed raw from all of her walking. The air was permeated with the stench of smoke and death. She had been watching these two for a while, sensing that she would be needed.

The girl's eyes were filled with a paralyzing terror as she looked at the man who had just been a dragon. Nova sensed her power choke, but a bright light was pouring from the old wizard, who was holding the enemy at bay. The boy was frozen with fear as well. She couldn't understand how they could be facing such danger, yet unable to act. She crept to a position where she would not be visible until it was too late; the time to attack was upon her. A growl rumbled in her throat, but over the screams, she was not heard. The hair on her back standing on end was the only evidence of the cool rage that flooded her. Her right eye glowed a deadly blue.

She lowered onto her haunches, stalking towards the circle, then leapt into action. Her teeth ripped out throats, claws slashing, and she won herself a few extra seconds of vengeance from the surprise attack. This seemed to wake the two from their sleep, their eyes clearing.

Nova's great jaw clamped on the neck of one of the undead, her eyes connected with the boy's, and a moment of mutual understanding was shared between them. In a great swinging motion, the boy crossed his arms against his chest, hands tight into fists, and then he flung them out to his sides. His hands unfurled like hemlock flowers, poisonous yet beautiful. A great darkness was unleashed upon the Shadow Walkers, and even Nova shuddered. He joined her in the fight, Nova used her teeth and claws, and he used his darkness. The Great Wizard fought alongside them as well, using his light, but surprisingly enough to all four, the darkness seemed much fiercer. Arietta began singing "Rain in My Heart" once more, trying to wash the streets of blood, trying to cool the fires that raged and devoured the once beautiful island. She then sent a blinding bolt of lightning into the Dragon King's chest, hurling him into the side of a building with a thunderous crash. Jerry's hands cut through the air, and his shadows were no longer whispers of the void that sung into the bloody night, but physical masses. They were great beasts that ripped and tore into the Shadow Walkers. They were death incarnate.

The tight circle that had once formed around the group had dispersed, and while there were still many close to them and roaming the streets, they were ultimately free to travel. The group sprinted towards the potion shop, and to their horror, it was on fire. The shop crackled and popped, and a figure moved frantically through the smoke-filled chambers. Gustoff blew the door from its hinges.

"Arkas!" he cried, covering his face. His throat was raw; a layer of smoke seemed to blacken it. He coughed. Though his eyes stung, leaking tears from the thick black smoke, he could still make out the old man limping around the shop, stuffing bottles into a large, burlap bag. The register had already been invaded, all of its money likely also in the bag of the shopkeeper. "Come out! This place is going to collapse!"

"I don't need rescuing, old friend. Everything I own is in this shop," the old man grumbled just loud enough to be heard. He let out a heavy cough as he picked through several of the unbroken vials on the floor next to a collapsed shelf.

"You may not, but we do, and a blackened corpse isn't going to help us at all. Your life is worth more than that." The building shuddered. The scraggly wizard sighed, and he hurried out the door to join the group. As soon as he exited the building, its roof collapsed, a cough emanating from the wood, and a large gust of hot air tickled Arietta's cheeks.

"I guess I owe you one." Arkas used a worn sleeve to wipe sweat and ash from his brow. He wheezed, coughing. "What do you need, old friend?"

"We need passage back. We need help remembering… remembering how to create a gate back to Earth," Gustoff said hurriedly, and Arkas' beady eyes scanned his.

"The gate has closed, but with our combined magic we should be able to reopen it for a short time. Join hands," he demanded clearly, and the trio joined hands. Arietta broke free of Jerry to lay a hand on the mysterious white wolf that had assisted them in their escape, and Jerry followed suit. "Now repeat after me--"

166

An explosion of fire, hot and pure, was released behind them.

"CEASE THIS!"

They trembled at the terrifying boom. An inky dragon soared toward the ground, but as he landed, he shifted. A devastatingly beautiful man continued a determined march toward the group in place of the dragon, his cloak trailing behind him. His eyes smoldered. Arietta's heart stumbled, Jerry's mouth gaped, yet dear old Grandpa Gus was deadly calm, as a viper prepared to strike.

"Take my place." His words were directed at Arkas.

"No!" Arietta cried, tears brimming in her eyes, and Jerry gripped her hands, both still touching the wolf's black-and-red-streaked hair. Arietta tried ripping her hand from his, tried charging after her grandpa, but Jerry's grip was vice-like. "Let me go," she screeched, her fury evident, as well as her fear.

"He's doing this for us. He will be okay. He knows what he is doing." Jerry's voice was soft, yet his eyes betrayed his words.

"You and I *both* know he's walking to his death!" As she struggled, Arkas began chanting, a blue glow radiating from his eyes. A soft, kind, and velvety darkness swallowed them. Arietta watched in horror as her grandpa was thrown to the ground and restrained by other members of the army. Her eyes were not on Lucius, but on the loving man that had guarded her, helped raise her, who was on his knees. His messy white hair obscured his frenzied eyes, but they remained on her as well, and his lips moved, sending a message her way. *I love you, Arietta.*

***

Arietta woke from her deep sleep, thrashing and screaming, her pulse creating green mountains on the monitor. Her parents immediately came to her side, their hands feeling as though they were suffocating her, and she fought against them with a wildness in her eyes. A nurse hurried in, followed by the white coat of her doctor, and seeing him only made her screams louder, more frantic. Tears were a river down her cheeks; she tore at the hands that were trying to subdue her. She still felt the blood on her legs, and the smoke still stung her nostrils. Where was she, again? Where was Jerry? Why had they abandoned Grandpa Gus? The other nurse wielded a knife--no, a needle. Arietta let out another shriek, cried and fought, but sure enough, the needle was inserted into her feverish skin, and the sedative seduced her into a deep sleep.

***

Present Day

Arietta's eyes fluttered open to a piercingly white light. Her blurred vision focused as she squeezed her eyes so that they were slits that shielded her from the intensity of the illumination. The room around her was white, and it reminded her of her childhood. The pain that had paralyzed her at home was down to a dull throb, which was the only thing that kept her in the moment. She reached over to the side of the bed and depressed the call button to summon a nurse. She closed her eyes and tried to swallow. Her throat was as dry as the desert sand, and if she wasn't careful, she would be getting a headache from the brightness of the room.

A short brunette entered with a bright smile on her face. "Hi, Arietta, how is your pain?"

Arietta tried to speak, but what she said sounded like a whispery growl rather than intelligible words. She closed her mouth, swallowed with a wince and tried again. "The pain isn't too bad, but my throat is really dry and sore," she croaked. "Could you be a dear and get me a glass of ice water?"

"Absolutely." The nurse smiled at her, but her eyes held a bit of pity.

Arietta had seen that look before, and she really didn't care for it one bit. When the nurse returned, Arietta asked her if she could sit up in the bed. She then took a long pull of ice-cold water, which numbed her throat and felt wonderful. She had an IV in her arm that probably delivered fluids, but nothing to keep her throat from drying out. After she had drained a cup of water, she asked for a cup of ice. She didn't want to drink too much too quickly. She sat in silence, munching on a small mouthful of ice when her throat told her that she needed it.

Arietta closed her eyes and went through the events that led up to her hospitalization. She had dismissed the muddy footprints in her house, thinking that she hadn't showered before bed that night. She could not dismiss the grass that was in her hand when she woke yesterday. She had to be traveling to Palidonaya in her dreams, but how?

The other thing that was bothering her was the strangers that she kept seeing that apparently knew her name and where she lived. The emerald green eyes reminded her of the Dragon King, but they were definitely not Lucius. Could they be sent here by him? Was that even possible? The last one had asked her for a weapon.

It was strange how the timelines had begun to blur for her. She had been immersed in the memories of her childhood to the point that it seemed like it had happened yesterday. The fog had been lifted that had blanketed those years. As it lifted, she had been experiencing strange occurrences that could only be explained by these events from her childhood. She closed her eyes and focused on how she felt once the panic had faded. Memories sailed her back to 1972 again, and she allowed herself to be swept away in the memories that she had once lost but were now found.

***

1972

The nurses had dismissed her incident as a night-terror-induced panic attack, and everything was back to normal. She was put through her regular dose of physical therapy, which didn't bother her at all, as the pain was a ghost of what it had been. The day had been long, but she knew it could've been months for Gustoff. Timelines were unreliable. She had to act quickly. She fumbled through her pocket and traced the grooves of the golden coin. She whispered the phrase over and over again, squeezing it until her fingers turned numb. The door to Palidonaya was indeed closed to her.

Arietta was lost in her thoughts as she made her way to the chemo room. As she entered, Jerry was sitting by a younger, dark-complexioned girl with curly dark hair, save one white streak that ended over her right eye, which was a brilliant blue that contrasted with her deep brown left eye.

"Hi, Jerry, who is your friend?"

"Um," she started uncomfortably. "Hi, my name, my name…" She drew in a frustrated breath. "My name is Nova. My sessions usually start a little later, but I asked to come in early today. You guys are normally not really here when I start."

"Not really here?"

"I've been there too. I was there when your friend was taken." A hand came up to her hair, taking one of the curly strands around her finger, a nervous tick she had developed at the hospital.

"Oh." Arietta hesitated, unsure what to say. Arietta sat down so that Nova was between her and Jerry.

"How did you... I don't recognize your face," Arietta stumbled, trying to connect the dots.

"When I go there, I can change into a wolf. We need to find a way back. I think that your friend needs help." The quiet girl's eyes narrowed, and a wolfish gleam was in her eyes. Recognition collided hard with Arietta.

***

Though little time passed on Earth while the Chosen were gone, months sped by under the Dragon King's fearsome conquest. From the ashes, his empire rose as he circled ever closer to Lenovia, the last stronghold on the continent. Clarette had been good on her promise to close the gateway, and the Chosen were separated from the land. Lucius took full advantage of their absence. His army ruled the darkness, and none could withstand their might.

There was, however, a spark of hope that remained. The wizard Arkas managed to evade capture on that dark night that Lucius's army had overtaken Belamoris. He faded out in Belamoris and reappeared on the mainland, where he decided to venture to the Great Beyond. He lived in exile in the sea of sand in a small hut, where he continued to search for a way to right the many wrongs that have been done to his great land.

Chapter Nineteen

A day passed with denied access to Palidonaya, and Arietta knew how much could change in a day. With a numb rock in her chest, she wondered just how much had happened. Around eight o'clock, after the sunset on the next day, there was a stir in the world and a rise in her chest. Deep inside, she knew that the gate had finally opened. She scrambled through the drawer in her nightstand, extracting the coin, then jumped in bed.

She tucked into the sheets, squeezing her eyes shut, and closed her hand around the coin. That all-too-familiar chant echoed through the chambers of her mind, and her hair whipped behind her.

The wind was brutal, and sand pelted her cheeks. The heat melted her, and she took time to open her eyes. The light stung, but the slow adjustment eased its steady assault. Where on Earth--well, Palidonaya--was she? She was nowhere near the lush grasses of Equus, couldn't smell the ports of Waterhaven, no woods within sight. There was only sand as far as the eye could see and a beautiful, crystal blue sky. She was delighted when Nova and Jerry appeared to the left and right to her. She immediately wrapped Jerry in a hug, nearly tackling him, and to Nova she gave a high five. Their eyes immediately set on a small, run-down hut sitting alone amidst the ocean of sand. It was its own oasis. Arietta led the small group to the door, knocking thrice and waiting in anticipation.

"Come in, hurry now," Arkas muttered conspiratorially. The hut was much bigger on the inside, filled with plants and potions. The color scheme was mainly yellows and browns, and while Arietta had figured the house would be hot, the temperature was perfect. Her eyes fixed on a bubbling Erlenmeyer flask on a small heater. "Don't mind my potions," he said dismissively before ushering them to sit at the small wooden table at the center of the room.

"Where are we, and how did we get here?" Nova questioned, her human form much less intimidating than her wolf form. Her short stature mixed with the soft smile was not the recipe to a threatening being.

Arkas smiled. "Your first question is...a little complicated. You are in the Great Beyond, though it is really difficult to tell exactly where we are at this time, as the lands are ever changing. I have been on the move, working on a way to open the portal long enough to bring you back." He directed the last bit to Arietta. "I need your help to free Gustoff."

"How long has it been here?" Jerry questioned, and his heart raced. He was beyond worried; he had grown to like the elderly man, and while he hadn't known him long, Gustoff was the father he never had.

"Gustoff has been missing for two months. I know that he is somewhere in Draconis. I don't know his exact location, or his state of being," Arkas explained kindly.

"He is in Draconis? Isn't that where all of the dragons live?" Arietta asked to double-check her suspicions.

"Yes, and that does present a problem," Arkas answered.

"Yes, it does. We couldn't even deal with two dragons. What good are we going to do against all of the dragons?" Jerry added.

Arietta continued, "Is there anyone who can help us? I am not leaving my Grandpa there, but I really don't think that we would last long against them."

"There is someone that may be of some use. We can ask the Keeper of Records," Arkas said warily, and Jerry narrowed his eyes. He could tell the man was being cryptic on purpose, baiting one of the children to ask the inevitable "what's the keeper of records?"

Nova, a slightly timid girl, fell into the trap. "Who's the Keeper of Records?"

"All answers come in time." He gave a mischievous wink to Nova. "We need to leave soon, preferably after the sun sets. That should only be a few hours from now. Would you kids like dinner?" Arietta's eyebrows rose as he lifted a boiling pot, revealing a bubbling, thick brown liquid. It made Arietta's stomach turn looking at it; however, she *was* hungry.

Arkas scooped portions into wooden bowls. There was a meat of sorts, which the brown liquid was poured over. Nova's eyes portrayed something of horror as Arkas dug into the messy meal with his fingers, a food that she had decided was definitely *not* finger food. Her nose scrunched up, but she figured she'd be hungry later should she not dig in as well. "Desert hare is quite scrumptious, don't you think?"

"This— this is rabbit?" Arietta instantly felt guilty at eating (and enjoying) the meat, and she was surprised at Nova, who had to take care not to devour the bowl.

Jerry stared at Nova. The once-hesitant individual, who hadn't wanted to dirty her hands, now had to restrain herself from licking the bowl. They finished their meal, relaxing and trying to get to know this odd old wizard named Arkas.

Arietta sat pensively as Arkas finished cleaning the dishes after eating. "Arkas, has anyone ever killed a dragon?"

The small hut was filled with silent anticipation as Arkas turned and considered the question. "Yes, a long time ago. Unfortunately, the weapon that was used has been lost, so there is no known way to slay a dragon."

"Wait a minute, when you say that there is no known way to slay a dragon, you mean that we can't kill them, right? So that means that we can't beat one of them, and there may be thousands! Why did you bring us back here!" Jerry raised his voice.

"There was a prophecy that spoke of a dark time when all hope would be lost. It foretold of a drawing of three from a distant land that would bring light to the darkness. I believe that you are the Chosen and that you will bring light to the dark."

"Oh, that makes total sense!" Jerry was beginning to get angry. "Let me see, we have a kid who is dying of cancer, one with arthritis so bad that she can barely walk down a hallway, and . . . uh, Nova, what are you like on Earth?"

"I have leukemia." Nova couldn't bring herself to make eye contact with Jerry. She really didn't like it when people started yelling.

"Oh, *fantastic*!" he drawled. "Another sad little dying kid. We are not a group of heroes. As a matter of fact, where I come from, I am a zero. I can barely take a crap without someone helping me to the restroom and wiping my butt." Jerry was losing it, and Arietta needed to calm him down.

"Jerry, we each have different abilities here. Whether I am one of the Chosen or not, I have to help Grandpa Gus. I really don't see where we have a choice anyways. Do you know how to get home, because I sure don't." This did not have the desired impact. Jerry's face turned red, and he continued to rant. Tears streamed down his face.

Arietta then began to sing, "Peace comes over my heart, when I am near you. You bring joy to my soul when I am blue. When my face begins to frown, I know that you will never let me down."

Jerry's face lost the redness. His breathing settled, and he smiled at her.

"Are you trying your witchcraft on me?" He then said, "Okay, I'm done. Now, let's find this library." He turned to Nova. "So, Nova, what kind of abilities do you have?"

"Wouldn't you like to know." Even after the outburst, she was starting to like Jerry. Her first impression was not good, but there was a lot going on in Belamoris. There would be time to show him exactly what she could do in this world, and it sure did beat the sterile hospital environment.

Arkas had finished cleaning the dishes and sat in a rocking chair facing the trio. "What is your home like?" He reached into a pocket and pulled out a small pipe, filling it with an odd-looking tobacco.

Jerry's eyes seemed to glaze over at the mention of Earth. "Back at home, I'm sick, really sick. Honestly, I think I might die soon," he said gravely, but then shook his head. "Sorry about that. Hate to bring down the table. I'm sure being back in Palidonaya will make me a little better." Arietta's hand clamped on his shoulder in an attempt to comfort him.

A somber silence filled the room. Arkas lit his pipe as blue smoke drifted from its end. He took a deep pull, wondering how sick children could possibly be the Chosen Ones that would lead Palidonaya back from ruin. Well, who was he to question fate? "Get some rest; we have a long journey ahead."

***

Across the desert and into the desolate, cold, and unforgiving mountains was a broken man. His once white, beautiful hair matted into a grimy, dull gray. His eyes stared at nothing. His heart shattered, the hope he once had nowhere to be found. There was dirt and blood on his face. Clarette, the woman that visited him every other day, brought a simple glass of water. This time he was careful to pace himself. Last time he had been so foolish, he ended up vomiting up nearly all the water he had greedily drank.

While olfactory fatigue had always been a blessing, it didn't seem to apply here in this hell. He always smelled the blood and the scent of excrement that hung heavily in the air. It was suffocating. Gustoff had been through a lot, but nothing could compare to this. He had daily sessions with Lucius, some lasting hours. Most of his fingernails were gone, and his arm had been shattered, then healed in several places. A few of his ribs were broken as well. His shoulders had both been dislocated, then relocated, which was done solely for the excruciating pain. There was no light here. There was nothing to hold on to, and the only thing in this bubble was suffering and darkness.

***

Arkas sat up with a start. He was beginning to feel frantic. He quickly packed the last of his supplies. He turned to the three Chosen, who were finishing up their meals, and said, "We must hurry, he knows that you're here."

"How could anyone know that we are here?" Nova cocked her head to one side. "We just got here."

"Lucius knows that you're in Palidonaya. I can feel him. You don't get it; the only reason I have not been captured is that I keep moving my hut. He is getting better at finding me. I barely had my stuff packed last week before I sensed them approaching. With your arrival, he will have sent them out after us."

"Okay, let's leave, but you have to fill us in on the road." Arietta didn't understand what he was babbling about, but the fear in his eyes spoke measures. Either they were on their way, or he at least truly believed that they were. With that, the four headed out the door. Arkas stopped at the doorway and spoke a few words, and the hut shrank into a miniaturized version of itself. He quickly bent over and placed it into his bag.

"We will start heading northeast. I have done the calculations, and the Hall of Records should be appearing just off the coast in two days' time."

"What do you mean that it should be appearing?" Jerry did not like the sound of this one bit. "Do you mean that you don't know where we are going?"

"I mean that the Hall of Records is not always in the same location. As a matter of fact, it is rather difficult to find. No worries, I have found it before, and I know that it will be there. We just need to keep moving."

The trip across the desert known as the Great Beyond was not an easy path. The sand was ever shifting, and the sun appeared to be moving in circles through the sky. Arkas would stop every hour or so and pace in a circle to get his bearings. More than once, the children asked him if he knew where he was going. Each time he nodded and would continue marching.

Jerry pulled up beside Arietta during one of these hourly sessions. "Ari, I'm pretty sure that we are lost. Look, he is headed off in the direction that we just came from!"

Arkas looked up at Jerry and exclaimed, "Which of us has been traveling this desert for the last two months evading the Dragon King? You would do well to be quiet so that I can get my bearings. The land is constantly in motion, as is the sun. I, and I alone, can get us to where we need to go!"

With that said, Arkas turned and strode off, with the others following behind. Arietta managed to catch up with him. She needed to diffuse the situation. "Arkas, I know that he can be frustrating, but we have never been to a land like this. It goes against our sense of direction. Now, can you tell me how you escaped and what has happened since we were last in Palidonaya?"

Arkas turned to Arietta and his expression softened. "I will do my best to fill you in on the last two months. Once you three had vanished, I turned to the incoming army and realized that there was no hope of me defeating them and rescuing Gustoff. I disapparated and appeared outside the city. I have been on the run since. I was able to gather bits of information as I made my way into Casparnia. By the time that I had crossed to the Silent Forest, Casparnia had fallen. My only choice was to flee to the Southern Sea, where I was able to book passage to the lands east of Draconis. My only safe haven was the Great Beyond. I fear that all of the Kingdoms now belong to Lucius and his army of the dead. With no known way to slay a dragon, his numbers are growing. There are rumors of a great nest that houses hundreds of eggs that are nearing maturity."

Arietta walked beside Arkas, taking in all of the information, then said, "We need to find a weapon. Do you think that the Hall of Records can help us?"

Arkas smiled, "The Record Keeper can either tell us where the weapon is, or he can tell us how to make a new weapon."

***

There was a rustle deep inside of Lucius's serpent's brain the second that the Chosen had been called. It turned into a searing pain when the three had stepped through the gateway together. He staggered, covering his eyes with the palms of his hands. With his eyes in total darkness, he could almost see them. He knew that they were with the Wizard from Belamoris. He had been tracking this wizard through the Great Beyond, and the old man kept one step ahead of him. He summoned Clarette as soon as the vision faded.

"Yes, My King." Clarette dropped to a knee as she entered his chambers.

"Rise, Clarette." Lucius had a way of drawing out the 's' so that everything he said came off as a menacing whisper. "I need you to send hunters to the wastelands east of Draconis again. He has called the Chosen, and they are with him. I feel that they are searching for something."

"Give the word, and I will have the hunters find it, My Lord." Clarette began to turn away, and he held her with his gaze.

"I cannot see what they seek, though we must prevent them from finding it." With that, Lucius dismissed Clarette to send the hunters. They would find the meddling old man and end him. Then he would finish the conquest of Palidonaya, and all would kneel before him! Lucius made his way to the dungeons, where the wizard Gustoff was held. He unlocked the gate and slithered into the room.

"Wizard, you will tell me what the Chosen seek." He placed the palm of his hand on Gustoff's forehead and focused his power there.

Gustoff's limbs began shaking uncontrollably as Lucius' power flowed into his brain. Spittle ran freely from his lower lip as he screamed in pain. Lucius was slightly impressed with the fortitude of the old man. Most would not resist him for this long. As he tried to force his way into Gustoff's thoughts, he again encountered a barrier that he could not penetrate. He doubled his focus, and the old man screamed.

"Tell me what I want to know!" Lucius bellowed as his focus intensified. Sweat began to snake its way down the scales where a human's temple would be located. His emerald eyes squeezed so that only a sliver was seen by Gustoff.

Through all of the pain, Gustoff held fast to his barrier. Lucius pulled back, sensing Gustoff either didn't know or wouldn't share the information he required. Lucius's hand ripped back from Gustoff's head and then crashed into the side of his face in a hard, open-handed slap that gashed his cheek where the talons had torn. With that, Lucius left Gustoff's cell, and Gustoff collapsed to the floor, completely drained of strength. A tiny spark of hope burst in his heart. Arietta, Jerry, and the wolf girl had finally crossed back into Palidonaya. At least he knew they were safe...for the moment.

Chapter Twenty

"Jerry," Arietta said softly. She touched his arm, wincing as he whirled around to face her.

"What--" he spat, then, upon seeing that it was only her, he softened. "Sorry. What's up, Ari?" The nights had grown incredibly cold; however, they were also very beautiful. She stared up at the navy sky, her gaze focused on all the beautiful galaxies that danced through the darkness.

"Are you okay?" She was quiet, as to not wake Arkas or Nova. He released a breath, the heat and cold mixing in the air. She lowered her gaze, her eyes now on him.

Jerry answered, "That's a hard question. I'm just... it's hard. I can still feel it, ya know? I can feel myself still getting weaker over there, across the gate. I always feel my mom's despair, the pain that she carries with her. I'm all she has left, and I'm not--" his eyes dropped, and his voice broke. He pawed at his eyes with frustration, wiping away the tears. He didn't want her to see him like this; he was supposed to be strong. She raised her eyes to the stars. "I'm not going to be there for her much longer. I always joke about her coddling me, but--" he choked. Arietta grimaced, wondering if this was the first time he'd actually been able to *talk*. To truly talk, to share the burden he felt. "She has been so sad, and I'm just so *angry* that I can't do anything about it. I think it would be best for her if I just wasn't around. I know it would be hard for her at first, but this disease that I have is eating away at her too. I don't know how much more of this she can take." His shoulders were shaking with the quiet tears, his voice wet.

Arietta didn't have words for this, didn't know what to do, so she simply opened her arms. He launched himself at her, burying his face into her shoulder.

"Don't talk like that, Jerry. You have been getting better." Her voice was as calm as a sunrise.

"No, I haven't." His words were muffled, but she heard the words with clarity, and her heart broke for him. She knew the struggle, feeling like she was making progress, but when she would return home, she was back to being bedridden.

"You're alive, though. I have hope for the two of us. Our story doesn't end here."

***

The sun rose an angry red, and the Hunters were racing across the desert. They were lusting for blood, hungry to serve their master. The scorching sand stung their paws, but they did not care. They did not pause to sleep, nor to eat. They scented the air, roaring through the sun's cycles, the thought of capturing the Chosen fueling the hunt.

"This scent is fresh." The beast projected this thought to her company, fangs dripping saliva. Her great emerald green eyes searched the waves of sand. Suddenly, the scent had lost its potency. "There has been a recent shift. This land is not the same." Anger burned in these thoughts, and the pride of hunters felt the frustration permeating this message. This group was the elite of the hunters, the most trusted by the king, yet the Great Beyond seemed to always be one step ahead. They pressed on despite their frustration, blazing a path through the sand to their destiny.

***

"My King," Clarette voiced, not crossing the threshold of his room. Her breath caught upon looking in at the splendor of his chambers. A massive bookcase was to the right wall, hundreds of books on the shelves, and trinkets of the finest quality were scattered about the room. His bed was the largest she'd ever seen, covered in beautiful damask blankets and a fur duvet. All of the bedding had glorious, ornate golden threads that Clarette had no doubt were genuine. The headboard was a tufted creme, and under the bed was a large rug that had been imported from Belamoris. The heart of the room was not the bed or the beautiful trinkets, nor was it the massive bookshelf. It was an excessively large chandelier with crystals dripping from it. The light refracted about the room, its gems casting wondrous sparkles throughout his chambers. Her heart pounded at the alluring room, not wanting to even *estimate* the price of the treasures within.

"What do you *want*?" He padded out of a set of French doors, hair still wet from bathing. He donned only a towel, and Clarette grew incredibly uncomfortable at this, her cheeks blushing a light rose. Three priests, two males and one female, exited the lavatory. They'd been tasked in bathing him, no doubt, and she counted her blessings that it wasn't her that had been given that chore.

"I know we have been focused on the conquest of Palidonaya…" She was nervous to ask him about this, but she knew it was for the best.

"Well, get on with it." He waved a lazy hand and called out to the three to bring him back a glass of wine. They scurried away like nervous mice.

"It is only a week before Diwa'Kahh. I believe we should take time out of the schedule to celebrate. This festival will raise spirits, reinforcing the pride all dragon-kind feels, and will serve to solidify your dynasty as the greatest king the dragons have ever known. Also, it *is* tradition. Every Draconis King has been welcomed into his reign through this festival. I hope I'm not crossing any lines saying this, but Diwa'Kahh is the greatest part of being a servant; I'm sure it's one of the greatest parts of being a dragon as well," she implored. Within the time she used to make her plea, one of the males had returned with a wine glass and a bottle of the lands' finest red wine. He nodded his thanks to the servant, and within the blink of an eye, he was gone.

Lucius stared pensively into the distance, lost in his thoughts. Every great king began his reign with the Diwa'Kahh celebration. The crown was placed on his head, his reign officially welcomed and recognized by his people. He had the ghost of a smile on his face, and finally continued. "This celebration must dwarf that of any of our past kings. Make the arrangements; it must be the most extravagant celebration our kind has ever seen. Paint the streets, set fires, do anything you must. Spare no expense; after all, I now control most of Palidonaya." He swirled the wine glass and drew its contents into his mouth, savoring the flavor. At this, Clarette could've sworn she'd seen a twinkle in Lucius's eyes, and she felt a stirring of excitement deep within her. This was all she'd ever wanted out of life, to serve her king, and to have an unlimited budget in planning the most decadent party anyone had ever laid eyes on, an unimaginably grandiose celebration.

"Make no mistake. I shall not disappoint you." She grinned, leaving the doorway, and Lucius to his thoughts. Lucius stamped at the butterflies in his chest which fluttered at the idea of the celebration of Diwa'Kahh. He loved the celebration as a child; it fueled his passion and pride.

"Lucius, come here darling," his mother's velvety voice called from within her chambers. He followed the voice, and his eyes finally laid on her. She looked like an angel, her hair intricately woven, and she wore a flowing, icy blue dress. Its lace was mountain frost, her skin fair and beautiful. Her fire-red hair seemed to blaze in its braid.

"Yes, mother?" His voice was still the voice of the child, and his eyes seemed to widen looking at her. She regarded him adoringly, her hand ruffling his hair.

"You've seen the preparations through all of the mountains; you've felt the excitement in the air," she started, grinning as he nodded enthusiastically. He silently prompted her to go on. "This year the Diwa'Kahh will signify the hundredth year of your father's reign," she explained, trying to keep still as her handmaidens fussed with her makeup.

"I love the Diwa'Kahh. When will I be able to participate?" He pronounced the word carefully, and it felt foreign on his tongue.

"Well, this year, you will take the first step towards the day that you will be honored in this festival. As the heir to the throne, you will be decorated and observe your father this

year." She raised a delicately painted hand to the ladies to get them to cease their painting. "Take off your shirt, darling," she cooed, and he obliged. "If you will, paint his chest. Make it as perfect, for tonight will be his first." Love permeated each syllable. "Diwa'Kahh celebrates the Birth of Fire. While you will not be participating in several of the events we have--"

Lucius's face dropped, and her laughter rang through the two corridors at that, as light as the tinkling of bells. "Don't pout, dear, you will have your time. You are far too young, nor do you have the crown yet. As I was saying, there will be a great feast, there will be the lighting of the skies, so many wonderful traditions! I won't spoil it, though; you will learn our customs through experience. You need to pay close attention to your father and his role in the festival, as some day soon, this festival will welcome your reign as king."

When Lucius looked at himself in the mirror that day, a mature male stared back at him for the first time.. Though he was still technically a child, a great surge of pride echoed through his bones in knowing that he would be able to observe his father this year. Flames were vibrantly painted on his chest showing his pride at being the prince of all dragon-kind.

Lucius shook himself out of his trance, the memory being one of the most important from his childhood. Its deep ache nearly crippled him. Why did the Council find it necessary to slaughter his mother? The kind and fair woman had done no harm to them… Lucius stood suddenly, that wrath that lit the fires of his heart coursing through his veins, and he flung his wine glass at the great bookshelf. Blood--no, wine--streamed off of its oak exterior, and glass decorated the floor. He dropped to his knees, face twisted as his old wound reopened, making his heart bleed once more. The Council deserved this, deserved the ravenous flame that devoured their cities. No longer would they suppress his kind; no more innocent dragon blood would be spilled. His people deserved freedom, and the Council would repent for their sins.

When the servants scuttered in, he was still on his knees with that haunted look in his eyes. He felt grateful that they didn't ask questions, that they never spoke. They wiped clean his mess, took great care in getting rid of the glass, and left him to his thoughts.

Once more, Lucius stripped off his shirt in preparation for the great ceremony. Just looking at the pyres that had been built in honor of Diwa'Kahh made his heart thump faster. He had bequeathed the finest artists known throughout the mountain kingdom to paint his chest for a generous price, and the results were quite stunning. Down his right arm, the histories of the Draconis had been elegantly illustrated. Down his left arm raced a great mountain range. Powerful dragon wings framed his eyes, and growing from his pantline upwards were blazing flames.

"My King?" one of the artists said respectfully, but not timidly. He fixed his eyes on her, and to his surprise, she did not flinch under his stare. "I have an idea, but I wanted your permission before doing it." He gave her permission before she even explained herself. Dripping red, orange, golden, and blue paint over her fingers, she looked him in the eye once, before running her fingers through his hair. He let out a muffled grunt at the surprise, but when facing himself in the mirror, he had to admit that it looked quite striking. The contrast in his raven hair and the effervescent colors streaked through it looked dashing.

He tipped his head, eyes not breaking from his reflection.

Today was the day a king felt closest to his people, a day where he walked among them. His court was small, but the expansion had gone well. As far as relations went with the Draconis, while he did not have personal relationships with them, he knew he had earned their respect. Walking through the streets, he couldn't help but to be pleased. Small fires burned throughout the city surrounding his estate, and they glittered like fallen stars. The city held a regality that none could parallel. Whispers of winter carried through the air, and he felt the gelid murmurs on his neck. Citizens passing by on the street attempted not to gawk while making last minute preparations. While usually at his estate, the servants collected the firewood to be displayed on the doorsteps; he collected it himself this year. No, he wouldn't venture into King's Forest, as he would as part of the tradition, but instead into the familiar woods that were open to all. Life breathed around him, the heartbeat of the forest ringing true in his mind. He enjoyed listening to the life force around him, cherishing the twittering of birds and the sputtering of squirrels. Not far from here, children were laughing in light tones, and he found himself lost once more in memory.

Chapter Twenty-One

Not far from their location in the Great Beyond, waves were crashing and lapping at the shores. They were *so close*, and yet they were not. The eyes and ears could not be trusted; the land would never stay the same. One night, when Arietta opened her eyes, a phantom hung over her, whispering what it called "secrets of the sand." Her scream had awoken Arkas, but by the time the old man arrived, the thing had disintegrated, swept away by the wind. According to him, this was nothing to fret over, quite a frequent occasion when one sought shelter in the ancient lands.

There were several rules that the children had been taught to follow in their time in the dreadful lands, and Arietta did not want to know what happened when one didn't abide by such rules.

"Rule one?" They always went over the rules before settling down to eat, sleep, or rest their tired legs. What was it with old men and their rules?

"If you get injured, don't bleed on the sand," Nova yawned, making the words barely understandable.

"Good. Jerry, rule two?" Jerry blatantly glared at Arkas, and Arkas paid no mind.

Jerry answered, "If you hear any strange noises, don't investigate."

Even Arietta could admit that his sullen routine was getting quite tiring. Nearly every word he spoke seeped with venom, save most of his words to her. She understood, yet his reasons didn't pardon the behavior. They *all* were tired. Arietta had gotten sun poisoning and had been sick, forcing them all to stop. Everyone's legs were sore, everyone was hungry, yet no one else subjected the group to their frustrations.

Arkas nodded. "Good. Arietta, third rule?"

"Don't take anything that isn't from the land. Take nothing offered from anything that speaks," she mumbled, trying to not think of how much she desired to sleep.

"Good. Rules four through six will be next round." Arietta and Nova shared a look of irritation, and Jerry let slip a rare grin.

"I need a nap," Arietta grumbled, directing the statement at Arkas. He nodded, considering it.

"I'd like a nap as well, but we simply don't have that kind of time to sacrifice. I am sorry." The difference between Arkas and Grandpa Gus was the discipline. While Gustoff tended to prioritize the comfort of the kids over the goal of the group, Arkas didn't mind hardship as long as the goal was being met. This was difficult on the group's relations as a whole, and the kids resented him for it.

The four marched relentlessly across the ocean of sand. Arietta shuddered looking at a massive dune ahead that they would have to climb. She turned to Jerry and Nova, who simply shook their heads in despair.

Arkas looked back at the children. "Once we get to the other side of this dune, we can break for a short lunch."

The children all groaned as they began the ascent up the dune. The footing was nonexistent, so Jerry and Arietta had to use their hands to help them climb. The sand stung, digging into the meat of their palms. Nova, on the other hand, simply changed into the wolf and scampered along beside them, unbothered by the slipping terrain.

They were almost to the halfway point when Arietta's vision swam, her head spinning like a top. Suddenly she was crawling down the incline instead of up it. She began to turn around before hearing Arkas' voice over the wind.

"No, Arietta, this way! The land has shifted; do not let the changing terrain fool you."

Arietta turned back toward Arkas, confused but willing to listen. After what seemed like an eternity, they had reached the bottom of the massive dune when all four dropped to their knees with another dizzy spell.

"What in the world!" Jerry exclaimed. They were now at the peak of the dune. "Weren't we just at the bottom of this hill?"

Arkas smiled. "There is a reason that some call this place the Wasteland. If you don't keep your bearings, then you will travel in circles. If we hurry, then we may make the bottom before the lands shift again. I really don't want to have to climb the rest of the way past this dune!"

***

Present Day

Arietta had spent two days in the hospital. She had called her neighbor to help take care of Cooper. The pain was finally at bay, and she felt stronger than she had for the last few weeks. She had to call an Uber to get home and was excited when the driver pulled in to pick her up. She introduced herself and told the driver her address as she settled into the backseat for the fifteen-minute ride home.

"Hi, my name is Drake, and I will be driving you home today. How is the temperature in the car?" The driver smiled as he spoke, but there was something about him that was unsettling to Arietta.

"The temperature is fine. I am really tired and want to go home so I can get some rest." Arietta couldn't place the feeling that was nagging at her, but she had seen him somewhere before. Maybe it was just a case of deja vu. The driver was very careful as he pulled out, and the ride was very smooth. Drake made small talk about the weather as he drove.

He had stringy brown hair that was covered with what she always referred to as a cabbie hat. It was pulled down so that the bill obstructed her view of his face. He had a neatly trimmed van dyke and a hawk-like beak for a nose. She then realized what was bothering her. She couldn't see his eyes. They continued with the conversation, never discussing personal opinions or anything of real consequence. He drove the conversation like he drove his car, careful and slow, being sure to avoid any danger. They finally pulled up to her house, and he opened her door for her. As she handed him the money for the ride plus a tip, she caught a glimpse of his eyes. He quickly turned away, but a glimpse was all she needed. His eyes glowed emerald green.

Cooper growled from the front porch as she settled up with Drake, who grabbed hold of her arm. Drake smiled and said, "We'll be in touch, Arietta. Give us the weapon and you will have whatever you desire."

Arietta jerked away from his grip. "I don't have a weapon, and if I did have one, I wouldn't be giving it to you or your king!" Arietta hurried up to the house to unlock the front door so that she would have Cooper to protect her.

Cooper let out a series of menacing barks as he saw the car approach. He did not like it when she was away. His job was to protect her, and he couldn't do that if she wasn't home. As the car door opened, Cooper watched the man exit the car to open the door for Mother. His scent was all wrong. It had been a while since Cooper had smelled that scent, and he was having trouble placing it. Cooper's yell translated to a series of barks followed by a low and steady growl. His drool hung from his jowls, but he did not shake it off. He wanted to sink his teeth into that man's throat. It was at that point that Mother seemed to realize that something was not right about that man, and she jerked her arm away from him. She turned and hurried up the steps as the man got into his car to drive away. Cooper's hackles raised on end. "Hurry, Arietta, open the door, he will be gone and I won't be able to catch him!" Again, this came out in a series of barks.

Arietta opened the door and grabbed Cooper's collar. "Good boy! I don't like him either, but it looks like he is leaving. This all feels like a dream, doesn't it? Men with green eyes and no hair asking me for some old weapon that I don't have." Arietta entered the house, making sure that Cooper did not bolt through the open door. She then did something that she didn't normally do in the middle of the morning. She turned and locked her front door, and then checked to ensure that the rest of the house was locked up.

***

1972

As they continued the trek through the endless sand, Arietta started to get a feeling that they were being followed. The only sound was the whisper that had been picking up over the past couple of hours as the wind brushed the surface of the sand. The sun may have been setting, but it had fooled her twice earlier when she suggested that they make camp for the night. Arkas roughly replied that it would be silly for them to camp for the night in the middle of the day. It may have just been the oddness of it all, as the group continued to walk in circles. She quickly turned one time and thought that she had seen the remnants of a black head duck under the dunes that they had passed several minutes ago. Another time, she thought that she saw a glowing emerald green eye watching as they descended from the top of another dune. The feeling was quite unsettling, as it was difficult to determine the difference between reality and illusion. Arietta didn't know how much longer that she could stand to be in this constant state of shifting time and direction. She didn't understand how Arkas could live here for the better part of two months without losing his mind.

"Okay," Arkas yelled. "This is far enough for today." The children looked at each other quizzically, as they were certain that there were at least two or three hours of daylight left. As Arkas built, or rather unfolded, their shelter, the sun had all but winked out of existence. Arkas had Arietta and Jerry build a fire. Jerry stacked the wood in a neat pile, and Arietta thought for a second, then began singing the chorus, "Set it on fire, burn it ever brighter." As she sang, her eyes glowed an unnatural blue, and as she finished the last line, fire erupted from the tips of her fingers, immediately igniting the wood that Jerry had so carefully stacked. Nova let out a whoop as the fire rose high into the night. Arkas returned from the other side of his now-erected hut carrying another desert hair. He entered the hut and seconds later came out with a pot full of vegetables, rabbit, seasoning and water. The temperature of the air plummeted, but the fire kept them warm as they settled down for dinner.

A good hot meal always raised the spirits of the group, but Arietta noticed that Arkas seemed distracted as he ate. He kept his gaze over their heads and off into the distance. Once everyone had finished eating, Arkas said, "We need to be ready tonight. It seems that we have some company that has been following us for a short while. I would expect them to pay us a visit sooner rather than later."

Arkas decided that he would take the first watch, as the three children were wiped out from the long day of marching through the desert. Arietta, Jerry, and Nova were sound asleep within seconds of lying down. Arkas grabbed a stool to sit outside of the hut and settled in for his two-hour watch. It was a beautiful night in the Great Beyond. There was a stir of magic in the air as he watched the stars spiral in the sky. This had to be the most magical place in all of Palidonaya. He knew that it was also the most dangerous, as many that had ventured out into the sandy wasteland were never heard from again.

He continued to scan the horizon for movement as that feeling of being watched crept up his spine. As he scanned, his mind wandered back to the day that he had first met Gustoff. They were both children at the time, and Arkas had gone to Waterhaven on a trip to collect supplies for the old potion shop. His father sent him to the outskirts to gather a bushel of fox wheat. This, his father had told him, was a great aphrodisiac that he liked to add to his infamous and highly coveted love potion. This was one of their biggest sellers of the non-healing potions. As he was daydreaming in the field, he happened upon a blond-haired boy wearing a white robe. The boy was rather skinny and had dirt smudged all over his face. Arkas introduced himself. "Oy there, my name is Arkas. Are you lost?"

Clean streaks trailed from the boy's eyes to the bottom of his chin. "Hi, I'm Gustoff. I am a little lost. I came here from Equus and am looking for a way back home."

"Where are you from? Maybe I can ask my Da' to help." Arkas was a little shocked that Gustoff had come from Equus all the way to Waterhaven by himself.

"I'm from Earth. I have been coming here for a few months, well, to Equus, anyway. I started to explore the forest and got lost. There were all kinds of ghosts and monsters in that place. I pretty much ran as much as I could, then hid at night. When I finally came out of the forest, I stopped in a town to ask how to get back to Earth, and the guy told me that if I made my way to Belamoris, I could go pretty much anywhere. I don't think he told me the truth. Everyone that I spoke to told me that they have never heard of Earth. I really need help. I think if I got back to Equus, I could make it home from there. I knew I should never have left." Gustoff was close to tears.

"Come with me, Gustoff. My Da' is a great wizard. If anyone can find a way to send you home, he can!" That was all he needed to say. It did take Martin the Magnificent, Arkas's Da', almost three days to find the spell to open the portal, but after that Gustoff made visits almost monthly for the next few years. Man, those two had a lot of great adventures and learned a lot of magic in those days. By the time they were teenagers, they had both made quite a reputation in the wizarding world.

Before Arkas knew it, it was time to wake Arietta for her watch. He quietly made his way into the hut and lay beside her and gently woke her from her slumber. Arietta was groggy, as it seemed that she had just fallen asleep. "Wake up, kiddo, it is your turn to stand watch. Here is a little potion that will perk you up for your two-hour watch."

Arietta drank the potion, the flavor similar to strawberries bursting on her tongue, and immediately perked up for her turn to stand watch. She hummed a jolly tune, trying to keep her mind on the positives and not dwell on the fact that she was alone in the darkness. She wouldn't say that she was afraid of the dark, but with the spirits that roamed the sands, she always felt as though there were eyes on the back of her neck. The rare times that Arkas referred to the mischievous spirits, he'd called them "The Lost." There was a veil over these lands, and the veil was much thinner in the Great Beyond. Spirits passed between realms of life and death, and they delighted in antagonizing the stray traveler. Arietta jumped at the sound of a distant snarl. *It isn't real, it's just sands trying to get a good scare out of me.* It was time for Arietta to trust her instincts and wake the others. She started with Arkas. He was a light sleeper, so waking him wasn't an issue at all. The fog of sleepiness cleared nearly immediately, his sharp eyes now scanning their surroundings. He nudged at Jerry with his foot, and Arietta poked at Nova.

"I'm not sure if I'm right or not, but I think something is coming," she admitted to Arkas, and she was relieved that none teased her about her fears.

"If you believe something is coming, it likely is. I'd rather you wake us up and give us a fighting chance than let us sleep through our slaughter," Arkas said gruffly, then, realizing he had been a little too blunt, threw her an apologetic glance. He rustled through his bag, extracting a small vial.

Arkas traced an eye over the vial with his pointer finger, then carefully uncapped it. The symbol glowed in the air before dispersing into their surroundings, and a butterfly of the darkest blue emerged from the vial. It fluttered onto his hand before a gentle breath from him sent the scout into the night. He kept the children close to him, a determined and cautious look over his face. His eyebrows were two daggers preparing to clash, and his lips were pursed unhappily. The Great Beyond had always put things into perspective for him. It was everything. It contained the mysteries of the universe, and it always reminded him how small he was. Though there was little of value in the Great Beyond, it had a calming effect on Arkas. The way the yellows and browns of the sand contrasted with the bright rich blues of the sky, the way the stars were constantly changing position in the nights due to the land's constant movement. The desert was as much alive as it was dead. It reminded him that it was easy to be dead, much easier than being alive, but it also reminded him the importance of that fight. His eyes sought out a burst of blue light not three hundred paces from their location. The wisp that had taken the form of a beautiful butterfly alerted him where the danger was, and that it was a valid concern. A deep frown set onto his face, and he looked to the kids. "Be prepared to fight; danger is close," Arkas said solemnly, and he received grave nods in response.

"I thought I smelled something; didn't trust my instincts," Nova bit out, irritated and sleep-deprived.

After a series of grunts and panting, Nova had fully transformed into the wolf and her eyes glowed a strong, icy blue, signaling her preparedness to tear her enemies down where they stood. Arietta's eyes flickered over the land, straining to see the danger, her pointer fingernail digging into her thumb as Jerry was locked on the horror that lay ahead for them.

***

Never had Lucius felt so content. His life mission was finally shaping; he had the control he so desperately lusted after. He had to plot every action carefully, but for Diwa'Kahh, he would finally be able to let loose a bit. Comparing the castle's firewood to the rest of the town, he had a fairly modest pile, but he didn't see that this was a problem. The sun produced a golden glow over the snow-dusted peaks of the mountains, and the scent of food the chefs were cooking made his stomach growl in anticipation. This was the one time that the entire Draconis Court would be in the same location, all outside in the cool air under a milky full moon.

The sun finally tucked itself away, and the moon rose on a joyous city. The pulse of the drums was his heartbeat, and while he had not yet had any wine, he was intoxicated. A lute was playing along to the thundering drum, and his citizens danced in the Commons. There were several tents of differing sizes, colors, and fabrics sprinkled throughout the walking paths surrounding the King's Forest, and his heart burned for them. They would be sleeping outside, waiting out here, living out here, all for *him*. All because they respected him and saw hope in what he was doing, even if it meant burning the rest of the world. His resolve grew at this, as he knew that they were trusting him to finish the job. A hundred generations of dragons would have the *entire world* to explore. Too long had they been prisoners to these mountains. The incredible surge of pride, of love he felt at this nearly crippled him.

The priests and servants enjoyed this celebration as well; however, they were much less involved. For the most part, the servants attended to the drunk and insured that all the plans had been executed to perfection, and if all of that was in order first, they would be able to celebrate. There was much responsibility in doing this, since any mistakes made would result in severe punishment. Oddly enough, when these punishments (usually beheadings, hangings, or the occasional roast over one of the great pyres) occurred, the blood always just stirred the air, filling it to the brim with excitement. The Draconis had always been a warring race, born of blood, fire, and ash. Seeing it spilled on this great day seemed to only be fitting. Seeing Clarette, he walked in her direction. She struggled with a ladder and what appeared to be replacements of torches that would light the main thoroughfare. He took the ladder from her, propping it up against the wall, as he was in a generous mood.

"Thank you, My King. Are you looking forward to the ceremony?" A feral green glow flashed in her eyes, but only for a moment.

"Yes. I look forward to proving my strength," he said simply.

"Hopefully I'm not crossing a line asking this, but what exactly happens when you venture into the King's Forest?" Her eyes searched his own carefully. Lucius pursed his lips, considering whether or not she should know. He shrugged to himself.

"My spirit and the Diwata of Flames will unite as one, and I will be influenced by Her fire. It will lead me into the selection of the flower, and if I'm worthy, she will present me with a fox to hunt. The fox will lose its coat for me." At this, Clarette's eyes flickered with mild distress for the fox. "I know, it's quite unfortunate for the fox, but I will be adding its spirit to mine by eating its heart." Lucius's serpentine smile went from ear to ear.

"Is the eating of the heart really necessary?" Clarette exclaimed, but Lucius simply studied her face.

"I'm not one to spit on tradition. It would be disrespecting the Diwata of Flames. Plus, that would be a terrible start to my reign." He preened his hair for a moment, then his hands returned to his sides.

"I suppose. Well thank you very much," she said, and was led off by several servants.

Seven drummers were at the head of the feast, hand-selected by Lucius himself, and the sound thundered in his head. A savage smile spread across his face, heart pounding. He never realized how powerful he would feel, and there seemed to be a fog clouding his vision, though he knew only he could see it. The magic in the air danced across his body. He felt Her presence with him, Her smoldering intent upon him. She was more powerful than he could ever have imagined. Her presence alone made him feel the need to burn. He would burn the whole world if that would satisfy Her.

The food was ambrosial, mouthwatering, savory; no words were adequate to describe how the food tasted to Lucius. He interlaced his fingers loosely, then flung them out to his sides, arms like his wings, and all the Great Pyres lit in synchrony. He was lost to the Diwata now; he was Hers and She was his.

Chapter Twenty-Two

The night was silent as the Chosen stood their ground, scanning the inky blackness for movement. Jerry leaned close to Arietta and whispered, "I don't see anything; why did you wake us up?" Arietta's cheeks burned a rosy red. As she opened her mouth to speak, there was movement out of the corner of her eye and pointed.

"Did you see that?" she spoke in a whisper, and Jerry heard the quiver in her voice.

Nova's vision had adjusted to the dark, her pupils fully dilated. She looked in the direction that Arietta had pointed and pulled in a deep breath. Whatever was out there was smart enough to remain upwind of her. "I am tired of waiting this out." She took off, low to the ground, with a snarl on her face.

Arkas called, "Nova, wait. They want to separate us. We need to stay together!"

Nova's instincts were now in control, and all rational thought had left her mind. She circled around the nearest dune and came face-to-face with one of the hunters. Nova's paws cut parallel trenches in the sand as she slid to a stop. She locked eyes with a creature that was close to six feet in height even as it crouched low to the ground. Its muzzle resembled that of a lion, with stiletto daggers for teeth. Saliva dripped from the longest of the creature's teeth as its lips pulled back in a snarl. It emitted guttural whumphs in short bursts as tendrils of smoke snaked from both of its nostrils. As the creature continued to utter this odd noise, a mane of long black quills stood on end, making the head double in size. The quills quivered in unison with the whumps. Two other creatures materialized, one on each side of her as the one directly in front began to blend into the background until all she could see was its glowing emerald green eyes. Adrenaline coursed through Nova's veins. Her legs stretched as she let loose a terrible growl. Her eyes shone brighter than all the stars as her body grew.

The hunters had finally caught up to their prey. Little did they know that Nova was no prey. She would never be the prey, for she was the great huntress. The Wolf bowed to none.

They were larger than anticipated, but that just fueled the bloodlust that pounded through her. With a howl that pierced the ever-shifting night sky, her eyes flashed angrily, and her hair stood on end. The howl was paired with a burst of energy, and the wolf continued to grow. She was a demon of the night, and one with the moon, and no hunter--no matter how large the fangs--could best her.

Her bones ached, but shedding their blood across the dunes of sand would ease the pain. It would make the expansion worth it. Muscles grew along with the stretching of her bones. Her vision blurred, then cleared as her eyes filled in the void left by the growing sockets. A grin stretched across her muzzle, and her upper lip quivered in anticipation.

The white wolf towered over the hunters, her hair on end and face warped into a menacing snarl. She was larger than a truck, fangs devastatingly sharp. She leapt, then clawed and tore through one of the beasts, but there was a factor she had not considered: poisonous fangs. Had the beings fought fair, she would've demolished them; however, with a quick bite to the nape of her neck pumping a sedative through her, as powerfully as she rose to fight, so too did she fall.

Her legs twitched aimlessly, coat melting around her to leave that same shy girl curled in on herself against the earth. While her eyes were closed, her face was contorted with that overwhelming rage, yet there was no fight left in her.

"Nova!" Jerry roared her name while racing towards the fallen girl. The remaining four beasts smiled Cheshire-cat grins at him. Clashing his hands together, he drew on the dark side of his power, unleashing several of his shadow beasts. A sharp slash from the claw of a hunter dissolved the shadow beasts into wispy trails of smoke that hung in the gelid air, and Jerry crashed to his knees, desperately trying to drag Nova away from the monsters.

Out of an instinct that Jerry never realized he possessed, he sent one of his daggers spiraling through the air towards the hunter to the left, still in his crouched position. The arc of the dagger flashed in the starlight, and with a thick squelch, impacted with one of the hunters. His screech made Jerry's ears pound, and he was delighted that the dagger had embedded itself between the beast's scales.

Launching its paws into the air with another devilish scream, its fearsome emerald eyes connected with his, and a dull throb of panic pierced through his thin veil of childish excitement for hitting the mark. It was going to charge him, and he only had one dagger left, and a sick friend he needed to protect. Close range was not a good idea for fighting one-on-one with a beast that size; that was one thing Jerry knew for sure.

"Jerry, move!" Arietta's voice ripped him from his head. His eyes were stuck on his dagger, and on the drops that were pooling down toward the handle. The hunter's blood was matte black, a startling difference from his own. Eyes glued to the blood, a perfect droplet finally release itself from the handle, falling like a raindrop to the ground. The moment the droplet hit, grains of sand raced out from under the hunter's feet, and the it was swallowed into the merciless sand.

"Don't bleed on the sand; rule one," Jerry said under his breath, amazement and horror coursing strongly through him. He shook his head a moment, refocusing himself to the fight. The hunter was furious, ripping its claws through the sand, orange light burning in its throats. Sand surrounded the hunter as it sank slowly into the earth. Soon, all that remained was Jerry's black dagger. He quickly retrieved it and slid it back into its holder.

Arietta took this all in coolly, drawing in a sharp breath. She knew what she must do, and she placed a calm hand on Arkas' arm as he frantically dug around in his pouch.

"It is getting late." Her crisp notes would be her weapon. "You cannot fight what we call fate." The hunters slowed, eyes drooping. "Even the mighty warrior must rest." She began to snap, a natural smile gracing her face. "The day is done, you've passed your test," she continued, skipping towards Nova and Jerry, while the hunters with drooping eyes couldn't help but to surrender to her siren song. "Let me have her, Jerry, I've got this," she said softly, and his eyes searched her own for a second before giving her the unconscious girl. "You cannot resist the call of the night, sleep the whole night through and give up the fight." Nova's face drooped to a peaceful calm, eyebrows no longer drawn together, face no longer disturbed.

Arkas quickly examined Nova's neck and wrapped a cloth around it to ensure that no blood touched the sand.

"Are you going to wake her?" Jerry questioned impatiently. Arkas began to protest, but Arietta simply lifted a hand, silencing them both.

"No, I am not. Not while the hunters are here. The best I can do for her is to relax her; it is far too much of a risk to try waking her."

Arkas nodded his silent approval, yet Jerry glowered in her direction.

"She was so *stupid*," he huffed. "Why did she risk that? We told her not to go, yet she did it anyway. She could die. We don't even know if she'll survive the night," he growled, then turned to Arietta, eyes suddenly much more primal. "Why won't you wake her? You can just put them back to sleep. Haven't you learned to control your magic better than this?"

She maintained eye contact, refusing to submit by looking away. "I will not wake her because it is dangerous to the rest of the group. You are right, it *was* stupid of her, because she wasn't thinking of the team. I am thinking of the team right now, and if you can't respect that, then I don't know what to tell you." Her voice was dangerously low, and Arkas had the sense to give the kids a bit of space.

"Who are you to make those calls?" He growled this, running a hand through his hair.

"Who are you to question them?" Arietta asked.

"I am part of the team, that's what I am! She could die in her sleep, and you don't even care."

"Of course I care, but I'm thinking about everyone. Just because I'm not using my dangerous and unpredictable magic that could possibly wake the death machines sleeping in the sand doesn't mean you and Arkas can't try."

"Okay, both of you cut it out!" Arkas finally broke his restraint, bellowing into the night air. "Who cares how we wake her? I'm doing it now with some Safrae flowers. I was *looking* for them when this fight broke out. I'm giving them to her, and we are leaving. It has taken me over two *years* to track down the Record Keeper, and I'm not allowing bickering children to stop me from finding it!" Arkas stalked aggressively toward the limp girl, chewed the flower into a paste, and spat it into her mouth. Both Arietta and Jerry agreed that it was disgusting, but Nova shot up a mere three seconds after the administration of the flower.

"My head is going to explode, it hurts so bad," Nova groaned, not attempting to stand. She pinched the bridge of her nose.

"You don't feel... poison-y?" Arietta grasped for the word she was going for, yet when it would not come, she made up her own. Nova laughed softly, white hair glowing ever so slightly.

"No I don't feel 'poison-y.'" At this, both Arietta and Jerry visibly relaxed.

"I hate to interrupt, but we need to leave," Arkas said, but not unkindly.

***

Lucius scented the fox, the pounding rhythm of its heart ringing in his ears as it darted from him. All life in the forest breathed with him. The essence of *everything* surrounded him, and he wondered how any mortal could give up such a beautiful gift. The trees were no longer trees, but they were spirits with faces, whose whispers echoed through the canopy. He was on all fours, legs and arms moving in tandem. They were watching him, the stars that peered through the treetops were old. Older than Palidonaya, most as old as time. They had smiling faces, and sensed peace from them. He wondered what it would be like to be so far away from everything--wondered if the silence would be deafening, or if it would set him free.

The fox was swift, and while she darted from him, he knew that deep within him she was prepared for her sacrifice. The great Diwata had chosen the fox for a reason, and the fox would humbly bow to the Diwata. All the kings of Draconis had their ashes spread here, all except for his father. His father did not deserve this honor, so his corpse had been left to rot. He would not spend the rest of eternity among Draconis's heroes such as Marak of Ash and Helio Death Bringer.

Lucius urged his limbs to go faster, his nose trailing the ground. He was in his humanoid form, but that didn't stop him from tracking. He neared the fox, closer and closer, and finally he caught her.

She did not yelp as he snagged a leg, did not fight as he snapped her neck. Her body went limp in his arms, and in the deepest pools of his heart, he felt sympathy. She had done him a great service, and he would forever be grateful.

"I'm sorry, little one," he whispered into the corpse's silky ear. "You will be of great use to me, to this kingdom. Your death was not in vain," he swore. On the ground, where her last breath was taken, a vibrant flower sprouted in its place. A deep maroon gladiolus rose, life replacing death. Lucius wrapped the fox around his neck, kneeling to the flower. Lowering a gentle hand, he dug into the soft soil, extracting the plant, roots and all, to preserve its life. A distinct, warm wetness trailed down his face, and acknowledged it to be tears. He'd been chosen as worthy. The Hunt was over, and he would meet his people as the officially recognized King of Draconis.

Their king emerged from the forest radiating, and those who had set tents out to be there once his hunt was complete stared in awe, every citizen falling to their knees for *him*. The bulk of his population were servants, only eight pure blooded Draconians, but deep down he now knew that was inconsequential, for all had the hearts of his people. Each and every one of them belonged to him.

A man of the Order of the Dragon kneeled before him, humbly turning his face to the ground. He balanced a dagger encrusted with emeralds between his hands: an offering. Lucius, tracing his pointer down the man's face to his chin, tilted his head upwards. The Diwata still danced in his eyes, and the man's mouth fell open. Lucius gingerly took the blade from him, plunging it through the fox to remove its heart.

Lucius raised the dripping heart, the blood splattering on the cobblestone beneath him, and the people roared. His teeth tore through the flesh, and dark maroon streamed down his face, two interwoven rivers of death and promise. Louder and louder the crowd roared, a chant, a plea, a cry… all his name. A female now came to him, and she placed a crown, *his* crown, on his head. Even the stars had been awakened by the noise, but their faces now faded, and the world returned to its normal state of being. The Diwata had left him, and yet She had not. She was not with him, yet he still felt her ever-raging presence. All was well, all back to normal.

Lucius paced, preparing his mind to speak to his people. He inhaled, the feast's scent still hanging in the air, the blood of the fox also clogging his nostrils.

"I have completed my Rite; I have claimed the fox. More importantly, I have returned with the Maroon Gladiolus. You might ask yourselves, why exactly is this important?" Murmurings blanketed the world, their velvet whispers and predictions sweet to his ears. He let loose a gentle chuckle. His eyes were glazed over with adoration, and the hearts surrounding him were pumping Draconis blood, black and true. All hearts beating for him, for the stars above, and for a world unclaimed. "Maroon, for our kind, is the color of success. Every great king that is carved into the histories had the maroon flower. The gladiolus also foretells the successful reign. It is a sign of great balance to come. The sword tail lily has two sides: swift punishment and mercy. Balance and good fortune are the predictions for my reign, but my reign does not just belong to me, but to all. You, my good people, are the heart and soul of this noble reign, I am the brain. Together, we will burn this planet and rule the ashes. Now, rise all. Rise a citizen, the heart and soul, servants and dragons alike, rise and claim your rightful place as one with Draconis." They no longer murmured; they all roared, a symphony of pride and love. In a wave, they stood and claimed their rights. King Lucius thrust a clenched fist into the air, and his name was the only word on their lips.

Chapter Twenty-Three

"I smell the sea," Arietta said, delighted by this. The salty smell of crashing waves and the distant cry of gulls was something she had not detected in months. That feeling of delight turned sour when her mind wandered and she thought to her grandfather's flashing eyes, fear and rage whirling in their never-ending gray. She remembered the revulsion that she'd felt by the cold and careful pace of the destructive king. It was funny how the smell of the salty air of the sea suddenly turned to fire and ash. That night would be forever etched into her memory. Arietta sighed and the grin dropped from her face as her mind raced through all of these thoughts in a flash.

Nova scented the despair; it tainted the sweet smell of ocean breeze. Nova furrowed her eyebrows as she felt overwhelmed by the memories of Belamoris. Her features softened as the realization hit her like a Mack truck; she had a pack. For the first time in her short life, Nova had friends, and this brought a smile to her face. No matter what waited for them at the end of this journey, she wouldn't be facing it alone. Nova looped her arm through Arietta's.

"When we get back to Earth, we should have a girls' day. I think that would be nice. Just you and me. We could go to an amusement park or catch a movie or something."

A look of genuine content spread across Arietta's face. "That sounds great, Nova."

A wolfish grin spread on Nova's face as she turned toward Jerry. "Don't get jealous, Jerry, maybe we could all hang out sometime." She had a devilish look in her eyes, as if she knew something. Arietta's head turned in question.

"Jealous?" Jerry let out a fake laugh. "Why would I be jealous of you? As soon as I can pull my skinny butt out of bed, I would love to hang out," he said with false bravado, and a light red spread on his face.

"Easy, fella, I'm not trying to steal her."

Jerry spluttered at this, looking back and forth between Nova and Ari.

"Steal her? What's that supposed to mean?" Arietta's brow was furrowed. It appeared that there was some sort of hidden meaning, but whatever it was completely went over her head.

"You can't *steal* her, we are all friends, right?" Jerry laughed nervously, but his eyes flashed.

"Faster, kids, we are losing daylight. I am not afraid to steal your voice if it'll make you move quicker," Arkas interjected brashly. Arietta's eyes flitted towards Arkas, and she shrugged, urging the rest to pick up their feet. Nova disentangled her arm from Arietta, hanging back to walk with Jerry. Once she was sure that Arkas and Ari were engaged in conversation, she turned a sly eye to the boy who was now just about as red as a tomato.

"So, you like her?" His head snapped toward Nova. Jerry couldn't help but feel unsettled every time that he looked into Nova's eyes, one icy blue and the other dark brown. He could never get a read on what exactly was going on behind those eyes.

"I never said that!" he whispered sharply, and Nova chuckled. He looked up towards Arietta, relieved that her focus was on the old fart next to her.

"You didn't have to," she smirked. Jerry searched her eyes, trying to find her intent, yet came to no real conclusions.

"Where did the shy Nova go? What did you *do* to her?" asked Jerry. She laughed again, a sharp yet charming sound.

"I don't know. Maybe it's the wolf in me showing through. So, why Arietta? What's got you all head over heels for my favorite songbird?" Jerry was flustered, his eyes bouncing back and forth from the girl ahead of them and the one next to him.

"I- uh…" he gulped, and Nova nonverbally prompted him to spit it out. "I don't know! I don't really want to talk about this…" He was promptly cut off by the wagging of a finger.

"Relax, I'm just messing with you." She covered up a laugh with a cough. "I like her too, but I think that someone has a crush!"

A grin spread on Arietta's face ahead as she inspected a map that had been produced from the bag that Arkas carried, and she pointed at it, questioning him. Jerry's look further betrayed his true feelings for Arietta, and as he turned his gaze back to Nova, she smirked at him.

"I feel something for her, but I really don't think it's any of your business. She is pretty, smart, and very brave. Why do you care so much?"

"This group," she motioned to the two ahead, to Jerry, and to herself, "this is my pack." She said this as if it explained everything, yet it only raised more questions for Jerry.

Arkas turned to them. "Faster! We are so close, but we are running out of time!" Arietta and Arkas traveled at a much faster rate, and after little thought, Nova shifted into her other form. It was faster and, luckily for Jerry, prevented her from asking more questions about something Jerry certainly did *not* want to think about.

That was when their eyes landed on it: a cottage made of wood, its roof spiraling up toward the heavens, the windows glowing a warm yellow. "The Keep," Arkas breathed. It was so much more beautiful than he'd remembered, so simple, yet even the walls were brimming with knowledge. Now he set out at a hobbled sprint towards their salvation.

***

Gustoff leaned forward, trying to rest his legs. Lucius had ordered that he would hang from the chains in the middle of the room two days ago. Gustoff hadn't slept or eaten for those two days. His shoulders felt as though hot embers had been inserted into them. His robe and shoes had been removed, so the cold chilled him to the bone. Each rib on his chest was more pronounced than the last. The guards did have a wet cloth wrapped around the end of a long stick that they thrust through the barred window two times each day so that he could suck the dirty water down his throat to keep him alive. As he hung there, he thought of Ari and hoped that she was safe. Gustoff had sensed when she was called here with the others. He knew that as long as Arkas had a beating heart, he would do his best to ensure her safety.

The guards approached down the hallway outside of his damp, cold cell. They were talking about a festival. Lucius was on some great hunt. Gustoff mustered what was left of his strength and called out to the guards. "I need food and water. If I don't get this, I will die. I am so weak; please bring me something."

"Shut your foul mouth, or I will remove your tongue, old man!" The guard rattled a stick on the bars of Gustoff's cell for good measure. "You'll get food when I decide!"

In a dry, raspy voice, Gustoff continued, "I don't think that Lord Lucius will be too happy with you if I die while he is away. All I'm asking for is a bowl of mead or a piece of bread with some real water. I won't say anything about it." Gustoff focused his mind on the guard who had rattled on his cell bars. The compliance that had been drilled into the guards throughout their lives reminded him of the late dogs in Gustoff's life that he had trained to sit when told and to speak for treats. Gustoff nudged the guards' thinking.

"I will bring you one slice of bread and a glass of water. After that, I don't wanna hear a peep out of your ugly wizard face!"

The guards left, and a smile covered Gustoff's face. He knew that he had them. Several minutes passed before the guards returned. One slid the bread and cup of water under the door. The guard kept his eyes down as he did this. Gustoff asked, "How can I eat when I can't even reach the bowl? I am a tired old man who hasn't slept or eaten for two days. My staff is not with me; please just untie me for a few minutes so that I can eat. You can hold your sword to the back of my neck while I eat. I am helpless as it is, but with a sword to my neck, I couldn't possibly hurt anyone. You can tie me back up as soon as I am finished." Gustoff nudged again, and the guard complied.

The guard unshackled Gustoff, careful not to look at him while doing this. Gustoff chose his moment, then doubled over and screamed in pain, grabbing his stomach. The guard studied Gustoff's face. His eyes immediately turned from green to white. "Oh my, something is wrong with your friend!" The other guard hurried over to see what had happened. He was not as careful as his commander.

Gustoff whispered into the guard's ear, "I need my robe and my staff. Where are they?"

The guard then turned and strode out of the cell and turned to the left. His partner stayed in the cell. Gustoff then asked the guard to close the door so that it would not draw suspicion. He reached up and grabbed the chain with both hands so that if anyone passed by, they would not notice anything out of place. Soon, the other guard returned with his staff and robe. "Now, I need you to chain my hands together and lead me to the back gate. If anyone asks, tell them that the king wishes to have the prisoner moved to a cell closer to his chambers so that he can question him when he returns."

The guard nodded, and off they went. Gustoff did not realize that to dragons, the back gate was on the roof of the castle. Once they arrived, Gustoff told the guards to return to their station. He also told them that they had already checked his cell and would not need to check it again today. The two departed, leaving Gustoff on the roof wondering how he would get out of Draconis.

He was too weak to teleport far enough away for him to be safe. He also needed food and water for his journey. He thought to himself, "Man, I should have brought the bread and water." As he paced the roof, he peered into a doorway at the other end. There was a large table layered with raw meat. He quickly grabbed the first piece off of the table and muttered "Ignis". The meat quickly browned with the flame blazing from his fingers. He crammed the dripping food into his mouth, nearly forgetting to chew. His stomach turned sourly, demanding more, so he grabbed two more large cuts of meat and wrapped them in a towel for later. His muscles screamed at him every step of the way, but he knew where he needed to go. dragging one foot in front of the next, he climbed the staircase that hugged the castle walls. It was a long drop down, and the trees from this height reminded him of the model trees he'd sit up next to the tracks of his favorite toy train set when he was younger. It was dizzying, being this high up, but the stars kept him grounded and gave him hope for a better tomorrow. The cracks in the staircase made his already-upset stomach roil, and his cut and bruised hands gripped the stone wall tightly. He knew who he needed, and focus was required if he were to even hope to escape these wretched peaks. They were the only beings in all of Palidonaya that could save him from more torture at the hands of Lucius.

Gustoff leaned against the battlements along the outer wall of the castle, waiting patiently, but not comfortably. Soon, he could sense her approach. Adrenaline shot through his body, afraid that others would see her gliding to his rescue. A shadow soared through the skies, giant wings cutting through the puffy clouds. His savior, he hoped; his greatest enemy, he feared.

"Gustoff, we assumed the worst once we heard that the king had taken you hostage."

A sigh of relief ripped through Gustoff as he laid eyes on the massive pegasus. Her snowy white feathers fluttered, moved by the eastern wind that ripped through the mountain range. "I have been outside of Draconis looking for a clue as to where they have been keeping you. I felt your beacon and raced here as quickly as possible. I stayed above the clouds so that no one saw my approach."

"Let's catch up later, Xersa; the guards might be on their way! Thank you for being here for me." With that, Gustoff climbed on top of Xersa, of the Aphrodite herd. Once Gustoff had a good hold on Xersa, the pegasus stepped off of the castle wall, spread her mighty wings, and soared away from the castle.

Chapter Twenty-Four

The quartet approached the Keep on wary feet, moving like shadows across the dunes of sand. Arkas drew in a sharp breath, tears pricking in the corners of his eyes. He couldn't even *begin* to explain the sense of joy and accomplishment he felt at seeing the house.

"Quickly now; I do not suspect that we have much time left." He placed a shaking hand on the small of Jerry's back, hustling him along. Finally, they reached the doorstep, anticipation thrumming through their beings. There was a distinct power pulsing through the Keep, which sent shivers along Arkas' spine.

He knocked thrice, holding his breath, trying not to dwell on his wrinkled old hands. The last time he had been here, his hands had been tight and smooth, the signs of age not showing as pronounced as they were now. A shaky voice called for the quartet to come in, the door swinging open at the knocks. The smell of dust, old books, and firewood graced his nose upon entering, and he noted the dim lighting. While on the outside of the Keep it appeared to be small, it was astonishing how large its innards truly were. There was a ticking coming from all around them, multiple clocks chiming at different hours, and rows upon rows of bookshelves were in his sight. In the middle of it all sat an enormous tortoise, his eyes closed behind circular wire-rimmed frames, moss growing on his large shell. All around the tortoise, floating in the air, were several pens scribbling on many scrolls.

"Um, excuse me, sir?" Arietta's honey-sweet voice cut through the sound of dozens of scribbling pens, hard at work. The pens simultaneously crashed to the floor, the papers drifting into a neat pile. The great tortoise slowly raised his head until his gaze locked on Arietta.

"Who enters the Hall of Records, and what is it that you seek?" Wisdom was in the tortoise's voice, as was aggravation. The travelers approached with caution, and the tortoise raised his hands; the pens lifted while the papers slid back into place.

"Horace, it is good to see you again. How are you?" Arkas said kindly, and the tortoise, to the children's surprise, sighed wearily.

"Wizard, you look familiar." Horace's glasses shifted as he examined the old man. "Though you were much younger when we last met. I ask one last time, what do you seek from the Record Keeper?" Another clock chimed, and Horace looked over his wire-rimmed frames at the nearest clock, eyes squinting in concern. Nova traced a finger down one of the books of an older breed, then examined her finger tip, rubbing her pointer and thumb together to brush off the dust.

Arkas said, "I come with the three Chosen warriors of the prophecy."

A harsh chuckle erupted from the old creature's beak.

"The prophecy of which you speak is one of muddled truth, though before my eyes stand four beings of great power," the tortoise replied.

"Muddled truth? Is Palidonaya at risk of losing to the darkness?" An icy fear had overtaken Arkas at the words of the Keeper. If they could not believe in the prophecy, in the idea that light always overcame darkness, then what else could they believe in?

"I know not of what lies ahead. I merely know the heart of the prophet who gave us these words. Worry not, wizard, you will find your way." Horace looked at each of the visitors as he spoke.

The children glanced to each other in silence. Then Arietta said, "Excuse me, sir, my name is Arietta, and I don't know much about prophecies. I do know that my grandfather has been taken by the Dragon King. I need to know how to kill a dragon. If you tell us, then we will be on our way."

"Interesting. Of all the questions that could be asked, you choose what is already known by the Dwarven King." Horace shook his head, moving quite slowly toward one of the bookshelves.

Arkas then said, "Horace, Palidonaya is running out of time. We have come a long way and must return to Lenovia with this knowledge."

Horace sighed at this comment, interrupting swiftly. He then moved to the nearest of the bookshelves and extracted a golden hardback with yellowing pages.

"I've kept the records for all time. To defeat a dragon in combat is very difficult, but not impossible. You will need a powerful weapon, wielded by a skilled warrior." Horace, taking his time, turned the pages, scanning one before turning to the next.

"The Dragon King has already taken most of Palidonaya. There are rumors of a nest with thousands of eggs nearing maturity. We must hurry or all will be lost." Arkas was losing patience, and Horace clicked his beak, looking pointedly over his shell.

"Patience, all is not lost. You still have the time that you require." Horace then motioned to another book that was on the top shelf as he moved toward a gold-plated ladder.

"Here, let me help you." Nova stepped beside Horace, helping him reach the book he was looking for, to prevent the tortoise from having to climb one of the many ladders. He thanked Nova, then used his beak to flip through the pages.

"You have that which you need awaiting you in Lenovia." He tilted his head, adjusting the glasses, and used one of his feet to keep his place.

"We do?" Jerry's eyebrows raised.

Horace continued, "Yes, a sacrifice must be made by a pure-born soul of royal lineage from the land of Equus."

"Less riddles, more words that make sense. What do you mean by that?" Jerry pushed as Horace crept back towards his chair.

"What you ask carries with it a great cost." His voice shook with his age, and Arkas' hands began to tremble. Was that great act of treachery worth it all? To spill a blood so pure would unleash terrible magic. This sacrifice surely meant eternal damnation. Horace laughed, a deep and throaty sound. "This sacrifice must be made willingly for the weapon to be forged." Arkas' eyes turned to the floor, unwilling to look into the tortoise's.

"We will do what is necessary, but I pray that there is another way. We could capture the king and force the dragons to surrender?" Arkas thought this all out loud, and the kids listened carefully, yet Horace closed his eyes and shook his head. "Maybe--oof!" Arkas fell through the floor of the Keep, and the building disappeared. Jerry let loose a cry of surprise as he fell through, onto the sand, and Nova looked purely befuddled. "The Keep moves automatically after an allotted time to a random location. All but the turtle and his dusty old books get kicked out right before the Keep moves," Arkas said bitterly. "We're lucky we got the information in time with the way that old bag talks." Nova nodded in agreement.

"He said we have to sacrifice someone from Equus. We can't sacrifice one of our own; there has to be another way," Arietta exclaimed, folding her arms. Jerry put a hand on her shoulder in an attempt to comfort her, but the sly look on Nova's face caused him to rip his hand off her and stuff it into his pocket. Arietta glanced at him out of the corner of her eye, curious about the action, but shrugged it off. She had too much to worry about to question her companions.

"I…" Arkas' eyes dropped to the sand. This was bad. "I'm not sure. We need to seek the Council's guidance. Let's pray that we are not too late. If the dragons have moved on Dragon's Bane, then the Council's forces will be scattered," he suggested. Nova perked up at this.

"That's amazing! Here I was thinking it was us versus the world, but no. There's an entire Council with forces! Beautiful. Well, we may have a fighting chance now." A wide grin spread across her face, and to the surprise of the quartet, where there were once human ears, large white wolf ears sprouted. "Little too excited, isn't that funny," she remarked offhandedly, tugging lightly on one of the ears. It felt soft on her hand, and she had to admit it was quite nice. "So, tell me more about the Record Keeper," she prompted, feeling a little self-conscious of the attention on her ears and wishing to redirect it elsewhere.

"He is one of the immortals that is tasked to keep track of all of the histories. All records are unbiased, all histories filed without error. You can find the answers to everything if you have the time to search through all the books. It is said that all worlds have a Record Keeper," Arkas replied.

"Do you think that Earth has a Record Keeper?" Arietta was intrigued with the notion.

"Yes, Gustoff assumed they would've been located in the Library of Alexandria," Arkas said dismissively, but at this bit of information, Jerry gaped.

"That is…" He grew starry-eyed. "That is the coolest thing you've ever said. How do you find the Keep? Do you think that it moves like the one here?"

Arietta chuckled lightly, Nova chortling along with her.

"I am not certain. I have only visited Palidonaya's Keep."

"I would definitely like to find it, assuming it isn't gone." His tone turned morose. Arietta looped an arm around his, a small smile on her face, causing Jerry to inhale sharply a moment before relaxing.

"If it contains all of the history, think about how much different the world would be." Those starry eyes of Jerry's turned to her.

"If mankind truly found it, they would destroy it. The violence of man is incomparable to any other species," Nova interrupted, her voice worn.

"What about the dragons?" Arietta asked carefully, concern flashing in her eyes a moment. Nova shook her head.

"Dragons don't drop nuclear bombs on cities. We have polluted our planet, killed millions of people in wars. If mankind found a Hall of Records, it would be destroyed," Nova retorted.

"Come on, Nova, that's not all, we have also done great things. Yes, we take and corrupt, but we give too. Life has a balance; humankind is no exception to that rule."

Nova shook her head, as if to clear it, and refocused on Arietta. She looked the blonde dead in the eyes to ground herself, seeming to return to her form.

"I suppose you're right." Nova laughed uneasily, and the group shifted.

"So, how are we getting out of this sand pit, Arkas?" Jerry leaned into Ari, getting her to break eye contact with the other girl.

"First, we sleep. Next, we go due east for about twelve barjinks, then north until sundown. We've had a long day, so a full night's rest is well deserved, I'd say." Arietta's face spread into a grin, as did Jerry's, and a closed-mouth smile came from Nova. Sleep not only was desperately needed, but terribly wanted as well. After bedding down, Nova sighed.

"Man, I can't wait to get out of this off-brand Tatooine." She closed her eyes, relishing in the warm sheets.

"You insult Tatooine by comparing this hellhole to it," Jerry snapped back, and the three kids laughed.

"I don't know what crazy moon language you all are talking in, but you better shut your traps. We have the gift of a full night's sleep, and I'm not about to be kept awake by your nonsense." There was a rustling of blankets as the quartet got comfortable, and light snoring was all to be heard from the hut by the ocean.

***

Far in the north, an unyielding cold swept through bustling mountains, and a queen claimed a throne unwillingly. The bitter cold nipped at her neck, yet she embraced it. The crystalline palace was flooded with her people, and her icy-blue eyes skipped over the crowd. She took a deep breath. She could do this; she didn't need anyone else. She knew that her parents shouldn't have made the voyage; now their names were just on the long list of casualties from the war, but their deaths would not be in vain. She would protect her people, something that they had not been able to do.

Chapter Twenty-Five

Gustoff had his arms wrapped tightly around Xersa's neck as the pegasus climbed higher into the clouds, soaring away from the cursed Draconis mountains. His strength was fading, but to loosen his hold meant certain death. He needed rest, water, and food, but it would have to wait a little longer. He closed his eyes and reached out with his mind. He had to know that she was safe, so he focused on Arietta with all of his mind and heart. His mind filled with a vision of the inside of a library. And then... a white blade smeared with blood. The blood glowed, thickly coating the weapon. With this vision in mind, his heart raced, and his grip on Xersa's mane tightened. The meaning of this, he didn't know, but what he did know was that Arietta needed him.

They were flying through thick billowing clouds, and as Gustoff looked past Xersa's neck, and there was a break in the clouds. They were over the foothills of Draconis and would soon be entering the prairie lands of Equus. What he saw in the distance forced a track of tears to slide down his weather-beaten face and fall like raindrops from the heavens to the scorched earth below. It was worse than the Wastelands, worse than any natural disaster he'd seen before. He forced himself to look down, forced himself to see it all. "When will we be able to rest, Xersa?"

"We will rest when we reach Lenovia. That is the only country that does not belong to the King of Dragons on this continent. I will need to eat and gather my strength for the final push to Aridol. The last of the resistance is housed there."

He relished the opportunity to lie down to sleep. His body ached from every joint, and his mind was still a bit foggy from both the lack of sleep and the mind-joining that Lucius repeatedly attempted on him. If not for the absence of Lucius, Gustoff would still be in his cell.

Xersa soared over the northern tip of Equus and into the southernmost reaches of Lenovia. There she found a large lake with a small island towards its center. "This should do nicely! We will be able to rest without having to worry about being spotted by the enemy." She circled the island from above to ensure that it was uninhabited.

Once she decided it was safe, they glided in for a landing just inside the tree line. Gustoff dismounted by falling off of Xersa and landing flat on his back, forcing all of his air to leave his body. He spent the next minute or two trying to just breathe. Once he had established that he would live from the fall, he removed the last two pieces of meat that he had taken from Lucius's chambers. He offered one to Xersa, who declined with a shudder. Gustoff summoned fire to cook the remaining meat. He then devoured it and lay down to sleep under the canopy of trees. Xersa then began to graze on the sparse vegetation on the small island to supply the energy needed for the final leg of the journey.

***

That night, Arietta's sleep was anything but peaceful. Her dreams were filled with hunters chasing them to the sea. The dreams then shifted to the Shadow Walkers, who devoured villages as they moved ever closer to the last bastion of hope. She dreamed of her Grandpa being tortured by Lucius and his men. And finally, she dreamed of a cold so complete that she could no longer move, of an evil that sought revenge and of a darkness that extinguished all light. As the darkness approached, her subconscious yanked her away from that awful truth, and she sprang up in the night, in the real world, far away from the terrifying dreams.

She got out of her bed and made her way to the door of Arkas' hut. She stepped outside to get some air and shake off the vestiges of her nightmare. She grabbed a water skin on the way out and took a deep drink from it. As she peered into the swirling night sky, the uncomfortable sensation of eyes on the back of her neck made her nervous. She turned and nothing but sand was in that direction. She did, however, know this feeling, and it was definitely time to wake the others up. She turned toward the hut and saw the great beast blocking her path. It was inky black with razor-sharp teeth. She tried to scream, but her voice was caught in her throat. The beast slowly stalked towards her, its emerald eyes locked on hers.

Arietta felt dizzy and lost, looking into the eyes of the beast. Her arms fell to her sides, and she walked slowly towards the Hunter. A dense fog had descended upon her mind, and after such a dream, it was difficult to think clearly. Though she knew that she was in danger, her feet brought her closer and closer to the snarling being.

Ari was within a few feet of the Hunter when she was knocked backwards to the sand. Her vision was blurred from the fall, but she could make out a figure standing over her, facing the Hunter.

***

Jerry was torn from his slumber when Ari pulled the door of the hut closed on the way out. He stretched and sat up in bed, looking around and listening for signs that others had awakened. He silently slipped on his shirt and crept outside. After peeping his head out of the door, a black blur in the dunes just past the hut scurried on.

Jerry closed his eyes and pictured himself standing outside the hut and in his mind's eye began to pull the light from that image. He continued weaving darkness around himself and then filled in the blackness with the colors of his surroundings. Jerry's body vanished. Quietly he crept along the path in the sand that was left by Arietta. Her silhouette shimmered in the moonlight; her visage was that of an angel. He circled around her silently, needing to see her face. As he got the first glimpse of her face, he noticed the dampness of tears that had been shed drying. What was wrong with her? Why was she out here in the cold rather than tucked in the warm bed? A blur just between Arietta and the hut put a stop to his questioning; a Hunter was blocking her way to the safety of the quartet. Ari turned and locked eyes with the beast. Terror gripped Jerry's heart at seeing Arietta go slack-jawed and stumble toward the Hunter. He had to act immediately, so he ran at her, shoving her to the sand. Jerry made himself visible, confronted the beast, and drew his daggers. The rubies inlaid in the quillon irradiated blood-red in the darkness.

The Hunter hissed, "The Daggers of Derge will not save you or your friend, boy." She then extended her senses and let out three loud grunts, shaking her mashta--the dark structure surrounding her face that most mistook for a mane--so that her

235

pack would surround the Chosen. The message was received, and the pack shimmered into existence, cutting off all routes of escape. "If you run, you will die," growled the leader.

Jerry forced a smile and replied in his best Scottish accent, "Every man dies, but not every man really lives." He then charged at the closest beast, slashing with each dagger in a move so fast that Jerry seemed to vanish and reappear at Arietta's side. Sparks flew from the daggers as they struck the beast on each side.

She roared and snapped her jaws at the boy, capturing nothing but air in the process. The leader sensed power in this lad. She advanced two steps, head held low, readying her fire. She would try to subdue them without burning them, but bringing back bodies was infinitely better than telling Lucius that they had escaped again.

Jerry's confidence faltered when the daggers did no damage to the beast. He moved to his right, keeping himself between the closest Hunter and a stunned Arietta. With his eyes never leaving the danger, he called to Arietta, "Could you come back to me? I could really use some help."

Arietta blinked. Before she could respond, he flashed out of existence again, reappearing in close range to the Hunter and, with sparks flying off of her hide, followed by a terrible scream, he appeared at Arietta's side again. When he reappeared, one of the long fangs had splintered from the impact.

"You will pay for that boy!" It charged at them, eyes blazing green.

Jerry quickly grabbed Arietta and threw her to the right as he lunged to the left. Jerry sprang upward, completing a flip at the pinnacle of his leap, coming down with both daggers aimed for the one part of the beast that frightened him most: her eyes. His daggers met the flesh, sinking to the hilt as the beast let out a startled scream, her mashta extending and spasming. Jerry was flung off of her head, landing ten feet from his initial leap. He was dazed from the fall and rolled to his side, attempting to fend off the other Hunters, but they were gone. Only the first remained, spasming in the sand. Once the flailing subsided, he cautiously approached and pulled his daggers from her lifeless eyes. "Daggers of Derge; I like the sound of that." Jerry let out a loud whoop as Arkas stumbled out of the hut to see what the commotion was all about and froze when he saw the body of the fallen hunter. The sand vibrated as the first drop of the hunter's blood splashed upon it. The swirling sand encompassed the hunter as it sank, becoming a part of the Great Beyond.

"How did you do that?" Arkas stared, watching the last of the hunters disappear into the ground.

"I used the Daggers of Derge on her. Stabbed her through both of her eyes. She didn't have a chance." Jerry smiled, wiped the daggers clean, and spun both in a circle before shoving them into the sheaths that he had fashioned in his vest.

"Are you certain that those are the Daggers of Derge? That would explain how you were able to subdue the beast. They were forged before the first war against the dragons. They possess the power that only one other blade has ever possessed: the power to slay a dragon. They have been lost for centuries." He took a breath, allowing himself to think. "The next encounter will not be won with such ease. If they know that we can hurt or kill them, they will be taking more lethal options next time."

"Um, they were using some pretty lethal options tonight. I just got lucky this time. We really need to put some distance between us and them."

Arietta spoke in a loud, awe-filled whisper, "That wasn't luck, Jerry; you were moving so fast that I couldn't even see you. You were amazing!"

Jerry's face turned crimson. He felt that his heart would leap out of his chest. "I thought that you were a goner. I had to protect my girl."

Arietta smiled and said, "Who says I'm your girl?" She then turned to Arkas and asked if he could pack up the hut. She was ready to get moving, and she could tell that Jerry was ready as well.

Chapter Twenty-Six

Examining the mural he had recently commissioned, Lucius smiled softly. It was beautiful; the sun shone through the window, hitting the wall and lighting the maroon gladiolus up perfectly. The artist, the same one that had painted his chest for the festival, made it for him, and he had to admit, he quite enjoyed her work. A small, mousy servant entered, disturbing his thoughts. While this irritated him, she seemed nervous, and he decided not to subject her to his frightening glare.

"It's Gustoff." Her voice trembled, and Lucius assumed she'd drawn the short stick out of his servants, having to deliver whatever news she had.

"What of him? Is he dead?" He waited a moment before hissing, "Well, spit it out."

"He's escaped."

His vision went red, the world no longer seeming whole. It was as if he'd blacked out and the rage had ridden him through the storm. When he awoke from it all, when the world looked as it had before, there was blood on his hands and paper rained down on his wooden floor. His desk had been flipped, and the servant was dead. From what Lucius could gather, he'd ripped her up with the letter opener at his feet. The scene was surreal; he was frozen, and all he could do was stare at his dripping red hands. That was one of his people, and it hadn't been her fault... He collapsed to the floor, bile rising in the back of his throat.

After a few minutes spent in a destroyed office with the coppery smell of blood permeating the air, he finally rose to his feet, brushing out the imaginary wrinkles on his pants. Grabbing at a kerchief on the floor, untouched by his storm, he used it to dab daintily at his eyes, wipe his nose and upper lip, and finally to remove some of the blood caked on his hands. Red gloves, that was what it reminded him of. He laughed humorlessly, shaking his head. He realized he looked quite unkingly, but he cared little as he strode into the hall.

"You." He jabbed a finger through the air at a male, smaller than average, and the boy cowered. "Get a team and clean up my office. Also, send bathers to my room." That smell, that revolting smell, still forced its way up his nose. One look at the bloodshot and clearly furious king had the boy quaking and sprinting off to find assistance for the task.

***

"I had to protect my girl," Nova mocked in a deep voice, smirking as Jerry rubbed at the back of his neck.

"Would you cut it out?" he groaned, fighting his own laughter. "She might hear you!"

"Well, you already said it to her face, so it's not gonna hurt her to hear it again," she sneered. Arkas turned around from ahead of them, raising a bushy eyebrow. "What are you kids bickering about?"

Arietta turned at Arkas' sudden attention to her peers trailing them. A look of panic settled on Jerry's face, turning to Nova with pleading in his eyes. The ghost of a smile came over her face, and her eyes left Jerry's, traveling to Arkas'.

"Oh, nothing, he just thinks that I would have met this group had we not traveled, and that's clearly wrong."

Jerry's brow furrowed in confusion. "Wha-" Nova jabbed at him with her elbow, and suddenly he understood. "Oh, yeah, I know we would've met. Maybe not you, Arkas, but we would've ended up meeting Nova. I'd already run into Ari before everything, and it's not like we were that far away; you were in the same hospital, just a different room. It's possible, don't you think?"

Nova quirked an eyebrow, flattered that he'd thought about the topic before. "Murphy's law, anything that can happen will, but it's just really unlikely. Yeah, you, Ari, and Gus could've been buddy-buddy, but I probably would've lived my entire life without even knowing your names. I'm shy, you know--we shared the same chemo room for two weeks and you didn't even notice me," she replied, and Arkas lost his interest.

"Crazy kids, don't they know about fate?" Arkas grumbled to Arietta, and she silently prompted him to explain. "Oh, come on, you surely know about fate, right? You know, the thing that controls *all* of the universe. The thing that popularized the phrase 'everything happens for a reason.' You all are destined to travel here and restore the balance; you were also destined to meet here. Whether you like it or not, there was no alternative path to go down." He chuckled at Arietta's wide eyes. "You can't tell me you don't know about fate. Goodness, Earth is so uncultured!"

Arietta argued, "We know about fate, it's just... It's not really something considered to be real. Some believe in it, but most don't."

"I am certain that fate is real. That's part of why you are all here, as the Chosen Ones; fate bonded you to this great responsibility." Arkas shook his head.

"I have been thinking about that too. Everyone thinks that we are the Chosen warriors that will lead the charge against these dragons. Who's to say that's true?" Ari asked.

"Our hope sits on a balance. We place faith in the prophet, and you have been working to fulfill the prophecy. As long as the people trust the prophecy, we are given resources to fulfill said prophecy, and should you start asking silly questions like that and break the trust of the people depending on us, you will topple our fine balance," Arkas said.

Arietta added, "Like a house of cards."

Arkas nodded. "Indeed, like a house of cards."

"The people of Palidonaya have to believe that they can win." Arietta had never bought into blind faith, but Arkas had a point.

Arkas said, "I agree."

"What if it comes down to us fighting a dragon? What if we get sacrificed because of all this prophecy stuff? Of course we should help these people of our own volition, but when prophecies are involved, all typical rules are allowed to be broken, and we don't get that choice." Nova spoke up, inspecting one of her claws.

Arietta paused. "I don't know. All I know is that it feels right to help them, and once I'm in, I'm all in."

Arkas stopped the group at what he determined was midday for a rest and a quick meal. He moved away from the others to eat in silence. He pulled a map out of his pack and began analyzing it, mumbling to himself as he traced possible paths. He looked up from the map as he listened to a noise he hadn't heard in several days: the children were giggling. As he watched them interacting with each other, a smile spread across his face. Hearing that beautiful noise, he decided they could take a few extra moments so that they could just be three friends enjoying each other's company. He could worry about how they would cross a land full of the enemy's forces.

Struggle was in Arkas' gaze and Arietta made her way to where he was sitting with the map spread out in front of him. "Hi, Arkas, it looks like you could use some company. What are you looking at?"

"This is a map of the known lands of Palidonaya. I'm trying to plot a course to Aridol, the capital city. We must share the information that Horace has shared with us. The problem is that we either cross Draconis or take our chances in Mirnalduhr."

"Well, I know that we need to avoid Draconis, but what's wrong with Mirnalduhr?" Arietta held Arkas's gaze.

"Mirnalduhr is the Dwarven Country and is not a land that you would want to travel through. The place is nothing but mountains that reach past the clouds. Unlike Draconis, it is bitterly cold, making it almost impassable. The route that we would have to take leads under the mountains through Derge. The dwarves have remained in isolation, untrusting of the other races. In other words, I don't think that they will welcome us with open arms."

"Okay, so Lucius has sent his Hunters to 'hunt' us down. It really seems that he doesn't like us. The dwarves don't like anyone, but they haven't tried to kill us yet, and according to Horace, they know how to make a weapon that would help us win against the dragons. Would it be possible to convince them to join us against the dragons?"

"The Dwarven Kingdom has never joined the rest of the Palidonayians in any of the wars against the dragons. I don't believe that they would harm us, but the trip itself may prove dangerous enough for us to avoid." Arkas was getting frustrated at his lack of options, and it was beginning to show.

"What is on the other side of the sea that seems to be just beyond the dunes? Could we go that way?" Ari thought she knew the answer, but wanted Arkas to start looking at other options.

"There are other lands across the water, but we have no way to cross it." Arkas closed his eyes and rubbed his temples. There had to be another way.

"Can't you just make us disappear here and appear over there like you did in Belamoris?"

"I could not teleport all four of us that far. The Great Beyond presents a problem with this line of thinking, as we could end up in the middle of the sea. If it were just me, I could perform a series of disapparations once I reached Draconis, making the long journey much shorter. I would need considerable rest in between, but I don't even know why I am wasting my time thinking about this, as there are four of us."

Arietta sat in silence for a moment, as she was getting an idea that could work. "Is it possible for you to send us back to Earth, and then bring us back when you arrive in Lenovia?"

Arkas looked up at Arietta in shocked silence. "I could definitely call on you from Lenovia. The gate is closed, but I was able to find a way to open it for a short time. I would have to peer into the dimensional realm, and if the conditions are right, this could work!"

Arkas quickly folded his map and started setting up his hut. He gave strict instructions for the others to give him complete privacy until he contacted them. Arkas then disappeared into his hut and began by creating a perfect circle of salt on the floor. He sat down in the center of it and began chanting the appropriate spell.

***

Xersa and Gustoff arrived in Aridol three days after leaving the dungeons of Draconis. He was tired, hungry and extremely weak, but he was alive. Raulin greeted him at the entrance to Dragon's Bane and immediately took him to a room to rest. He arranged for a hot bath, food, and clean clothes to be prepared for Gustoff. The Council asked for him to give a debriefing, but Raulin insisted that Gustoff rested before they pushed him to talk. Gustoff was in far worse condition than he had thought.

It took two baths to clean him fully; the first had been stained a muddy brown from the dirt and sweat that coated his body like a primer. The second, a bubble bath, helped to loosen the muscles that had been pushed much farther than they had ever been pushed, both in the dungeon and during the flight. The stew that was brought to his room along with a loaf of bread was the first substantial meal that he had eaten in days. Gustoff almost broke down to tears when he laid down in a real bed to rest. It would be several hours before he would be talking to anybody. Raulin also had a draught of sleeping potion delivered so that Gustoff could have a restful sleep void of any nightmares. As Gustoff drank the potion that tasted like warm apple cider, his eyes became extremely heavy. He placed the cup on the nightstand and was fast asleep as soon as his head hit the pillow.

***

Arkas called for the group to meet him in his hut before nightfall. "I need you to gather inside this circle." Arkas stepped out of the circle as the three Chosen entered it. He then began to chant and leap into the air as he danced around, throwing some sort of powder over the children. Jerry giggled at how ridiculous Arkas looked as he pranced around. Arkas then commanded that all three of the children close their eyes and think about home. They did so as an intense light began to illuminate the circle. There was a blinding flash, and then, Arkas was alone to make the journey to Lenovia.

Chapter Twenty-Seven

Present Day

Arietta lay in her bed quietly, trying not to think of the loneliness that consumed her. A solitary tear streamed from her left eye, and she thought of her grown children and her grandchild, wondering if they were thinking about her. Pressure settled on her arm as Cooper laid his head down on her with a soft whimper.

"Guess it's just you and me, kid." She squeezed her eyes shut, the pain in her body still present, though she knew that she could tolerate it. She stroked Cooper's boxy head, thinking of days gone by. She sat up, made her way to her nightstand, and opened the bottom drawer. The case was sitting in the same spot that it had occupied since the day that she and Joey had moved in. Then, she wasn't sure why she felt the need to protect and keep this small gold coin, but she knew now. She carefully removed the coin from its case, the gold hue dulled by time.

"It's been a long time, old friend," she said into the velvety darkness, squeezing the coin in her hand and concentrating with a laser focus. "Palidonaya... please. Take me home." Her voice was shaky and sad. "Palidonaya, please take me home," she whispered. She felt her soul move; the heat in her hand was a welcome sign. She squeezed harder, a single thought echoing through her being, illuminated by the ethereal light. The smell hit her first, the sweet, fresh air. She opened her eyes, hesitant at first, and began to cry. The tall grass tickled her arms, and she dropped to her knees. It was… it was beautiful.

A powerful voice from behind startled her. "Why do you cry?"

"Who… who are you?" Arietta turned and a brown spotted horse with a long golden horn protruding from the center of her forehead stood looking at her.

"My name is Malachia. I am the Lead Mare of the Zeus herd. Who are you?" she questioned, and Arietta bowed her head.

"I am Arietta, but my friends call me Ari. Am I in Equus?" Ari said softly, and the horse tilted her head.

"Yes, we are in the land of Equus. Did you say that your name was Arietta? Our legends speak of a powerful warrior that is named Arietta."

"I don't look like much of a warrior, do I? You are of the herd Zeus. Do you know of a stallion named Dimitri? He was the leader of the herd that was left outside of Waterhaven." Arietta trailed off.

"Dimitri was the legendary king that led Zeus to take back the homelands that had been stripped from us. He was laid to rest last winter, I'm afraid. He knew it was his time, and took the eternal sleep. It was peaceful and dignified."

Arietta searched her mind for the traditional saying that they used. "May his legs run strong, and may he be one with the wind."

Malachia nodded gratefully at the words, a small part of her flattered that Arietta had remembered such a special part of their culture.

"Are you alright, Arietta?"

"I cry tears of happiness for my return to Palidonaya. I have felt so alone the past few years. My only true companion is my dog, Cooper." Arietta took a tentative step towards Malachia, suddenly wanting to verify that she was indeed real. Arietta stumbled with a groan, grabbing her hip as pain shot through her leg.

Malachia strode forward and touched her golden horn to Arietta's hip, the warmth enveloping her lower body. The pain dissipated. She stood and hugged the mighty mare.

"Malachia, I am not from this realm. I have not been to Palidonaya for years, and I have just begun to remember my travels here from my childhood. There have been people that I believe are from Palidonaya in my world asking me to give them a weapon."

"Are you certain that they are from Palidonaya?"

Arietta cocked her head slightly as she considered the question. "I really don't know for sure. These people know me by name, though I have never seen them before. They have the emerald green eyes of the King of Draconis."

"There is one who may be able to help you. The Lady of the Black Hallows deals in the mystic. She leads the order of the Black Robes, and if the king is sending emissaries to your world, she would know."

"Where would I find the Lady of the Black Hallows?"

Malachia lowered her head. "She resides as far south as you can travel. That is all I know."

Arietta thanked Malachia, then vanished from her sight, only to awake in her bed the next morning with Cooper's heavy head resting on her left hip. A hip that no longer ached.

***

1972

"Jerry?" Arietta approached his bed, eyebrows drawn together. Jerry opened his eyes, and even such a small action seemed difficult.

"Ari, what are you doing here?" He appeared to be upset, yet also relieved. "You really shouldn't be seeing me like this."

She sat carefully on the side of his bed, grabbing his hand. "I knew it was bad; I didn't realize it would be this bad, though." She felt sick. He was a skeleton, all the healthy fat he had melted away to expose bones. She could count his ribs through his hospital gown. His hair was gone and his face was gaunt, eyes and cheeks sunken in. He looked like the shell of a person.

"I never wanted you to see this, see me so broken." He closed his eyes, shaking his head. She brought his hand to her lips, kissing it lightly to comfort him.

"It's alright, Jerry. You are my friend, and we will fight together no matter what we are facing. I brought you flowers to brighten the room," she said quietly, hating the smell of alcohol that the hospital seemed to be bathed in.

"Thanks--"

His mother interrupted him before he could get anything else out. "I'll give you kids some alone time. I'm going down to the cafeteria; do you want anything?" Both Arietta and Jerry shook their heads.

"You look beautiful, just as beautiful as you do in Palidonaya," he said quietly. No flirtatious tone, just truth.

"Thanks, Jerry, I-"

"I don't know if I'm going to be able to make the whole journey, but I'll stick around as long as I can, got it?" He squeezed her hand, and she felt like crying.

"Don't say that. You are going to be fine, you hear me? After this is over, you'll be fine. I promise," she said weakly.

"Don't make promises we both know you can't keep." His voice was soft, and that was when she began to cry. He reached a tired arm up to her face, swiping away the tears that dappled it. Then, at that moment, the pull told them that it was time to return.

"Jerry, I have to return to my room so that I can use my coin. Is there anything that you need before I leave?" Arietta stood, wiping the tears from her cheeks.

"I just need the blinds closed so that Mom doesn't try to wake me up."

Arietta quietly and quickly closed the blinds and darted off to her room and toward Palidonaya.

Arietta lay down in her bed with her coin in hand. She couldn't stop the flood of tears as her mind kept returning to Jerry and what he had said. "I'll stick around as long as I can, got it."

He looked much worse than any other time she had seen him. Together, they would find a way to heal him, they had to. She squeezed her eyes tight and began the process that would rocket her through time and space to Palidonaya.

She was still crying when she crossed over, and while she was upset, she was relieved that Jerry was restored on the other side. He wrapped a tentative arm around her, pulling her to his chest, and she cried harder. Through her tears, she punched him, swift and hard.

"You jerk, don't say stuff like that." Her voice came out wet and nasally. Nova looked back and forth between the pair, one eyebrow quirked. Jerry turned to her and shrugged.

Jerry quipped, "Oh, cut it out, Nova. I know what you're thinking: yes, I am a jerk and deserved that."

Arkas surveyed the two, wondering what had Arietta in tears. Then, he stepped aside, and to their surprise, Gustoff stood in all of his glory.

"Ari." He tapped on her shoulder, trying to get her to turn around. "Ari," he insisted, finally getting her to look over her shoulder. She gasped, immediately detaching herself from the boy.

"Grandpa." She fought the urge to weep once more. She took careful steps and wrapped her arms gently around Gustoff. It was Gustoff's turn to begin crying, and he squeezed her tightly.

"I missed you, dear. I missed you so much." Her shoulders were shaking with quiet tears, and Gustoff pulled her away from him to see her face. "You look so... different." His voice broke.

"I missed you so much, Grandpa Gus. I wanted to save you, but we couldn't return. When we finally made it back, we were with Arkas in the Great Beyond. He took us to see Horace." She was swiftly interrupted as Gustoff inhaled sharply.

"You saw the Record Keeper? What information did you find?"

"We asked him how to kill a dragon," she replied.

"Is there... is there any hope of defeating King Lucius?" He was quiet, sorrowful even, afraid to keep the flame that was his hope burning.

"Grandpa, there is *always* hope. We have a chance, and I know that we will defeat him."

Chapter Twenty-Eight

Lucius sat at the head of the table in his chambers, which were now serving as the war room. The festival had come to an end, the crown officially placed upon his head. It was time to bring open war to all of the lands of Palidonaya.

He had called all of his generals in for this meeting, entrusting the Shadow Walkers to hold the lands that have been conquered. Each of the dragons had taken their human forms for this meeting so that they could have a seat at the table. "Let us begin," Lucius said in a quiet, yet commanding tone. "Scarlett, what is the status of Equus?"

"Yes, my Lord, I have taken and held the region of the Zeus herd. I was not able to turn any of the herd into Shadow Walkers, so I have been destroying any who cross my path. Their numbers are decimated, but the remainder have been eluding me. They use the Silent Forest as cover, though I am confident that the dwellers of the forest have been further culling their numbers. I would estimate less than a hundred remain."

Lucius stood from his chair and folded his hands behind his back, making his way to Scarlett's seat. With cold precision, he drew back his hand, striking her across the face. It left an angry welt, his claws lengthening with that cold rage before meeting her face.

"You forget that several hundred managed to escape your initial attack! This herd had the first contact with the Chosen. Should that be not enough to condemn them, they led the charge against my father's army and won. They must be destroyed." Lucius had once again let his anger get the better of him.

"It will be done, my Lord." Scarlett's eyes never strayed from the king as she calmly responded. Any other response may have ended in her death, so she chose her words carefully. "I will need a small group of hunters to speed the process up, my Lord."

"The hunters just returned from the Great Beyond, their queen slain by the Chosen. I will have to raise a new queen before they can be sent out, and I have plans for the remaining pack. Have you been able to make arrangements with the forest dwellers?"

"The dead serve no one." Scarlett's blood began to heat.

"The dead will serve the rightful King of Palidonaya!" Lucius bellowed as he slammed his fist to the table.

"I will continue my palaver with the oldest, the one with the strongest claim to the land, my Lord." Scarlett knew that there would be no negotiating for reinforcements.

Lucius strode back to his place at the head of the table. "Fynnossa, what news do you have of the Artemis region of Equus?"

"My Lord, their numbers are few. I have been removing all food sources from the region with my flame. Those that remain have fled to join the Apollo. The region known as Artemis is now fully under your control."

"Excellent! Frorsa, what is the report from Aphrodite?" Lucius could feel how close he was to controlling the entire continent. Once this was accomplished, then he could attack Fændell.

"My Lord, all living beings that once dwelt in Aphrodite have fled to the south. I am all that remains in that region."

This put a smile on Lucius's face as he moved the dragon pieces into place on the map that was etched into the great table. The lands of the Apollo were almost entirely cut off from all allies. "The time to strike Apollo is upon us! Scarlett, you will enter Apollo from the north, while Fynnossa and Frorsa will enter from the west. Deiphonei, you will attack from the east. The herds of Equus will be no more!"

"Hestia, you will continue to hold Belamoris. Armess, I am sending you north to Mirnalduhr to the dwarven capital of Derge. There you will proclaim that land in my name."

"My Lord, with all respect, the dwarves of Mirnalduhr have never joined in the fight against us. Why would we provoke them to fight us now?" Armess was not pleased with the prospect of attacking the dwarves in their tunnels deep in the mountains.

"They supplied our enemies with the tools for our destruction." He didn't care that they'd also provided Draconis weapons. "They created the Sword of Atonement as well as the Daggers of Derge, which were quite effective against our armies during the Great War. I will not make the same mistakes that my father made! I will send a pride of hunters with you to aid you in the mines of Mirnalduhr."

"The Era of the Dragon is upon us. As we speak, Shadow Walkers are among the people of Casparnia and Lenovia, slowly draining the fighting spirit of the Council. After we have secured the east and the north, then we will suffocate the remaining stronghold." With that said, the meeting was adjourned, and the room cleared of all but Serafina, Clarette, and Lucius.

"My lord, what tasks will you assign me?" Serafina asked quietly.

"Your task is the most important. You will guard the future of our kingdom. We have rained fire upon this continent with eight dragons. When the eggs hatch, we will take all of Palidonaya. Now, leave me, as I must plan the final push to Lenovia. That is the final piece to our conquest of this continent. Next we shall move on to the bigger picture: world domination."

The High Priestess and Serafina left the War Room as Lucius sat down at the table. He was very close to reaching his first goal. There was but one obstacle that remained in his path: the Chosen. He would have to deal with them before he could claim what was rightfully his to rule.

***

When the Chosen arrived at the castle, they were immediately granted access, and given the finest rooms and food. Three maids had been assigned to each of the travelers. In the dining hall, the leaders conferred.

Neoma leaned over the table, scanning the letter. Arietta's penmanship was quite beautiful, that she had to admit, and the lead mare hoped desperately that graceful lettering and kind words would sway the Queen of Ice to their side. Timara rested a gentle, glowing hand on Neoma's neck.

"Neoma." Her voice rang through the quiet room, and the mare lifted her eyes to the blazing stare of Timara. "Are you sure you should be here?" Neoma snorted, flicking her braided aqua tail.

"What are you implying, Timara?" The mare's voice was sharp, as if to warn the woman to tread lightly.

"You can leave if you'd like. We all know where the king is focusing the next attack: on your herd. You can lead your people to safety… We can manage this situation." Javaron knew what it was like to have loved ones in danger.

"I do not need your pity. It matters not if I fight here or in Equus. My sister is quite capable of leading the remaining herd to safety!"

"I mean no offense. I am well aware of the duplicity that you are feeling. Loved ones in danger on one end of the continent and responsibilities on the other. We are simply saying that it would be okay if you went to tend your herd."

"Enough of this talk! I will not shirk my duties with the Council. As I said, my sister is quite capable of getting the survivors to safety. Now, I will not continue discussing this."

"Look, Neoma knows exactly what she risks staying here," he said evenly, slowing down his words. "We need to be discussing a plan of action, not sending away valuable members of the Council!"

"Queen Timara, I'm afraid Lord Javaron is correct. I do know exactly what I am doing here. I acknowledge that many I care about could be wiped from Palidonaya within the next few weeks, but I also know that oftentimes innocent blood is the price of war. Our hope of victory resides here in Dragon's Bane, and if my staying here will further the cause, then I shall stay. A true leader puts the lives of the many over the lives of the few." The crescent moon glowed a soft blue on her forehead, and moonlight seemed to be dusted over her soft words. All in the Council exchanged grave looks before continuing to draft the letter.

***

"Princess," the noble breathed in sharply, "*Queen* Kaelin, my apologies."

Her eyes glowed darkly at this, the gaping wound that was her heart being prodded at.

"*What* do you *want*, Sir Devon? I have had enough of your incessant chatter. Start speaking with meaning or be gone." A hand clutched at her chest, and she forced herself to breathe. An image of her family burning and being slaughtered on foreign grounds flashed in her mind. The connection in their blood had forced her third eye open, made her watch the flames melt their snow-kissed skin.

"You... you forgot the Contribution. It was due a few moons ago." His voice shook, and some emotionless part of her produced a feral grin at the scent of his fear. She pulled heat from the air, eliciting a shiver from Sir Devon as he awaited her reply.

"Right. I will make the formal call for the Contribution, give the country a few days' notice."

"Very well, very well." He took a bold step toward her, and she raised a hand, producing an icicle. It danced through the air, light refracting as it hit the ice. He took a step back out of respect, and she snapped, causing the icicle to shatter. "I was curious," he stammered. "When will you begin the courting process?" She laughed harshly, the sound echoing through the crystalline chambers.

"I will do no such thing. You, and all the other power-lusting nobles, will give me my time to grieve. You will respect the fallen souls of my--the king and queen, and the two princesses before me."

These imbeciles had no idea what it was like to lose a family. Third in line, destined to elegant libraries, luxurious food and parties, and nothing more. She would've been thrown the scraps, what was left over of the power, being third born, and with that she was happy. Thrust into power, a position she had not bothered to learn with enthusiasm, and thrust into grief, she claimed the crown. An ice throne built on the bones and blood of her family, her tears, and the fire that had pierced the western skies.

"My Queen," he purred, "I mean no disrespect, but you have been sitting on the throne for a century now. It is time that we name our future king. Should you need someone to talk to, someone to advise you, know that I am always near." She narrowed her eyes at him. He was a leech, a blood-sucking leech that would suck her resources and time if she allowed him.

"I'm sure you will be." She did not hide the disdain that dripped from her voice, and he took the cruel tone as his cue to leave.

Chapter Twenty-Nine

Javaron sat in the War Chambers alone, gazing at the large map of Palidonaya that was etched into the mammoth circular table. How could the Dragon King have gained this much territory? Once Belamoris had burned, Shadow Walkers overran the coast of Casparnia. The herds of Equus were under constant attack from the Dragons, their plains ablaze. The only stronghold was located on the southern coast of Apollo. The Council would be convening shortly, and he needed some sort of plan. As he sat pensively staring at the map, the clapping of a single set of hooves echoed throughout the chamber. His eyes turned to the door as Thauleon, King of Apollo, entered the chambers.

Thauleon bowed his head as he entered.

"There is no need for formalities, Thauleon. Enter and tell me of Apollo."

"There is no Apollo. The Dragons attacked from all land borders, pushing the herd to the south. The herd was unable to take flight with the Dragons upon us. Those who escaped used the underground tunnels to reach the coast. They were forced to leave the mainland to the south. I alone was able to make the journey here to report."

"How many remain?"

"A hundred, maybe less. All of Equus now belongs to the Dragons. Lenovia is the last country left on our continent."

Thauleon's eyes burned with anguish, his ribs protruded in waves. Soot, dirt and blood soiled Thauleon's body. Javaron dropped his eyes to the table and moved a stone figure of a dragon to each of the countries of Equus. "Lenovia may not stand alone. We have sent word to Faendell and Mirnalduhr."

Thauleon let out a crazed laugh. "Hope is lost. The Dwarves will not venture out of the mountains, and while Faendell has been plotting its revenge for a century, it also has been in a self-imposed exile. Our only hope is to find a land that the Dragons cannot reach."

Javaron bowed his head. As he sat in silence, the War Chambers began to fill with Council members. He was acutely aware of how his response today would shape his legacy. Great leaders were born through great adversity, and he would not fail his people in their greatest time of need.

"Leaders of the Seven Kingdoms, we meet today to decide the fate of all who follow us. The Dragon King has taken all land east of the Silent Forest. We are the last stronghold remaining."

There were murmurs throughout the chamber as the news of defeat sank in. Whispers of doom filled the chamber as the murmurs turned to bickering. Xersa, the leader of the Aphrodite herd, was the first to address the room. "What hope do we have? The dragons are not vulnerable to any of our weapons. They kill all who oppose them."

Javaron stood, slamming his fist on the table. "Silence! We *always* have hope. We will stand and fight to the last one of us if necessary. Yes, the weapons that we have will not harm the dragons, but there is a blade that was forged that could aid us."

Brannan of Casparnia stood. "My King, that blade has been lost for a century. No one knows its whereabouts. Some say that the Blade of Atonement was destroyed as a part of the agreement that ended the Great War."

"Aye, I have heard these stories as well. They are not true. The Blade of Atonement is gone, but it was not destroyed. It was taken to the city of Derge in the Dwarven country, where it was remade to form two daggers. These Daggers of Derge are in our possession, as well as the knowledge to forge a new weapon that can be used against the dragons." Javaron summoned Arkas, Arietta, Nova, and Jerry into the room.

"Jerry, will you show the daggers that you used against the hunters?" At this request, Jerry drew the daggers from their hidden sheaths. Javaron continued, "I give you the Daggers of Derge. The last remnants of the Blade of Atonement."

Again, murmurs traveled around the room before Timara rose to speak. "How can we be certain that those are the Daggers of Derge? Furthermore, what use are they against a full-grown dragon?"

Jerry met Timara's gaze and replied, "The hunter that I faced called them by name before I killed her."

Javaron continued, "We all know that the hunters are smaller versions of wingless dragons. They were created by the dragon king to hunt any that he desires. They have the same body armor that a full-grown dragon has, therefore these daggers could be used to slay a dragon."

Jerry interjected, "I had difficulty penetrating the body armor. I had to go for eyes." He shivered at the thought of the other hunter he had not killed himself that had been swallowed by sand.

The room again erupted in murmurs. How would this help? Which one of them could ever get that close to the mouth of the beast, and would they have the same effect?

Arkas stood. "We know how to create a weapon to use against the dragons." The room fell silent. "We visited the Record Keeper. He shared the secret to the creation of the Blade of Atonement. Though the price is high, we can and will forge another weapon."

Neoma was the first to ask the question. "What price do you speak of?"

"We need a sacrifice of the purest blood in all of Palidonaya. The sacrifice of the King of Equus. The weapon must contain both the horn and the blood of the Royal Line." Arkas's eyes turned to Raulin as he made this statement. "This sacrifice must be made in the mountains of Mirnalduhr so the magic can be immediately captured during the forging of the weapon. The price is great, but it is the only way."

Javaron spoke next. "We must plan our next steps carefully. We need allies if we are to drive the dragons back to Draconis. We have sent word to Faendell, but we must follow the letter with an emissary to meet with the Queen of Ice. We must also send a party to Mirnalduhr to forge the weapon. Finally, we need information from Draconis. Rumors abound that Lucius is cultivating his offspring. Enough dragons to overrun all corners of Palidonaya. If this is true, we must find his breeding grounds and destroy the offspring before they hatch."

Javaron continued, "Gustoff has volunteered to travel to Faendell with a small party to plead with the Queen. Thauleon. Once you have had adequate nourishment and rest, will you take him to meet with the queen?"

"It would be an honor, Your Majesty." Thauleon bowed his head.

"I volunteer to go to Faendell as well," shouted Arietta. "We need to have another female along to help relate to the queen, and Grandpa Gus, I mean, Gustoff. He could also continue teaching me how to use my powers."

"I'll go too." Nova turned to face Arietta. "I go where you go." Arietta nodded solemnly, with appreciation.

"I can take three, but no more, as the journey will be across the sea with no stops. Belamoris is now enemy territory."

"Very well, Thauleon will take Gustoff, Nova, and Arietta to meet with the queen."

"I will go to Draconis to gather information." Jerry couldn't believe what was coming out of his mouth. "I can make myself invisible for periods of time. This will give us the best chance."

Javaron sighed, turned to Xersa, and inquired, "Could you accompany Jerry to Draconis?"

"I cannot take anyone with me. My powers do not hide others, just me," Jerry said, hoping that no one would catch his lie.

Javaron responded, "You will need passage to the capital in the mountains. Xersa could wait in hiding for your return."

Xersa replied, "I will take Jerry to the capital and wait there for his return."

Raulin was the last to speak. "I will need a group to accompany me to Mirnalduhr to forge the weapon. Dimitri will be one, as he is my most trusted. Who else would accompany me on this quest?"

Arkas stood. "I will, as I have the information that the dwarves will need to forge the weapon."

Javaron nodded his approval. "The rest will remain here to fortify the capital. The Shadow Walkers draw closer each day. Raulin, you must make haste, as each passing day brings the dragons closer to our doorstep."

The Council adjourned, representatives from each state filing out, making their way to begin preparations. There was no discussion as they left that War Chamber, no joyful banter that usually followed a meeting of the Council. The somber mood that had fallen over them would remain for many days to come, as all knew that sacrifices would be made and friends would be lost. The survival of the Seven Kingdoms balanced on a razor's edge, and the failure of one mission could be the tipping point that would cause the downfall of the entire realm that the Council ruled over.

"Xersa?" Jerry said, the mountain range in sight.

"Yes, Jerry?" She turned her head away from her white-feathered wings, as she'd been preening her feathers before being interrupted.

"So, how does this work? I've never ridden a flying horse."

Xersa laughed. The boy was covered with a layer of dirt and grime that had accumulated on his skin through his journeys. "The first thing that we are going to do is to get you a bath. I don't need that dirt on my coat." Her pastel-pink fur had finally been cleaned after saving Gustoff, and she was not interested in having to bathe again so soon.

While Jerry was bathing and getting a clean set of clothes, Xersa began planning their trip to the dangerous mountain region. She decided that she would alter the route that she took to bring Gustoff to Dragon's Bane so that she could avoid any unwanted attention from the patrols of the Dragon King.

Jerry returned for inspection by Xersa. She was amazed at the difference in his appearance. His skin was two shades lighter and his new clothes were not tattered, each piece relatively new. The final addition to his uniform was a long, hooded, black cloak that would hopefully keep him sheltered from the biting wind. They were ready for the trek to Draconis. He climbed onto her back, and she groaned before stretching her wings and racing forward. They spread gracefully, and she leapt to launch herself into the air. Jerry let out a loud whoop, seeing that they were airborne, but the joy did not last as they rose higher and higher into the sky.

"Ease up, kid!" Xersa yelled over the wind, the sensation of pain at his fingers gripping her hair bringing her out of focus. She banked around a tree, striving to get higher to avoid most of the trees embedded into the massive mountain. Jerry's eyes were squeezed shut, and he buried his face into her mane, wrapping his arms around her neck. "Relax! I'm not going to drop you, just try to enjoy the view," she suggested lightly, and he shook his head.

The capital city of Aridol was magnificent from the air. The stone structures reminded Jerry of the books that he had read that described Camelot. His heart was racing; he did not like heights, and they were approaching the level of the clouds. He squeezed his eyes shut and buried his face in Xersa's mane. He remained in this position for the rest of the trip that lasted through the day and into the night.

They were nearing the main city, where the castle was located, and Xersa knew she would need to get out of the air. "Look," she demanded. Although his heart was racing, veins spreading icy fear throughout his whole being, he could not be happier that he looked. From above, the city of Draconis was quite beautiful. The dim glow of fairy lights made the city emit such a pleasant feeling, it was like a home away from home. This seemed odd, considering that nowhere else on this planet had he been at peace. "We're landing," Xersa said uneasily, her legs kicking a bit as she steered around trees gliding gently to the ground. Her feet hit the soft underbrush of the forest, and Jerry cocked his head, inhaling deeply.

"Mint?" he asked softly to himself. An animal comparable to a deer leapt only a few paces away from the pair, scurrying out of sight, and birds chittered happily all around them.

"For Dragon country, this is incredibly beautiful. It still feels… it feels wrong." Her words were but a whisper, something that Jerry chose to ignore. He felt nothing wrong here; everything was right and good in these woods. "I'll tuck myself away into a thicket; you have a week before you have to check in. If you don't, then I leave to get help," she said, and Jerry absentmindedly shook his head. He inhaled once more, relishing the scent, then worked to raise all of his shields for protection. He would be entering the heart of the enemy, and there was no room for error.

Chapter Thirty

In the darkness of his campsite, Jerry shot up, panting. He had so many nightmares on this side of the universe. He still had these nightmares on Earth, but when he would wake up in his bed, he always faced a less confrontational death with no escape. He wasn't certain which was more horrific, only sure of the pounding war drum that was his heart. It skipped a beat when he saw her, but quickly he'd realized it was not the real Arietta. She was cruel, somehow even more beautiful than before.

"Gerald," she hissed in his ear, nails like claws dragging down his face. The hot sensation of his blood trickled down his skin, and he'd been horrified that he'd merely drawn closer to her. The pain was dull, fleeting even, and the ache inside his chest was far worse than any physical pain she could inflict on him. *"You disgust me." Jerry inhaled sharply at this, and she'd laughed lightly, a lover's laugh. "You always did, you know. I never saw you as my hero, never saw you as an equal. I saw you as you were back on Earth. You are dying." She swallowed, taking a breath. "I will never love you. You aren't capable of receiving love. You are selfish. You've never deserved it." He whimpered, a pathetic sound.* Jerry shivered.

He watched her burn, consumed by the flames of gentle savagery, her eyes wild with terror. Her beautiful hair at his feet in piles of ash. The hair was what smelled the worse, the smell stuck to the inside of his nose, causing his stomach to twist. He stood, watching helplessly, unable to move, speak, or act. Skin melting, screams ripping from her, yet something new arose from the ashes, something terrifying. In her place stood the king of the dragon race, and the king embraced him carefully. "*I think you are very capable of being loved. She will never love you. Don't you realize this? I will take care of you if you let me.*"

Jerry shoved the king roughly away from him, and the king cocked his head, a feline smirk on his face. He smelled like gladioli, a bright and fresh smell that reminded him of life. "I look at you, and do you know what I see?"

Jerry shook his head dumbly.

"Potential." He smiled, "I see so much potential within you. You could help me turn the tides, save this world, and preserve a dying species. We can't survive in the mountains alone, and it was unfair to condemn us there. You could be our savior, my *savior."*

Jerry's eyes turned milky, lost in the effervescent ivy of the Dragon King's. "Do visit me soon, won't you?"

Though Jerry knew it was a dream, the lasting fear had stuck with him. Sadness dominated his other feelings, a deep well of sorrow in his heart, yet he didn't know why. Dreams weren't real. He laughed, trying to brush off the feeling of deep upset and unease, before dressing himself. He needed to be more careful about his powers now that he was in this strange land. He could tell the energy depressor he'd shielded the room with the night before had weakened, and that soon his mental guard and effort to stay hidden would both determine if he left these lands alive.

At the border of Faendell, Arietta held her breath. They'd sent a letter ahead, because even peacemakers entering without permission could warrant war, and they now were waiting to see if they would be granted passage. The mountain range was far more beautiful than that of Lenovia and was far more vast. Clouds prevented Arietta from spotting the usual baby blue of the sky, and snow hugged around her knees. She wore a heavy, fur-lined cloak, yet the wind managed to bite through it to her skin. Snowflakes tickled her eyelashes, and she was curious as to how these people could stand such an overwhelming, bitter cold. She released the breath and it came out in wispy tendrils that curled in the air.

The guards chattered in a language foreign to her, yet with the spell that Gustoff cast upon her, she could understand their conversation. They seemed nervous and cold. They glanced to each other, then looked upon the travelers . Nova suppressed a shiver, melting into her wolf form, a seamless transition that would shield her from the cold.

"We will let you in, but beware, the land is old and has its secrets. Stick to the paths, respect the wind, and by the Gods, you must respect the queen." *They are polytheistic.* Arietta made a note of that, making sure she wouldn't offend them at any later time. Gustoff nodded, needing no spell upon his ears, surprisingly to her, and she was curious about the history behind that.

"Thank you. May the mountain judge you fairly," Gustoff replied. Fluent in not only interpreting, but speaking; that was another surprise. As called by tradition, the guards crashed their staffs together, then lifted their hands to the mountain.

The castle was in the heart of the country, in the highest peaks of the mountain, and was far too cold for any pegasus to fly to without risking hypothermia. With the assistance of a team of four snow oxen that were offered at a relatively low price of just four gold coins, they were up and at the palace doors within two days.

Gustoff turned to Arietta and smiled. "Are you ready, honey?"

Arietta smiled back and said, "Hey, I am one of the Chosen. I was born ready." He chuckled, glad she was okay and that the trip hadn't lain too heavily on her heart. Gustoff slipped a hand up the sleeve of his robe, withdrawing a purple elixir. This would help the aches that never seemed to leave after his descent from the Draconian range. His body always felt heavy, and while the elixir was bitter and foul tasting, he drank all of it in a smooth gulp.

"What is that, Grandpa?" Her eyes were bright and unconcerned.

She had put him on a pedestal as her hero, and he didn't want to tarnish her view of him. Even heroes felt pain, and they had nightmares too. Just two days passed on her end, but it stretched to a lifetime for him.

"It…" He didn't like lying, so he forced his mouth into a crescent moon smile and grabbed her hand. "It's nothing, honey. Just keeps me on my toes and ready to go." A half lie, just a sin of omission off of his tongue.

"What does it taste like?" She didn't prompt him further on the use, and thank everything for that.

"Genuinely terrible, so bad it curls your toes." He laughed. Her sunshine smile was blinding, and she squeezed his hand, turning her eyes to the crystalline palace that forged through the sky. The light bounced off the clear walls, and the building shimmered with anticipation for its new guests. Something about the palace told them that visitors didn't drop by often, and that they should be traveling with trepidation. One of the oxen raised his voice, directing his words more to Nova than the others.

"Wolf, the queen was once kind, but through cruelty and loss is now bitter. She is much like the coiled snake: one wrong move and she is ready to strike. I tell you, as she has a penchant for furs, and would love nothing more than to have a reason to take your coat should you say the wrong thing." Nova shook herself out, smoothly transitioning to her human form. The sting of the transition was a welcome thing, and while the words of the ox made her nervous, she figured it was better to meet the queen in her human form anyway.

"Furs? That is terrible." She wrinkled her nose, and the ox blanched at her new form.

"You're a Chosen One." He immediately averted his eyes.

"Sort of, that's what they've been telling me," she said offhandedly, feeling the suffocating crush of speaking to someone new in her lungs. A large part of her wanted to stay in the form of a wolf so she would not have to speak to anyone. She wondered if that was why she was given the power she had, if that was why she was allowed to be completely unhinged and fearless here.

"I apologize for bothering you with my warning; forgive me." He lowered his head in a humble bow. That was weird.

"Please don't apologize," she stammered. "I appreciate the warning. I like my fur in my wolf form; it would've been pretty upsetting had she decided she didn't like me and wanted to skin me." The ox, thoroughly shaken, nodded curtly and forged through the snow, back to his other three companions.

***

Raulin, Dimitri, and Arkas sat down for a small lunch before the entrance to the dwarven city of Derge beneath the great Mount Astoria. The two unicorns used their noses to brush the snow aside and nibble on the grasses surrounding the small pond that lay at the foot of the tallest known mountain in Palidonaya. Arkas took the last bite of bread and returned to the mountainside, studying the runes, looking for a way in. The writing that was etched into the stone spoke of a test that they needed to pass before entering the tunnels that led to Derge. This troubled Arkas, as he had no way of knowing whether or not they would pass this test. He sat pensively, his mind racing through possibilities. The only real option that he could see was to proceed through the gateway to face whatever lay beyond.

"Raulin, Dimitri, time is not on our side. We must enter the mountain, but we have to proceed with caution, as there is a test that we must pass before we will be allowed into the city of Derge."

As the three travelers entered the gateway to Derge, a frozen fog surrounded them. Arkas's beard instantly gathered a frosting, ice crystals sparkling in his thick hair. He found it more difficult to move as he crossed the threshold into the mountain. His mortal body froze in place, and a cool, slimy sensation wriggled in his insides. Once his spirit was pulled out of his body, he could again proceed into the mountain. He looked over his shoulder to see that the unicorns were frozen. Their spirits were quite beautiful. Raulin's red coat had a silvery frost covering his entire body. Once all three had left the physical realm, they proceeded together into a large golden chamber. A throne made of granite sat proudly, located at the far end of the chamber. They moved to the foot of the throne, where a mighty celestial being appeared suddenly, sitting upon it. A loud baritone voice echoed throughout the chamber, shaking the ground in its cadence.

"I AM THORUNDALL, FIRST KING AND PROTECTOR OF THE GREAT DWARVEN CITY OF DERGE! BEND THE KNEE, THEN REQUEST ENTRY INTO THIS CITY!"

The three travelers quickly dropped to one knee and bowed their heads out of respect for the dwarven king. Arkas was the first to look upon the fully materialized dwarf. His ebony beard flowed down to the middle of his stomach like the waves in a mighty river. His broad nose had a rather reddish hue, and his eyes were a deep brown with large pupils designed for seeing in near-darkness. Upon his head perched a golden crown filled with every type of jewel that one could imagine. His thick black hair draped over his shoulders, equaling the length of his beard. He was adorned in the dress of a king, with a crimson top, black pants, and boots that ended just below the knees.

The immense projection of the king overwhelmed the mind, but Arkas knew that in life he would have stood no taller than the middle of his chest. Thorundall had thickly muscled arms and legs, as did all members of his race.

Arkas looked at the boots of the king and spoke in a loud but humble tone. "King Thorundall, we wish to enter the city of Derge and request that your people forge a weapon that will allow us to defend our kingdom against the Dragons of Draconis."

The king glared at the travelers, unimpressed. "WHAT HAVE YOU TO OFFER THE PEOPLE OF DERGE?"

Arkas pulled a small pouch from his pack, set it on the ground in front of him, and mumbled a verse in the ancient language, waving his hands above the pouch. It began to grow until it stood as tall as Arkas and three times a wide. The king stood from his throne and approached the bag, opening the top. A smile came across the king's face when the light of the gold coins glowed on it. He needed no more gold, but his nature drew him toward it. He clapped his hands twice, and both he and the bag vanished.

The three looked at each other, wondering what had just happened. The room spun, and with a satisfying pop, they were sucked back into their physical forms, drained and disoriented. They fell to the ground, heads aching from the ordeal. Raulin was the first to speak after shaking his head to force clarity. "Do you believe that our offer of payment was accepted, or did we offend the ancient king?"

Arkas smiled. "That is no ancient king. Thorundall is the current king of the Dwarves of Derge. We will know soon enough if the offer is acceptable."

The ground shook as the giant throne began to move to the right, exposing a passageway behind it. The opening was around five feet tall by three feet wide. Arkas, Raulin, and Dimitri slowly approached the doorway, peering into the darkness to see what lay in wait beyond its opening. As they neared, a dim light flickered in the depths of the exposed tunnel. They decided to wait to see what was approaching the grand entry. Soon the light grew in strength, and they could make out several figures following a lit torch. Dwarves filed out of the tunnel with Thorundall leading the way.

Raulin looked at Arkas. "What magic did they use to make him appear so vast?"

Arkas smiled and snorted. "Dwarven magic is both ancient and powerful. To pull one's spirit from their body requires a powerful spell, but to do this with so many is an impressive feat."

The door groaned open, and at this the three were compelled to drop to their knees. Strange and powerful magic haunted these halls, and Arkas found it incredibly amusing that a spell had been cast that made all drop to their knees when the king entered.

"Rise, we are done with formalities. What weapon do you seek?" Thorundall refused to acknowledge the spell, just dismissed it verbally to prevent the spell from working again on the pair. Thorundall's voice was not as booming, but carried the same authority in its tone.

"Your people once made the Blade of Atonement that our people used during the last Dragon Wars to defeat the enemy. We wish for you to make a similar weapon." Arkas kept his tone humble as he addressed the king.

"The price for that blade was great indeed. Are you prepared to make such a sacrifice again?"

Raulin stepped forward. "I am Raulin, King of the unicorns of Equus. My blood is both pure and of the royal line. I will make the sacrifice that will save my kingdom. My son Dimitri is present to assume the throne when I am gone." Dimitri stamped his front hooves, an act he did when he was nervous.

"Very well, I have seen the payment that was offered and will take your request to the Dwarven Council."

"But I thought that you were the king. Can you not make such a decision without consulting?" Raulin looked from Thorundall to Arkas in confusion.

"Please forgive us, King Thorundall. Raulin knows not the ways of the dwarven people. We will wait here if need be until they have made a decision." Arkas again bowed to the king.

"Nonsense, you will come with us and feast while the council meets. We are not barbarians! Your comments offend me not, as we haven't been in contact with your people for a hundred years. I doubt that your grandfather was alive the last time a dwarf and a unicorn met in council. Now, come and eat. We will prepare a meal that will include several different meats and grains so that everyone can enjoy good company and food while the Council discusses your payment."

With that, the dwarves led the travelers into the opening and toward the great city of Derge. Arkas, Raulin, and Dimitri all had to duck to fit into the dwarven-sized tunnel. As they made their way deeper into the mountain, Raulin asked Arkas why Thorundall could not decide whether or not to make their weapon.

"While Thorundall is the High King, there are kings for every city in Mirnalduhr. Each king has a seat on the council, which in turn makes decisions for all dwarves. The dwarves adopted this form of government so that no dwarf wields too much power."

The group emerged from the other end of the tunnel, which allowed for the three travelers to stand upright and take in the wonder that was Derge, the capital of Mirnalduhr. The cavern opened up so that one could not see all the way to the ceiling. Buildings of stone surrounded an enormous castle. White granite was used for most of the buildings, while the castle walls were formed from gold. Torches made the city glow in the vast cavern. The streets were filled with dwarves who were in the process of performing various jobs to maintain the city. As the group approached, the dwarves in turn stopped what they were doing and bent the knee for Thorundall, resuming their duties after he passed. They were led straight to the castle of gold, where they were taken to a vast chamber with a giant table that stretched more than fifty feet in length, though it was only two feet tall. The guests of the king were shown to their places around the table as food was brought in and served to all.

Arkas's mouth began to water, and his stomach reminded him he hadn't had a decent meal since the group left Lenovia.

There were roasts of many different beasts accompanied by mounds of vegetables, most of which were roots similar to potatoes. There were also great bowls of soup provided. The dwarves wasted no time digging into the food, slurping, chewing, and belching their way through the meal. Raulin and Dimitri were brought great bowls heaped with grain, which they devoured, as they were as hungry as Arkas. Roasts, vegetables, and soups were followed by mounds of dwarven desserts made with heavy cream and custard. Raulin and Dimitri were provided with oats and alfalfa, which were the preferred desserts of the unicorns.

After the meal was finished, the three were led to a sitting room, where Arkas was offered a pipe and tobacco, which he accepted as well as a strong dwarven brandy that he sipped while smoking his pipe. The dwarves were a merry people that worked hard and played just as hard as they worked. They sang, danced, and told stories to entertain the guests. As the night wore on, the party began to thin out. Arkas, Dimitri, and Raulin were shown to their rooms to rest. Thorundall sent word that the decision would be made after everyone had a good night's sleep. Arkas and the others fell asleep as soon as they settled down into the beds that had been made for them. They slept a dreamless, deep sleep, as they hadn't had a good rest since they left Lenovia five days earlier. They would soon know if their trip was for naught or if they would have a weapon that would install fear into the hearts of the dragons. A night of peaceful rest followed, and Raulin thought he could stand to die here. He would like to see the sun one last time, to graze upon lush grasses, but for his people, he would die in the darkness of the dwarven mines.

Chapter Thirty-One

He should've known to stay out of the Priest's tavern. There was a shift in power; it thrummed deep in his chest, and Jerry looked out the window to the raging sky. It was angry, deep gray nimbus clouds, swollen, prepared to spill back onto the earth. He shivered, paying the tab he'd opened at the tavern. A figure moved in his peripheral, and the hair on Jerry's neck stood on end. This was bad. The room silenced as the figure moved closer, tucking himself into the chair across from Jerry. Jerry looked up slowly to confront the attention of the stranger.

"Gerald, how are you?" The serpentine eyes were fixed on Jerry's. A horrific realization hit Jerry: he knew the creature sitting across from him. The gaze that pinned him to his spot was the gaze of a murderer and torturer. Of a dreadful, vile king. His heart seemed to stop, the world blurring. "Don't worry, you are safe. You may drop your energy shield if you'd like. I know where you are now." Jerry obeyed this command, his power now thrumming and mixing with the air. Lucius inhaled deeply, a moan humming in his throat, and he closed his eyes. "So much power from you, so much potential." Jerry knitted his eyes together, shifting uncomfortably.

"Let us get to the business at hand." He grinned, bracing his hands together and leaned across the table. "Gerald, there are many things to consider, many things that you need from me. I can give you the world, you know?" Jerry sighed, fidgeting nervously. He tried thinking of Arietta's face, to the kind soul of her grandfather. He tried picturing Arkas, the grumpy old potion master. He tried remembering why he was here and to not be so horrendously tempted by those words. He couldn't stand himself. He wallowed in self-loathing by being so intrigued with this simple statement.

"What do I need from you?" Jerry said this thoughtlessly, surprising himself.

The king let loose a dark smirk, leaning forward. He saw an opening, and the opening spoke of opportunity. Chosen or not, people were corruptible.

"Many things. You crave power. You crave freedom, justice for the hand the world has dealt you. Am I right?"

Jerry stared at his hands, nodding slowly.

"Boy," the king sighed. "You reek of death." He propped his head up with a loose fist. "Your poor mother weeps for you at home. She cries, she prays, she pleads. She already lost your dad, and that nearly ruined her. If she loses you too, she won't survive."

Jerry inhaled sharply at this. "We both know it, do we not? She is reliant on you. I know you love her, but I see a much darker emotion concealed under that love." The King looked pointedly at him, and Jerry shrank.

"And that is?"

"Resentment, my dear boy. You resent that she cries for you daily. You know the amount of pain that you have caused her. You can't have what you want with her still in your life." Jerry's eyebrows lifted; a look similar to rage flashed in his eyes.

"That's not true! I love her," he insisted, and the king chuckled in a rich undertone.

"Of course it is. I'm not here to judge you, but to help you. I know that you love her, but she is your only tie to the world that has given you nothing but grief and pain. Without that attachment, you could stay here permanently and be strong. No more pain or weakness." Lucius took a deep breath. "I can feel your power, see your true potential. You could be a ruler here. There, you will die soon. I can make her forget you. You can still see her, check in on her, but I will give her the life she always wanted. I'll give her wealth, give her a husband that has the strength to protect her, give her a boy that isn't dying. On top of that, I can give you strength beyond your wildest dreams, and cure your ailing body. No ties, no death looming over your head; all your wildest dreams will come true. All you have to do is--"

Jerry interrupted, "Sell my soul, I suppose. Betray my friends, help you murder innocents, a small price really." The sarcasm lashed at the king, and he slowly shook his head.

"No, I would never ask you such a thing. Instead I will present you with an offer. A clear conscience and a life of luxury. As I said before, you could rule over one of my new provinces. I could give you immortality and everlasting peace. I'm asking you for so little, in exchange for the world." Jerry held his breath, studying the features of the snake.

"I..."

Jerry awoke covered in a sheen of sweat. The dreams were becoming more vivid each day that he spent in Draconis. Was he on the verge of accepting the Dragon King's offer? He violently rubbed his eyes. Of course not! It was just a dream. He knew that time was running out. He needed to gather the information that he was sent to find before he was discovered.

***

Lucius sat up in his bed. A smile snaked across his face. Entering the boy's mind was becoming easier each night. This kid, Gerald, was here in Draconis, searching for something. Lucius couldn't read what he was seeking. Though the risk was great, he had decided not to alert his guards of the boy's presence. The power that he could feel emanating from the boy could be of great use. He must tread carefully with Jerry.

***

Raulin awoke startled by the clash of swords and axes, the roar of a mighty beast. He snorted, eyes widening, realizing he was alone in the room. Where was everyone? What was happening?

"Raulin!" Dimitri's voice boomed outside the room. "Raulin! The dragons are here! We need to leave!" Raulin gripped his battle armor in the quarter of the room with his teeth, slinging it haphazardly over his back.

"We shall not abandon these people in their time of need! We will fight!"

"Father, your life is far too precious to risk! We need your essence, your blood, for the blade! We cannot aid them now!"

"Check your priorities, boy. They can soak up my blood from the battlefield if need be; we must fight with the dwarves. They would never join us if we allowed them to be slaughtered." He exited his room to join his distressed son, looking regal as ever. He nearly glowed in the dark hall, eyes burning. It sounded like a hell symphony, the screaming and clashing and roars melting together to create a song of the damned. If the stallion had to pull on his inner demons to end the cacophony of noise, then that he would do. Contrary to popular belief, he could dance with the darkness.

***

Armess stood at the foot of the great mountain with three of the hunters at her side. After a brief assessment of her surroundings, she concluded that the entrance was too small for her dragon form to enter, so as she made her way to the door, she morphed into her human form. Her auburn hair billowed in the cold mountain breeze; her slender body was midnight black with an emerald green cape flowing from her shoulders. As she entered the gate to the mountain, a frozen fog surrounded her as she felt the pull of the dwarven spell on her spirit. Her eternal self exited her body, producing an inky black cloud that filled the room, taking the shape of her dragon form.

"I AM THORUNDALL, FIRST KING AND PROTECTOR OF THE GREAT DWARVEN CITY OF DERGE! BEND THE KNEE, THEN REQUEST THY ENTRY INTO THIS CITY!"

"I bend the knee to Lucius, the true king. I will not bow to a pretender!" Armess's raspy voice echoed in the chamber as the dwarven king appeared atop the throne.

"THEN BEGONE, VILE CREATURE! YOU ARE NOT WELCOME UNDER THE MOUNTAIN!"

Armess focused her energy on her physical self. Dwarven magic was strong, but it was no match for dark magic that she possessed. The dark cloud that was her eternal being began to swirl and slowly move towards her frozen body. It took all of her focus to maintain control of her spirit as she battled the dwarven magic. As the inky blackness began to enter her body, there was a blinding white burst of light in the chamber as Thorundall winked out of the room. Following the flash of light, Armess's spirit slammed into her body. She quickly called for the hunters as she rose to her feet. The room was not large enough for her to take her dragon form, which was unfortunate. She would have to have the hunters do most of the early work. The three hunters moved to her side as she pointed to the granite throne, the only break in the smooth structure of the room. Armess's tongue flicked through the air, sensing the warmer section behind the throne. She closed her serpent eyes and sent a thought to the hunters. "The throne holds the key to entering the mountain. Destroy it!"

Thorundall immediately ordered his army to the entrance. Hundreds of dwarves adorned in body armor, carrying their battle axes in hand, sprinted to the entrance. He then quickly made his way towards the chambers that had been reserved for their other guests.

The hunters made quick work of the throne that blocked the entrance. The three of them together had been able to rip it from the structure that allowed for it to be moved from the opening. They were able to fit single-file through the opening as they made their way to the city of Derge. Armess followed them, hoping that the opening at the other end would allow for her to take her dragon form.

The first of the hunters exited the tunnel before the dwarves could move into position. Godrin, general of the army, ordered for the entrance to be blocked as the dwarves surrounded the hunter. A loud crash echoed through the city of Derge as the dwarf miners pulled the keystones and collapsed the opening to their city. The second hunter bellowed in pain, entombed in the falling stone.

The remaining hunter roared in rage, her eyes glowing a dark emerald green as the army moved in on her. She opened her maw, and a brilliant green flame erupted. Armor and axes clanged to the ground as the first wave was turned to ash. The dwarves behind them who were unlucky enough to feel the secondary heat screamed in pain as their armor was melted and fused to their bodies. Godrin roared in anguish as he watched his brothers being incinerated, their bodies turning to ash before his eyes. He ordered the throwers into action as the beast began to recharge its fire. The hunter made quick work of those closest that had survived the flame, slashing with its claws and whipping its tail.

The throwers had loaded their trebuchets, and boulders were being hurled at the beast. The hunter charged the line of defense, rubble piling up at the entrance. As the dwarves reloaded, they made adjustments to their aim. The beast was simply too quick for this tactic to be effective. Godrin ordered his next line of soldiers into the fray.

The beast's eyes glowed that deep emerald green again as Arkas' voice boomed throughout the city, magnified tenfold by magic. "MOVE AWAY FROM THE BEAST!" he bellowed. He then focused all of his energy to the newly loaded trebuchets. "LET LOOSE THE STONE!"

The dwarves launched a second round of stones. Once they were in the air, Arkas altered their path so that the aim was true. The beast was crushed under the weight of twenty large rocks, and she panicked. Releasing another terrible burst of flame, the rock melted together, and she trapped herself inside the tomb that would bring her demise. The army cheered in victory, as Arkas' voice boomed once again, "The beast is not yet vanquished! Only a dragon blade can do such a deed."

Godrin hastily ordered his troops to regroup and surround the beast that was entombed in the stone. Dreadful scratching noises sang through the caverns as the other hunters continued to claw their way towards the city.

Thorundall joined Arkas and said, "We must begin forging the weapon immediately. The dwarven army will continue piling rocks to block the entrance, but eventually, they will enter our city. We must be ready. The Dragon King will rue the day that he awakened the sleeping giant under the mountain!"

***

Arietta bowed before the Queen of Ice, and the woman of great power looked upon her. Her eyes snapped to Gustoff and to the rest of their party, before landing back on Arietta.

"Girl, rise. I tire of speaking to old men who think that they are wise. The young will rule this world, so that is why I must hear from you."

Arietta rose quickly, looking the woman in her icy blue eyes. Her face was ivory, hair frosted a snowy white, as were her eyelashes, and the eyes that Arietta fell into were blizzards of their own right.

"My name is Arietta."

"Confident," the queen noted, and smiled. "I admire confidence. Go on, tell me why you visit me."

"I visit you, my Queen, because we need your help. I was summoned here to protect Palidonaya, yet the Dragonkind's force is too strong. I watched them light Belamoris on fire, watched them slaughter *children*. I am frightened of what will happen, but likewise I will not back down. I ask you to join us. I ask Faendell to join our fight, and to put an end to their reign of terror." Arietta felt as though she held the heart of a lion in those moments, and she held her breath under the cold eyes of her queen.

"My family was slaughtered by their kind. I was the third in line." The cold queen's face twisted into an icy half-grimace, half-smile. Arietta's eyes widened, and she gulped, forcing her face back into a neutral expression. Nova, now in human form since they were within the castle's crystalline walls, shuddered. "I was never supposed to rule, and yet the dragons made my reign a reality." Arietta was horrified by those words, and the queen tittered sharply. "Girl, by the look in your eyes, I can tell you misinterpret me. I never wanted to rule. Either of my sisters would have been twice the ruler I was, until now, of course. My soft heart has now hardened like the ice-covered mountains we reside in. I resent the dragon that brings terror. My eyes still see the hellfire raining down upon those I held close to me."

Arietta gulped, her eyes stinging. "Join us, then. Prevent this from ever happening again, ensure the lasting line of your blood is unfamiliar with the terror of the dragon. Fight with us."

The ghost of a smile graced the Queen's feral face. "I will join you under one condition." She quirked a silvery eyebrow, and Arietta waited with bated breath.

***

The room was filled with a musty, thick smell, and Lucius, in his dragon form, was bathed in sweat. The light knock at the door made him hiss, but still he invited the individual in. Clarette, donning all her robes, entered and shut the door quietly. She padded over to his side, supplying a cool wet rag from within her robes, gently dabbing his forehead.

"How do you feel, my king?" He groaned, opening his eyes, the pupil slits adjusting as they focused on her.

"Do not *dote* on me, priestess. This task will bring a glorious reign of fire to all of Palidonaya." He had a fever, and as long as he could stay conscious through it, the eggs should survive. The eggs had to survive.

"I'm not doting, I'm checking in on our future." She nodded at the large sack at his back. The membrane was heavy against his skin, and he groaned.

"Five new dragons could be the difference between world domination and defeat. The pain that I feel at this moment is inconsequential. I just need to stay awake." He paused for a moment, stretching his scaled neck.

"Are you in pain?" she asked quietly, and he closed his eyes with a sigh.

"Yes. All the great dragon kings have endured this same pain. My ancestors smile down on me, knowing that I continue my line. Yes, I am in pain, but it is with great honor that I endure it."

"What will they look like? I've never seen dragons hatch before," she said quietly, and she could've sworn she saw a faint smile on the king's reptilian face.

"They will be beautiful. After the eggs are freed, it will be another few months before they hatch. The egg color tends to be the color of their scales. The young dragon is neither in their humanoid or dragon form. They are somewhere in the middle. Their shape is that of a human infant, yet their arms and legs are decorated with scales, tiny limp wings on their backs. Until they are able to shift, you will be looking after them." Clarette, a woman of schemes, without a single maternal bone in her body, shivered.

"I'm... I'm not sure that is a good idea, my king. I am not a woman of children, I--"

He cut her off with a hiss.

"Priestess, raising a Draconis child is the highest of honors. You will do it, and you will do it with care. You wanted to serve, and so you shall serve our kingdom. I do not trust the other priestesses like I trust you, and you will look after the infants until they are able to transition to a member of the Draconis race. It is my command for you to do this," he said quietly, yet sternly, and she dipped her head.

"If that is your wish, then I shall do it without complaint, my king." He muttered his appreciation, dismissing her from the room. When this was all said and done, the world would be brought to its knees, but for now, he would have to suffer through the night.

Chapter Thirty-Two

Jerry had been in Draconis for six days before he found that for which he came. There was an opening in the mountain below the great castle that housed the king. A massive stone carving of a dragon etched into the side of the face of the rocks encircled the chalice-like gateway that led deep into the hea. He stayed out of the line of sight of the guardians of the tomb-like structure. From the wooded area beyond the heart of Draconis, he had seen Lucius enter yesterday and he still remained inside. There were two priests stationed outside the entrance. They did not seem formidable, but if they raised an alarm... well this *was* the land of the dragons. He decided that tonight, he would venture into the tunnel to see why of all the areas in Draconis, this was the only one that required guards.

Just before nightfall, Jerry watched the king exit the chamber, and in a flash, he had transformed from his humanoid form into the giant black dragon that they had faced in Belamoris. The Dragon King then soared into the air, the breeze created from his mighty wings sending Jerry's hood back, his hair billowing in the wind.

Jerry liked the fact that his hair now trailed past his shoulders. Back on Earth, Jerry's head was shiny and completely hairless from the continual barrage of chemotherapy that was required to keep his cancer at bay. In this land, he was a great thief and a mighty warrior. Back at home, he could barely take care of himself. Jerry knew that if it wasn't for his mother, he would never return home.

He needed to stop focusing on the negative and finish the task at hand. He had been all over Draconis and had found nothing that would help the Council. It really didn't make sense that Lucius had taken as much territory as he had. Jerry had counted six dragons, including Lucius, and there was no way that they could hold the lands that they had conquered with so few. This place had an ominous feel about it. If there were any secrets that Lucius held, they had to be here. No one came or went from this area, save the guards that changed four times each day.

He had to time this right. The two replacements headed towards the entrance. Jerry took in a deep breath and, with a laser-like focus, his body disappeared from the visible spectrum. He silently tucked in behind the two as they made their way up the trail to the entrance in the mountain. The guards were an odd lot. They looked more like monks than soldiers. They wore full length black robes with hoods covering their bald heads. The sleeves wrapped around their hands, which were clasped in front of their stomachs. They moved with a subtle grace, walking with perfect posture, heads bowed in silence. The changing of the guard was done without any acknowledgement shared between the pairs. Two simply made their way up, while the others made their way down. They passed each other a few feet in front of the entrance as Jerry darted around them and into the opening. He didn't dare breathe as he passed the quartet, using the newfound agility that he acquired each time he ventured to Palidonaya. He stayed out of the visible spectrum until he was deep within the cave.

A velvety darkness encapsulated him as he made his way along the passage. Far ahead, a pinpoint of light interrupted the inky blackness. A dry heat seared his cheeks as it blew down the tunnel from the opening ahead. His heart was pounding as he drew nearer to the light at the end of the tunnel. As he approached the aperture, the blistering breeze swept his brown locks from his shoulders. He stepped towards the entrance, eyes watering from the brimstone in the searing breeze. The enormous chamber beyond the tunnel was lit by the magma that flowed in rivers below.

Jerry stood at the entrance, viewing an obsidian path that led from his position to a large platform that was created over the molten rock. The heat in the chamber was almost unbearable, but he continued down the path, leaving the visible spectrum once again. As he carefully made his way to the large platform at the center of the chamber, the seventh dragon of Draconis sat patiently, looking fierce and intimidating. It was positioned at the end of the path standing between Jerry and whatever it was guarding.

Jerry froze in place as the mighty dragon took in a deep breath. He refocused to remove his scent from the room, praying that he wasn't too late. If the dragon sensed him, he would die. There was no hope of him reaching the tunnel and making his way to safety. He reached the place where the path ended and the platform began. The great beast lay several feet in front of him, yet he could not see beyond. He slowly inched along the edge of the platform, careful to not disturb the dragon. It took all of his focus to remain hidden from it. As he circled past the beast's tail, his breath caught in his throat. Jerry had to report back to the council everything that he had seen. There was no hope for Palidonaya, as beyond the dragon lay hundreds of eggs waiting to hatch. The day of the dragon was almost at hand.

Jerry thought back to his dream, and while it felt wrong, he could not see a future in which the dragon race would not reign supreme. He knew he had little time, knew that once the last states and countries in Palidonaya were taken over, he would not be able to accept all that Lucius had to offer. He could have the world, but was it worth selling his soul for? He shivered, despite the heat that hung in the air.

***

Javaron paced, raking a hand through his red hair, and directing soldiers around his court. He sighed heavily, looking out to his great city. Each night the gates were surrounded by what were once citizens of Aridol, but now served a dark master. The night was lit by the glow from their unnatural emerald green eyes. Each night, more appeared, if he didn't act soon, there would be no hope of victory. Yet they could not penetrate the shield that the wizards of Dragon's Bane had created to protect what was left of his people. There was a hum in the air, an energy that suffocated his citizens. He knew, as did they, that many would fall in the upcoming battle. Soldiers manned the large crossbows and lined the walls of the castle. Many more were assigned to evacuating the women and children to the underground tunnels and to safety. It would be unpleasant, but as long as they stayed undiscovered, it would be far better than burning to death.

Timara placed a comforting hand on his shoulder, and he turned anxious eyes upon her. "It will work out. The people of Lenovia always recover, and they are a people that are designed to survive." His brows furrowed, taken aback by the kindness in her eyes, and frowned.

"I am worried that our spirit will not be enough," he declared quietly, voice barely above a whisper. "One dragon can decimate a city in an hour, there are whispers on the wind that six are on the way, in addition to the army of Shadow Walkers, which can infect our own soldiers." One of Timara's hands went to her curly ebony hair, trying to think of what to say.

"Then we shall fight to the end." He searched her eyes, nodding solemnly. Not for pride, not for glory, but for his people would he die.

***

The powerful wings of the dragons cut through the air, and the city was in their sight. Lucius was leading, with the others following, creating an enormous arrow-shaped fleet that would soon rain death upon his enemies. This day would be a glorious one that will be recorded in the histories of dragon-kind. He would paint the capital in blood and smoke and flame. Lucius felt exhilarated. On this day, where his father had agreed to be placed in chains, he would finally have his revenge. This was the first great step in world domination. He would slaughter and enslave these people, and they would begin to pay for their crimes.

The dragons circled the great walls of Dragon's Bane silently from above, the night hiding their arrival. They would rest tonight in order to be fresh for the coming battle. They followed their king beyond the city to the valley below to feast and rest. The next evening would end the reign of man and begin the reign of fire.

Concentrating, he sent out a thought to the others, ensuring them that after the next sunset, they would have their revenge for the last century of cowering in the mountains of Draconis.

"The descendant of King Antonin is mine." And within the walls of the great palace, Javaron shivered, sensing the arrival of the true enemy. He knew that the coming battle would more than likely be his last.

"A man can only die once." He said this thought aloud, and it brought comfort to him. He would not die a coward.

***

The armada cut silently through the waters as the sun crested the horizon, creating a beautiful sea of pink over the lands of Casparnia. Arietta and Gustoff were standing side by side on the bow of the lead ship next to the queen, and Nova, still in wolf form, was bathed in the morning sunlight.

Arietta squinted as the sun continued to brighten the morning sky. "This may be the most beautiful sunrise that I have ever seen." She could just make out the tops of the buildings of Waterhaven. Though it had only been a few months since she had visited that city with Jerry and Grandpa Gus, it seemed that an eternity had passed. So much had changed.

Gustoff sighed as he noticed that there was not much activity in the city for even this early in the morning. "I fear that we are too late."

The queen turned to the two, and in a regal voice she said, "We made this journey in record time, Gustoff. Your spell has kept the wind in our sails the entire journey. We will avenge all that have fallen to the abomination that you call the Dragon King. Lucius will kneel the day that fire meets ice."

As they drew near the shores of Casparnia in the town of Waterhaven, they grew quiet, bearing witness to the decimation that was left by the Shadow Walkers. The buildings were beginning to show the effects of ill repair. The streets were littered with trash. There were no people in sight.

As the queen's army filtered into the city from the ships, one thing became painfully clear. They would not be replenishing any of their supplies in Waterhaven. They spent the better part of the day unloading their vessels. Two hundred ships in all were docked along the shores of the city. The queen's army was twenty thousand strong, with more ships scheduled to leave Faendell as soon as they were stocked with supplies.

"Tonight, we will camp here. Tomorrow, we make our way to the capital city to join the others and plan for war!" Her eyes shone bright with vengeance as she entered the royal tent to begin the plans for tomorrow's trek. The bustle of soldiers setting up camp and organizing supplies continued late into the evening.

As Arietta and Gustoff finally were able to sit down to rest, Ari looked into the deep blue eyes of her grandfather and said, "What if Lucius is waiting for us at Aridol? If Arkas and Raulin are not able to make a weapon, what will we do?" She wrung her hands, and Nova rose, pushing her massive head under Arietta's arm.

"Fear not, Ari. Arkas will not fail," Gustoff said. "These are dark times, but remember that the night is darkest just before dawn. The Chosen will unite, and I know we will win." He did his best to sound sure of himself, but if he was being totally honest, he was afraid of what the near future would bring. "Let's try to get some rest, the next few days will be long."

Arietta looked to the ground and began, "Grandpa, there is something that I haven't…"

Gustoff frowned. "Honey, what is it?"

"You know how everyone keeps calling us the Chosen?" Gustoff nodded.

"What if we fail? The prophecy never had a resolution, it just spoke of people of great power fighting a great evil. Everyone who has known of our gifts has these expectations but I just… I'm not sure I can meet them. I'm not a hero, I'm just a girl swept up in a dream." Arietta could not look her grandfather in the eye.

"People aren't heroes because someone chooses them. They are heroes because of the choices they make. You could have stayed in the hospital, but you came back." Gustoff smiled at Arietta.

"I came back because you needed my help." Her eyes met the shimmering water, and the violent memory of the smell of charred flesh and smoke clogged her mind.

"Yeah, but you stayed, and you chose to go to Faendell."

Arietta nodded and gave Gustoff a hug, burying her face deep in his robes.

*****

Javaron, the King of Lenovia, stood in silence on the top of the highest tower of Dragon's Bane, looking out over the city of Aridol that surrounded his keep as the sun eased its way beyond the western horizon. With the absence of sunlight came a darkness crawling with death. The last remnants of the sun disappeared from view, casting a beautiful blood-red horizon that would signal the beginning of the great battle of Dragon's Bane. The protector of the Realm took one last look at his city, noticing the movement as soon as the sun had passed the horizon, bringing darkness to the land.

He turned to Alexandra, his trusted general. "What do you think that they have been waiting for?" Though the question was rhetorical, he would soon get his answer. Alexandra shook her head, and the two turned, heading for the war room to make final preparations for the defense of the castle.

The silence of the night was interrupted by a roar that seemed to shake the walls of stone that helped to fortify the castle. The ebony sky was lit up with a violent burst of the red and orange hues of flames, a signal to attack from Lucius and his fleet of dragons. The Shadow Walkers that had been passively gathering at the base of the castle over the last several days began throwing themselves at the shield created by the King's greatest wizards. Sparks of white burst as evidence of their force, like sparklers in the night.

The Walkers fled from the expansive area that surrounded the front gate of the castle. Javaron turned to Alexandra. "The army is yours to command!"

She shouted to the men manning the outer walls, "Archers, nock! Crossbows ready!"

Instantly the first line of archers manning the walls placed arrows at the ready, picking their targets from the sea of enemy soldiers, many of whom were friends and family of the king's soldiers. Six dragons hovered above the gap created by the departing Walkers and at once let loose flame so bright that it would blind anyone who didn't avert their gaze. Fire spread over the energy field, lighting up its surface. The flame roared for what seemed like an eternity, though it was only a minute or two. After a moment of rest, the dragon fire returned to the shield.

Javaron tore down the stairs to the lower levels of Dragon's Bane, sweat running freely from his brow. He found Brannan, the high liege of Casparnia, helping the last of the women and children into the tunnels.

Brannan turned to face the intruder that was running towards him in the dimly lit stairway, sword drawn and ready. Javaron turned the corner, seeing the business end of a sword waiting for him at the entrance to the tunnels.

"Brother, our time has run out. The enemy has begun the attack." Javaron was out of breath as he delivered this news.

"Javaron, you must leave with the others to protect the Realm," Brannan pleaded with the king.

"That was not what was discussed. You will take those who were not selected to stay. You will flee Aridol through the tunnels and be the leader that Palidonaya needs. We have no weapon to use against them. I am the king, and I will stay with my soldiers and fight." Javaron clutched Brannon's right elbow and pulled him into a hug.

"I am not the leader that you are. Let me stay and fight." Tears streamed down Brannon's face as he made one last attempt.

"There is greatness in you; people will follow you. I have chosen my path. I am still the King of Lenovia, and I have chosen you as my heir. This is my final command to you." Javaron then turned and began climbing the stairs to the main floor of the castle, passing the remaining soldiers, who were handpicked to protect those leaving through the tunnels.

The energy field finally gave, the blast from the flames searing the castle walls, the gate smoldering from the heat. The Walkers charged forward and began scaling the simmering wall, hungry for flesh.

Alexandra's voice boomed, "Loose!" and hundreds of arrows found their mark, slowing the pace of the Shadow Walkers, but not stopping their approach. The soldiers manning the crossbows began firing at will, aiming for the dragons that circled the castle. The few bolts that found their mark bounced harmlessly off the dragon scales and fell to the ground.

"Ready infantry!" Alexandra drew her sword, as did the soldiers stationed on the tops of the walls. "Go for the head and take no prisoners!" She turned to scan the horizon as Javaron approached and drew his sword.

Walkers cascaded over the tops of the walls, falling on the archers. They would not be adding to their army, for Lucius had commanded that all in Dragon's Bane would die tonight. They had been ordered to fast for the past three nights; their bodies screamed for flesh, and the air was ripe with the smell of fear.

Javaron bellowed "For Aridol!" and charged, swinging his sword with reckless abandon. The Walkers, who were devouring what was left of the army, circled away from him, and he hacked desperately through the necks of what were once his people. He was heartbroken, and wasn't sure when he had started to cry. Tears streamed from his eyes and disappeared into the forest that was his beard, giving him a crazed look as he continued his advance. There was no honor in this. From above, a roar split the night sky. The dragon flame cleansed the wall of soldiers that were manning the crossbows. The Walkers continued to gorge themselves on his army despite the many that fell to the sword.

Javaron looked onward, catching Alexandra's wild eyes. The razor-sharp teeth of the Walkers flashed brighter than the sun, ripping, tearing, chewing and swallowing as they devoured her hands. Each of those long pretty fingers were bitten off as easily as one would bite into a carrot. He was sick then, vomiting off the balcony. A strong wind danced through his hair, and he turned on his heels to face it. His stomach twisted painfully again, watching the ebony beast land. Its wingspan was massive, its eyes holding death in them. It shifted, turning humanoid, but that terror associated with the massive beast only seemed to intensify, those fearsome deadly eyes still that same awful green hue. In his heart, Javaron knew he would die today.

Lucius approached the descendant of Antonin with a sneer on his face. Javaron shaking drew his sword and charged at the king, swinging to take off his head. Lucius calmly caught the sword in his hand, crushing the blade in his grip. The evil sneer etched into Lucius's face slowly spread to a smile when he glanced down at the broken sword. The moonlight bounced off the shattered sword, and Javaron dropped to his knees. He refused to look at the vile creature that loomed over him, his shaggy hair obscuring his face.

"I guess you've won." His voice was broken.

"I have waited a century for this day of retribution," he said this quietly, the victory not as sweet with the man's spirit already shattered, much like that useless sword that had likely never seen a day of battle. He drew back his arm and swung, clawing Javaron's head from his body, sending it rolling along the battleground. He then dropped the lifeless form that had once ruled Lenovia and strode over to claim the prize. He smiled as his Walkers finished off the rest of the army that had tried to protect the castle. The night was long and gruesome, and the Walkers did exactly as they were asked. Not a single soul that had remained behind escaped that night. Many Walkers lay on the cobblestone roads, stomachs too swollen to move.

Lucius made his mark on the castle, collecting Javaron's remains to hang on display for all to see. "Some king you were," he spat, holding the head by its hair. He chuckled, humor gone from his voice. "Look at you now." He felt a beast similar to pity twist in his heart, looking into those milky eyes and watching the lolling tongue. This man was supposed to be great, the leader above all leaders. Lucius knew now that his will was the greatest, that no man was better or more fearsome than he. He would not be confined to the mountains, and *this* was the taste of freedom! This is what it meant to truly *live,* cutting down those who had wronged you. He studied the face before throwing it to one of his subordinates. Hestia caught the head with an oof, and it thudded against her chest. She laughed, joy and pride dancing in her eyes, but once she caught his gaze, she knew he was not yet ready to celebrate. "As I ate the heart of the fox, so too shall I eat the heart of the man who shared murderous blood." Though Javaron did not commit the crimes of his father before him, Lucius made certain that those crimes were paid for in full. The priests who had fought with them, the Walkers, the hunters, and the dragons all cried in celebration as he drug the headless, seeping body by the arm. He hauled it up the great staircase of Dragon's Bane to look upon his people. "People of Draconis!" he roared, voice boosted by the acoustics of the castle. All activity stilled, and they turned to him. "My people, today is the day we celebrate!" A cry from the crowd boomed, and he continued on. "Together, we have taken down this continent's *greatest country*. We took down its oppressive rule! Now, we feast and we wine, and most of all we *celebrate* the Dragon Kind!"

Chanting was in his ears and a song was in his heart as he planted his clawed hand deep into the chest of the headless corpse, an explosive splash of blood hitting his cheek as he ripped out its heart. Stringy blood and flesh clung to his hand, and he held that tiny heart in a clenched fist and examined it a moment. He buried his teeth into the raw meat, tearing, and the crowd erupted into cheers. He grinned with his chin dripping with blood, teeth stained red, and bloodlust flashing brightly in his eyes. His breath quivered with ecstasy. That was this wonderful feeling.

***

Thorundall walked with a purpose as he led Arkas and the others through the tunnels to the great forge. He walked quickly, for time was precious. He knew that his army would keep the dragon and its hunters at bay to the last man if necessary, but that may not offer them the time that they needed to complete the ritual and forge the blade. The dwarven priestesses would be in place by now, with the forge lit and the iron melting. The crystal was being hollowed out with the final preparations in place.

The chamber was lit by fire, the intense heat battering their faces as they entered. The ceiling was low at the outer wall, causing all but the dwarves to stoop as they entered, though the ceiling sloped upward toward the center of the room where the hot air was vented and oxygen allowed to help fuel the fire. The room was dark, with an orange glow emanating from the molten iron that would soon become the weapon that was so desperately needed. Seven dwarven priestesses were evenly spaced around the smelting pot. A heavily muscled dwarf worked the forge that seared the metal to its liquid form. He had a protective leather apron covering most of his chest, with thick gloves and a mask that protected his face from the intense heat. There was a steady deep hum in a language that none entering could speak.

Arkas took in the room as he crossed the threshold to the chamber. A language that had not graced a human's ears in over a century echoed throughout the room. He was almost overcome with emotion as the last of his group entered, with Dimitri followed by Raulin, who walked with his head held high. He pranced, every connection of his hoof to the ground filled with pride, along the circumference of the room, knowing that these were the last living beings that he would see with his physical eyes. Though he was afraid of what lay ahead, he trusted that his sacrifice would lift his people out of the dark shadow that Lucius had cast over the lands of Palidonaya.

An ancient dwarf with a flowing white beard hobbled into the chamber with what appeared to be a crystal made into the pommel of a sword, a needle-thin point protruding from the handle. He made his way to a stone table, laying the pommel into a groove cut in the center of the stone. The groove fit the crystal perfectly, and at the top of the stone table was a basin.

Raulin made his way to the head of the table and, in the powerful voice of a king, said, "What I do now, I do of my own free will. Let a weapon be forged that will lead our people to victory so that my sacrifice will live on in the hearts of all the peoples of Palidonaya." There was no fear in his heart, no hesitation, only determination filling his being. He had expected a great many more years to rule; however, knowing he died a servant to his people gave him purpose.

One of the priestesses approached Raulin and began chanting, the volume increasing as her speech progressed. Raulin lowered his head as the priestess removed his mighty horn with one flick of the wrist. Deep in his throat, Raulin grunted, closing his eyes and tipping his head. He slouched into the white-hot table, unable to stand on his own. The horn was placed in the melting pot, adding its magic to the steel that would become the blade that would be known to all as Raulin's Oath. With his horn removed, the blood flowed freely from Raulin, gathering in the basin. Dimitri snorted, wanting to look away as his father's blood was spilled, but he knew, to honor his father, he must watch. He owed his father, more importantly his king, the respect of watching the ceremony to the end. The chanting grew in volume and Raulin's sacred blood illuminated the basin. Slowly, the crimson liquid followed the channel cut into the stone, filling the hollow crystal.

Arkas stood mesmerized by the scene. He was sad to lose a friend, but simultaneously, the cold fascination of a magician's curiosity numbed his pain. The chant reminded him of a nursery song, something sweetly familiar in the priestesses' cries. Their voices blended to a crescendo, and two more muscled dwarves lifted the melting pot. The great stone vat was held over the table, and all in the room fell to their knees, prayers echoing in the chamber. The liquid was carefully poured into the groove surrounding the blood-filled crystal. The seven stood swaying from side to side in unison. Energy, bright and powerful, stirred in the room, and the last of the metal was emptied onto the table. The two returned the melting pot to its original position, then moved to the outer edge of the chamber. In a bright flash, the chamber was filled with white light. Raulin's lifeless body slipped from the table, and with a loud crack, the table split in two The sword remained, suspended above the table. Thorundall strode to it and grasped the sword in his right hand, lifting it high above his head. "I give you Raulin's Oath!"

He turned to Arkas and handed him the weapon. Raulin's Oath was surprisingly light, though Arkas could detect great power within the blade. "With this momentous sacrifice comes a gift that in life Raulin could not give to his people. The gift of hope."

Epilogue

Present Day

The grasses at the cemetery swayed in the gentle breeze. The old oak trees planted in the resting ground wove their roots around the gravestones, many of which were too old to decipher the names that had been etched on them so many years ago. Some had toppled over and moved away from the graves to which they were assigned.

The white lilies that Arietta clutched quivered in the wind, and though her heart was heavy, a smile shone on her face. It was his birthday, and she always brought him flowers to remind him that she loved him and that she hadn't forgotten him. Two rows down, three stones across, lay her grandfather in his eternal slumber. She knew he wasn't really there, that his soul had moved on, but this was his last tie to earth. Hallowed ground.

"Hi, Grandpa," she said softly, laying her flowers at the head of his spot. She lowered herself to her knees, resting her head against the gravestones. "They're back, but I'm big now. I'm stronger and smarter than I was before. Still just as terrified, but we can only ask for so much improvement, right?" She laughed, shaking her head. "I never stopped missing you. It never stopped hurting." She closed her eyes, letting the sun warm her cheeks and make her feel sleepy. "I'm all alone. I hope that when it is my time, I'll find you again." Tears pricked at the corners of her eyes, and her lungs weighed with grief. The gravestone was warm and coarse under the sun, but it wasn't comforting. Her phone chirped at her, and she was pleased to see one of her sons had called her.

"Hey, Mom," the boy--man now--said tenderly.

"Hi, baby." She tried to sound like she wasn't crying. A heavy sigh sounded from the other end of the line.

"I just wanted to check in on you and ask you something." What did he want? She should've known he didn't simply call to talk to her. He never just called.

"What is it, honey?"

"There have been some... suspect... gentlemen poking around down here, asking about you. Are you okay?"

That turned her blood to ice.

"Whatever you do, don't let them near you or your family. They are bad business, and I don't know what they want from me. I've had my house broken into, I've been followed... just be safe."

"Mom? Why didn't you call us?" A long stretch of silence ensued after the innocent question, and her son swallowed heavily on the other side of the line.

"I didn't want to be a bother. Stay safe, okay?"

"Okay, you stay safe too. If you need, you can stay down here with Sarah and me." It was an empty promise and she knew it, but she smiled and told him she would think about it. She traced a hand over the top of her grandfather's headstone and said her goodbyes.

Arietta clinched her hands into fists, anger boiling to the surface. The sharks were circling, looking for a weapon, and they thought either she had it, or someone in her family did. She couldn't face this alone anymore. It was time to call an old friend.

Made in the USA
Monee, IL
11 March 2021

61397924R00184